HOT RAVES FOR PYNK AND HER NOVELS

SEXAHOLICS

"Raw, gritty, and...shocking...explicit. Pynk dives head first into sex addiction and its players...and she works it."

—BibliophilicBookBlog.com

"Hot and steamy...Pynk's down-to-earth and fast-paced writing style keeps the story moving and entertaining. The sex scenes are plentiful and titillating...Pynk delivers."   —TheBlackUrbanTimes.com

"Intense...unbelievable...raw and real."   —SimplyStacie.net

EROTIC CITY

"Steamy."   —Library Journal

"No-holds-barred...you may want to keep this book under the covers."
—StreetFiction.org

"Sure to enchant the freak in all of you...open the spicy pages...and leave your inhibitions in reality...I really enjoyed every moment in *Erotic City*. It punctures erotica's envelope...And I mean that as a compliment."
—ApoooBooks.com

"Quite a standout for this genre...the dialogue [is] lively and fun, and the plot moves quickly...No matter where you fall in the sexual spectrum, this book is sure to meet you where you'd like [to] get off."
—FeministReview.BlogSpot.com

"Five stars! Excellent...entertaining yet highly erotic...Fans of both erotica and contemporary literature will enjoy."
—UrbanBookSource.com

"Entertaining...erotic...enough sex between these pages to keep a person hot and bothered, but there is substance there as well."
—ImaniVoices.com

POLITICS.
ESCORTS.
BLACKMAIL.

PYNK

GRAND CENTRAL
PUBLISHING

NEW YORK   BOSTON

Grand Central Publishing
Hachette Book Group
237 Park Avenue
New York, NY 10017

www.HachetteBookGroup.com

Printed in the United States of America

RRD-C

First Edition: December 2012
10 9 8 7 6 5 4 3 2 1
Grand Central Publishing is a division of Hachette Book Group, Inc.
The Grand Central Publishing name and logo is a trademark of Hachette Book Group, Inc.

Library of Congress Cataloging-in-Publication Data
Pynk.
Politics. escorts. blackmail / by Pynk. — 1st ed.
    p. cm.
ISBN 978-0-446-56334-5
1. Prostitutes—Fiction. 2. New York (N.Y.)—Fiction. I. Title.
PS3616.Y565P65 2012
813'.6—dc23
                                         2012014123

This book is dedicated to all sex workers who want to quit the game but get pulled back in for that one last gig. I pray for your salvation and repentance as you deal with past demons and work to overcome temptation. You are more than your bodies—you are queens, worthy of happiness, respect, and love.

ACKNOWLEDGMENTS

Here we are—my fourth full-length erotica title! I want to thank the readers first, for reading my works, sticking with me, and for spreading the word about Pynk. Your support is the reason I continue writing in this genre. Writing erotica is not easy and sometimes society has a hard time accepting it because of the taboo topic of sex, but in spite of those who claim not to read it and who judge those who do, readers seem to be asking for more and more erotica nowadays, for both the entertaining story content and the turn-on factor. I do think that readers are embracing the genre more and more, and for that I say, "Thank you!"

To Hachette Book Group for believing in me and for publishing my titles, I am thankful. To Latoya Smith, my editor, your revision letter on this story made a huge difference. Your editing skills and knowledge are what brought this title together. To the rest of my GCP family, Jamie Raab, Linda Duggins, Anna Balasi, Miriam Parker, Renee Supriano, Nick Small, Brianne Beers, Jihan Antoine, the art department, publicity team, sales team, production staff and copy editors, and others; thank you very much for putting out such quality Pynk books.

To my loving family and amazing friends, for your support and patience, especially when I need to escape into writer's heaven—thanks so very much! To my fellow authors who offer tons of camaraderie and love, I cherish your support.

Thank you, Karen Thomas—you acknowledged my work twelve years ago, and then I was finally able to sign with you, in 2004, 2007, and 2009. Without you taking me by the hand and guiding me with your expert critiques, I would not be writing at the level I am today.

My agent, Andrew Stuart, I appreciate you for keeping it real, being optimistic, being patient, and for adding me to your list of amazing authors. There's more to come.

KP, for being my sounding board, enduring countless hours listening to me read my rough-draft scenes out loud, for being patient and caring and loving, and for offering sound advice. Thanks for taking the time to show you care with actions, not just words, proving that love really is a verb. Love you!

My bestie, Mary HoneyB Morrison—S. B. Redd—Yolanda Gore—Antoinette Gates—Deborah DivaDee Walker and the Divine Friendship Bookclub—Carol Mackey with Black Expressions—the Fort Benning staff—Cindy at Urban Knowledge in Columbia, SC—Jessica Reese at the Pynk Butterfly in Columbia, SC—Jeanette Sapphire Best-Charrette—Patricia Crowe—Vonda Howard—my webmaster, Bryan Cleveland—Carol Taylor—my fellow GA Peach Authors, Jean Holloway, D. L. Sparks, Gail McFarland, and Electa Rome Parks—Michelle Gipson—Cydney Rax—Mocha Ocha and the NAACP Author's Pavilion—Radiah and Charles Hubert with Urban Reviews for their support and for their Fall Fiction Fest—the amazing Ella Curry and BAN Radio/EDC Creations—Brian W. Smith and Trice Hickman for their *On the Air with Trice and Brian* show—Cyrus Webb for his *Conversations LIVE! With Cyrus Webb* show—Linda Jordan and the Central Library in Atlanta—the Southwest Regional, Washington Park, East Atlanta, and South Fulton libraries in Atlanta—Renee at Zahra's Books in Inglewood, CA—TaNisha Webb and Fall Into Books—the Bukh Law Firm in New York—Sadia and the Escort Times—Antoinette Gates—Stacy Smith Baron for the interview about New York City—Sonya Ward—Nellie George—The Heat of the Night authors, Lorraine Elzia, LaLaina Knowles, Niyah Moore, Elissa Gabrielle, and Ebonee Monique—Diamond Black—Curtis Bunn at the NBCC (National Book Club Conference)—Naleighna Kai and the Cavalcade of Authors—the African American Literary Awards Show for the nominations of *Erotic City* and *Sixty-Nine*—the Decatur Book Festival—all of the book clubs who are indeed the heart of the book-buying industry—my devoted Facebook and Twitter followers—THANK YOU.

My next title, *Sin in the City*, is about two best friends, Mercy and April, who find themselves so desperate for money that they head to Las Vegas for one night only, but end up staying for thirty days of gaming and sex, documented in thirty different scenes, day by day. I hope you keep an eye out for it.

Also, if you enjoyed *Erotic City*, the swinging drama continues and you'll want to check out my novella, *Erotic City II: Miami*, which is part of a four-part anthology series called *Insignificant Others*, with bestselling author Carol Taylor, and which debuts in May 2013. The many shades of Pynk just keep on coming!

Remember to live your sexy dreams responsibly—without guilt!

Smooches,
Pynk
xoxo
www.authorpynk.com
authorpynk@aol.com
www.facebook.com/authorpynk
www.twitter.com/authorpynk
www.sex-see.blogspot.com

AUTHOR'S NOTE

Escorts

My first Pynk title, *Erotic City*, focused on swinging; the second, *Sexaholics*, was about the oversexed and sex addiction; the third, *Sixty-Nine*, was about the undersexed and sexual repression; and now I've tackled the subject of escorts, bringing you *Politics. Escorts. Blackmail.*

Prostitution, escorting, and sex trafficking are all very serious problems in our society. Opinions vary on whether or not prostitution should be legalized. In this story, which is set in New York City, it is illegal. Prostitution was once considered a vagrancy crime, comparable to sleeping on the street or begging, but it is now a public-order crime, and mainly an issue of morality.

There are three categories that define the types of prostitution in the United States: (1) street, or streetwalkers, like hookers, (2) brothels or massage parlors, and (3) escorts or out-calls. Here are some facts: Most escort agencies have their own websites. Some advertised on Craigslist, but the Craigslist adult section was shut down in 2010 after pressure from law enforcement and anti-prostitution groups. Nevada is the only U.S. state to allow some legal prostitution (mainly brothels, and only in certain counties but not in the city of Las Vegas). In Louisiana, convicted prostitutes are required to register as sex offenders. One poll suggests that 30 percent of single men over thirty have paid for sex. A large percentage of prostitutes are said to have been abused as children. Some view buying sex as a form of addiction. There are John schools to examine and rehabilitate solicitors of prostitution. Brazil, Canada, Germany, France, Italy, Mexico, Portugal, and Switzerland, among others, have legalized it and believe sex for sale to be a legitimate and necessary service (for the complete list of countries go to www.prostitution.procon.org). Some call it a bartered service, even within a marriage, and that in the U.S., if we have freedom of speech, religion, and trade, why violate the premise of the Constitution by prohibiting sexual relations between consenting adults? Courtrooms are overburdened, and customers and prostitutes pay fines but are then back on the streets with no impact on the problem.

There are groups who would prefer that the act be managed as opposed to ignored, that legalizing it would prevent underground rings that recruit and abduct young girls, and that legalized and controlled environments will improve health and curtail underage prostitution. Legalizing it would involve government. But wait—our governments are supposed to solve the problems our county faces, not contribute to them. But, as is apparent in the news on a regular basis, government officials often pay for sex, and even if they get around the charges, there's still the morality issue again because most of them are married, so the fact is that they committed adultery.

Adultery is a big part of this novel. Whether we legalize prostitution or not, there is still the issue of morality. If a candidate for president of the United States pays for sex, legally or illegally—even though some say this is a private matter and no one else's business—his moral compass would still be questioned because he is running for president, hoping to lead our government and our country. But is what politicians do between the sheets really our business?

As you read *Politics. Escorts. Blackmail.*, you'll notice it's not written from the point of view of the politicians who are running for president. I did that on purpose, though you will see political news headlines at the beginning of each chapter to keep you abreast of the ongoing presidential race. I wanted to explore the lives of those who sell their bodies for a living. It's about the lives of one madam in particular, named Money, and her three escorts, Leilani, Midori, and Kemba. I wanted to see what their worlds were like, what it looked like for them to live knowing they sexed up men and women of privilege, public figures, lawmakers, actors, athletes, and politicians. The time period of this book runs right along the timeline of the Republican presidential primary, beginning in the spring of 2011 and running right up until the final candidates are decided and the winner is voted upon during the fifty-seventh United States presidential election on November 6, 2012.

You'll get to see what escorts are paid to do, how much an agency charges, what the escorts must endure, what their private lives are like, where they've come from, what the benefits are, and what the downsides are. You'll see each escort's issues and missions as they all take you on a journey into their world of sex for money.

I enjoyed writing this book, and I learned a lot as I researched what prostitutes go through, what the laws are, what the risks are, etc. I interviewed two escorts, talked to criminal attorneys, a city councilman's assistant, and several individuals who live in New York City. I did not want to glamorize the business itself, but I made certain to focus on creating flawed characters with specific journeys, letting them get as raw as they needed to. It wasn't about what I would do or not do because it wasn't about me. I didn't judge. I tried to make it all about the escorts and the people they encounter over the year and a half in which this novel takes place, no matter how intense it got.

It is my desire that you enjoy the rawness of it all, and understand that rawness, as well as the softness, from an emotional and a heartfelt standpoint. The erotica factor is here, being that a lot of people read erotica for the sex scenes—but more important, I want people to keep coming back to my books because of the story. While my books are character driven, they also show a side of life we may never get to know or see, or that might make us feel uncomfortable. But at the end of the day, when we turn the last page we're fortunate enough to close the book and go back to our everyday lives. My goal is to make you think back to at least one of the characters in this book and wonder just how they dealt with it, why they did what they did, and how they're doing. I want you to remember them—I hope Money, Leilani, Midori, and/or Kemba are unforgettable. Then I'll know my mission was accomplished.

Get ready to be eroticized Pynk-style.

I give you *Politics. Escorts. Blackmail.*

Notice from Pynk:

If you are erotica squeamish, especially when it comes to what a client will ask for from an escort, be prepared to squirm.

Consider yourself warned!

PYNK DEFINITIONS

Politics: A process by which a group of elected representatives make collective decisions for all the people to abide by.

Escorts: Individuals who accompany people to social events and/or for private conversation in exchange for money. Sometimes sex is involved, sometimes not.

Blackmail: A crime committed by a desperate person who wants something, and is holding something over someone else's head to get it.

"Integrity is doing the right thing even
when no one is watching."

—C. S. Lewis

POLITICS. ESCORTS. BLACKMAIL.

Prologue

Dear Mr. Big,

I'll bet you think this book is about you, now that it's all said and done, right? Well, you're wrong. It's not. It's about me, Money "Queens" Watts, pimptress-slash-madam, and how the world of politics, escorts, and blackmail came to a head, all in one day in 2012. It's about my side of the escort coin. The side of running a business, Lip Service, that provided sex for money. Hooking. The oldest profession ever.

This is my own version of sex and the city. Sex in the Big Apple. Sex with big names. Sex for big money. Sex that made big news. You were Mr. Big. But now...well, like I said, this story is not about you.

As you know, I was the provider, or organizer, of this money ship. And they, the clients, were also called hobbyists. Some called them Johns. I think the word John is too generic when

you're dealing with greedy men of power who seek uncomplicated lust, oh excuse me, uncomplicated dates, at all costs.
Especially when you're talking about political figures. What you
don't know is that I knew the mind of politicians, and their
need for sex, like I knew the back of my hand. Politicians might
be in an arena of lawmaking and legislation, but they still fuck,
oh sorry again, date. And as long as someone is willing to
"date" them undercover to feed their entitlement hunger, there
will always be sneaky, unfaithful men or even women who get
some on the side, simply because they're in a position of power
to do so. Most are the guys who didn't get laid in school but
now that they have fame and fortune, they feel entitled, married or not.

I did it over the Internet on my own exclusive escort website, but most times, for the regulars and VIPs, it was over
the phone to my booker, who took information and processed
calls. We had two hundred different 888 numbers, routed to
one main number. You couldn't join my website and post a pro-
file page like you were on some dating or adult site, hoping
for the hookup. My site was informational only. You'd go there
and look it over, and pick who you wanted for a date based
on their photo and description, and then call us. Hazel eyes,
five foot nine, one hundred thirty pounds, with a body shot
from the neck down, or five foot six, one hundred forty-three
pounds, chocolate brown eyes, dressed like a businesswoman,
leaving much to the imagination, and so on. No slutty shots.
Classy all the way. And those pictures were nothing more than
stock photos.

My shit was no street corner operation. These were not har-
lots, or escorts of ill repute. This was not a brothel or some
prostitute strolling the streets. This was about arranging for a
sophisticated man or woman to escort you to dinner, and then

possibly going somewhere after for an intimate evening. If the two of you skipped the dinner, that was fine, your call. It always comes down to what two consenting adults choose to do. That's it. No different than a first date with someone who doesn't call the next day. Only there's a nameless booker who gets ten percent off the top. I'd split the rest fifty-fifty with my escorts. And at anywhere from one to three thousand dollars per hour or more, sometimes even thirty thousand per weekend, we did very, very well.

I provided a necessary service, and my escorts were excellent at what they did. Even better at separating the thin line that stretched from the legal end to the illegal end. The loophole in the system gave us a tiny bit of wiggle room, and that wiggle room was our friend. I could smell a rat, or a raid, a mile way. That's why I dealt with high-profile hobbyists and not just your average Johns. Attract the politicians or celebrities, or the most elite businessmen. They have a lot to lose. They'll stick to their story of innocence while being strapped down for a lie detector test. If you have a video of them caught dead in the act, they'll swear on their momma's grave it wasn't them.

Funny how the very people who make the laws are sometimes the ones who patronize the offense. Laws? Please. I made my own.

I guess you think you got me, huh? You think this is a damn game? This is my world. I came from a place of espionage and government cover-ups. I'm made from my father's stock. I worked hard to charm and seduce and gain the trust of wealthy political figures to build my impressive clientele list, and you think you're gonna come up and do this? Yeah, you must think this a joke.

Everyone who turned their backs on me is going to get theirs.

And you, you better watch out because you might end up with the same fate.

Strap on your strap-on, I mean seat belt, and listen up.

Because you don't know the real story…

Ciao

Republican presidential candidate Philadelphia mayor Kalin Graves took an early lead in the polls with New York senator Darrell Ellington on his heels. However, the entry of several new candidates this month has drawn an interesting mix of contenders.

One

∽

Money

Tuesday—May 10, 2011

The skies were dark on a cold morning in late spring, though the sun was sure to show its face by seven and warm things up about twenty degrees, into the fifties. The cold chill of the below-zero weather of winter had ended months earlier.

It was very early, 5:01 on a Tuesday, after Money—her actual birth name—exited her large, brick, six-bedroom, red roof Tudor home in the exclusive Forest Hills Gardens area, a neighborhood in Queens only fourteen blocks long. She held a NY travel mug with her last few sips of black coffee and hopped her frame into the back of a yellow cab, sat back against the faded leather seat, and told the dark-skinned driver simply, "Belvedere Hotel." As she crossed her long legs, she felt the strain in her defined

calves, brought on by her regular, forty-five-minute elliptical workout.

The driver nodded, pulled the flag to start the meter,
and took off down the sloping, curved street. He was the
one whom the taxi company would send whenever Money
needed to go into the city. She was claustrophobic and
hated the subway, so she didn't mind the fifty-dollar one-
way ride, and she knew he wouldn't try to stiff her by taking
the long way. What he knew was that she'd tip him 50
percent of the fare. His only question was, basically, which
hotel?

She was on her way to play the part of Queens, the name
her hobbyists knew her by.

The cab driver turned down the radio just as the story
ended about the Republican Party presidential primaries and
the candidates who had declared thus far. To her surprise, two
out of the six were on Money's client list, disguised as Mr.
11 and Mr. 51 in her little pink book—Philadelphia mayor
Kalin Graves and New York senator Darrell Ellington, re-
spectively. She wondered how that would play out. Just one
more reason to keep things in line.

She had expected her company's bookings to slow down
with the elections about to gear up, but experience told her
that pressure breeds needs, and that could prove beneficial
to an agency known for guaranteeing privacy and discretion.
Which was why she wasn't worried. She sipped her brew and
made the backseat her temporary office.

Money glanced at her gold Movado watch. It normally
took her half an hour to get to midtown Manhattan to meet
her very regular client for their 6:00 pre-work sex appointment. He was so regular, in fact, that sometimes he'd come
to her home for an in-call. But being that her on-again, off-

again boyfriend, Jamie Bitters, was back on again, Money decided it would be best to have an out-call for now.

Jamie was a client who, after their first time together, couldn't wait to come back again. By the second and third times, he paid to extend the dates. He'd share pictures of his kids and talk about his childhood. By their fourth time together, he asked her out. He was a former chief deputy sheriff for New York who had been fired for using a county credit card for personal use. One week after he lost his job he filed for bankruptcy, and due to his questionable reputation he found himself unemployable.

Money knew the deal. She was his cash cow. She admitted it to herself and to him. But Jamie's affections were at times a much-needed escape from the realities of her world. It still amounted to sex for money, only he was escorting her in her life.

In the meantime, he also stood in as the bodyguard and driver for Lip Service. He was always on standby, but was rarely called. Yet she still kept him on the payroll just in case.

Money was the eldest daughter of her half-French father, Arthur Watts, who worked as a French diplomat in London. He was accustomed to the world of politics and keeping things undercover. He spoke three languages and had also moonlighted as a spy for the Russians.

She and her family had lived in London for years and then moved to Atlanta after her father got caught red-handed with Russian hookers in a hotel room in Moscow. Funny thing was, he never got caught giving away government secrets to the Russians. But his greedy penis and the world of hookers brought him to a fast halt. He was caught on tape receiving oral sex, and was blackmailed for money. He gave up every red cent the family had to keep the tape from being leaked. But a copy was sent to government officials anyway, and he was soon fired. It was also sent to the Mrs. Life was funny that way. The same act that brought him down years ago now made his daughter, Money, a multimillionaire.

Through the fallout of the scandal, he and Money's mother, Beverly Watts, stayed together. She was a retired high-fashion model from Sudan who traveled across the world before Money and her baby sister were born. He'd stayed with her in spite of her indiscretions as well. She'd slept with a possessive married designer who caught her and two other models in the act of a threesome. In a fit of jealousy, he fired her from fashion week in Milan, but let the other two stay on. After that, her modeling career was pretty much over.

Her mom and dad claimed not to know what she did for a living, but she knew her father's greed and love of money wouldn't allow him to object. Cash was what he claimed made the world go round, which was why he named his oldest daughter Money. It's what he hungered for. He was distant when it came to anyone but his wife, which also included his daughters.

Money glanced out the window of the cab to check on their location. She looked down and pressed her middle finger along the touch screen of her phone, thinking back to her tough conversation with Midori, her independent contractor, or IC.

Four days earlier, they had talked in the lobby of the Algonquin Hotel on Club Row. During that conversation, Money had a look on her face like she was pissed off, upset, and disgusted. Midori, also known by her escort name of Brooklyn, looked both sweet and worried.

As they sat on the sofa in the lobby, Money turned to Midori and said, "So tell me what happened and don't give me some lame-ass, cockamamie story, either."

Midori replied, "Bailey's just jealous. He's making up stories."

"Oh really? What's he jealous of?"

"He knows about Virgil."

"And how does he know anything about your private life, Midori?"

"I guess he followed me. Maybe he's been watching me." Midori acted stumped.

"You guess? Midori, listen to me. This is a problem. Are you laying up with him, talking about you instead of listening? Are you breaking the rules?"

She said, "No."

"No rule breaking, huh? Then answer me this: How is it I send you to meet Bailey at the St. Regis, and you take money from him on the side?"

"I did not."

"Then tell me what happened in the hotel room? Why was it damaged?"

"It wasn't damaged when I left him there."

Money asked, "So, you didn't tear up the room and threaten to accuse him of roughing you up?"

"No. He said that?"

"I said that."

"You know I make enough money. I wouldn't do that just to get some extra cash from a client. He's the problem, not me. What I didn't tell you is that Bailey's guilty of escort bonding. He said he loves me," Midori explained.

"When did he say that?"

"A while ago."

"See, that's something you should've told me as soon as it

happened. I wouldn't have assigned you to him. He's good money, but he won't be requesting you again, I guarantee you that. He's no longer a client. I smell trouble."

"Okay."

"What's up with you and Virgil, your little whiz kid from MIT? Please tell me you two aren't still serious?"

"It's coming along."

"And he still doesn't know what you do?"

"No. He thinks I'm a Realtor."

"It's too close for comfort, Midori. He's Senator Ellington's stepson."

"Yes. And that's something I wanted to talk to you about. See, the other night, Virgil was talking about playing around on the computer. He's doing this tech job and with his IT training, he said he knows how to hack into e-mail. He's talking—well, joking—about hacking into Mayor Graves's personal e-mail account." She gave a slim laugh.

Money shook her head. "Midori, that geeky mama's boy is looking for something on Mayor Graves that would embarrass him and his family and cause damage to his political career. That's called blackmail, not a joke or prank. And he'd do it just so his own mother can be First Lady, and you know I'm right. But he could also do years in prison for wire fraud and identity theft, and more. He really thinks he'd be able to get away with something like that?"

Midori replied, "He wouldn't really do it. He was just talking. Sometimes he acts like he's a young Bill Gates or something." She laughed again, a nervous laugh.

Money kept a straight face. "I see nothing funny. What the hell is it you see in a nerd like him, anyway?"

"He's nice."

"Look at you, Midori, still looking for your knight in shining armor? Still looking for love to take you away, like in the movie *Pretty Woman*, huh? You're a love junkie."

"No, I'm not."

"It's sad that your little boyfriend has no idea that the dirt he'll uncover could be his own. If he goes through with this, he'd not only uncover evidence linking Mayor Graves to escorts, but he'd open a whole ugly can of worms that would expose his stepfather's other life. I'm sure nobody knows that Ellington pays for sex. Not only would it expose him, but Lip Service as well. And that's not gonna happen. I won't let it. Virgil had better watch himself. Your boyfriend's so busy trying to blackmail the enemy, he'll end up destroying his own political family."

"I've got him, Money."

"Yeah, well, you'd better."

"I do."

"Handle it."

"I will." Midori then asked, "How'd you know about the room being torn up? I mean, did the hotel complain or did he tell you that mess?"

Money only said, "Don't try to change the subject. Look at me."

Midori did.

"You'd better handle this, and quick before I have someone else handle him. I've been at this for years, and I have a lot to lose. My clients have a lot to lose. I'm not going to let anyone ruin this. If you don't fix it, I'll do it myself with one phone call."

"I'm begging you, no. Please tell me you wouldn't do anything to Virgil."

Money crossed her leg toward her. "Midori, just because you're my sister, doesn't mean I'm going to let you fuck this up. We're deep in New York City politics, and right now, there's porn and kinky sex on tons of government comput-ers as we speak. It's the perfect place to make money for the service we can provide. And it's gonna stay perfect. Before I let some amateur, sorry-ass blackmail scheme happen, I'll do what I have to do."

Midori was silent.

Money continued, "You could learn a thing or two from Leilani. You need to stay clean—and keep this simple and easy." She held out an envelope. "Brooklyn has been re-quested, so get your shit together. I'm flying you to the Florida Keys for a late dinner, and then two full days with a Long Island physician. Meet him at the Little Palm Island hotel tonight at nine. Your flight is at four. All of the info is in there."

Midori took it. "Four?"

"Yes, four. This is a five-figure weekend for both of us. Don't be late. And tell your little nerdy boyfriend whatever you need to in order to make this happen."

"I'll be there in time for the flight." Midori stood up.

"And?"

"And I'll keep Virgil in check. Bye." Midori walked away, switching her grand hips.

Money shook her head, as if to shake away the memory of that conversation, and gave a long sigh, sipping her last bit of coffee. It was painful to put her foot down like that with her sister, but she had to let Midori know she was no-nonsense, and that she would not risk her freedom or her life for anyone.

She knew her sister had arrived back from the Florida Keys the previous evening and thought about calling her, but de-cided not to, just to give Midori a little more time to let the seriousness of it all sink in. She had already informed the booker not to respond to requests from the Navy vet, Bailey Brenner, who was catching serious feelings for Midori.

Money looked down at her phone again and saw that her booker had just sent a text that all three ICs were booked for the day. In order to give Midori time to rest up after her trip, Midori was assigned a late evening with her regular, Mr. 91.

Leilani had two appointments, one with Mr. 51, her usual. And Kemba had one with Ms. 101, a high-paying, bisexual professional basketball player who preferred pussy but liked a little dick every now and then.

Money realized it would be a good day financially, and she was prepared for the work ahead of her. Her job was to fulfill fantasies, plain and simple.

She put her empty travel mug into her oversized purse that had its usual contents; bottled water, her iPad, ID, credit card reader, regular and large condoms, lube, makeup, baby wipes, cell phone, a device to detect cameras and wires, and Altoids. She was plucked, waxed, lotioned up, and dabbed with subtle body oil between her breasts. She never wore anything potent enough to leave a scent on her date. She was ready to perform.

By 5:34, Money looked up. The cab driver had already made a right at Sixth Avenue and slowed to pull up to the small, elegant hotel in the theater district.

"Fifty-two dollars even," he said, as he turned off the meter.

Money had her regular seventy-five dollars folded up and ready. She handed it to him, grabbed her bag, and exited, wearing her tight, white skirt suit. She headed into the hotel as the cab pulled away.

One thing she knew about going to a place of business, as

opposed to a private residence, was that the employees, door-men, whoever, would see it all. Money knew that the more confident and nonchalant she seemed, the quicker she could check in, get the keycard, and head up to the room as though she was on routine business. She never dressed too flashy. No loud colors. Just a business suit or conservative dress and high heels, hair up in a bun, smiling.

She engaged in insignificant chitchat while paying for the room at the front desk, then took the keycard and headed up in the elevator. Same old same old.

As far as the cost of the date, she'd already run the trans-action through the credit card scanner on her iPad. She preferred credit cards as long as the hobbyists didn't have a problem giving their billing information. Since 80 percent of her clients were regulars, it worked because most had special personal-expense accounts set up. Besides, she considered Lip Service too high-end for the risk of cash exchanges like solo escorts or girls on the street. Every now and then she'd let her ICs take cash from a client, but the rule was it needed to be in an envelope and in clear sight as soon as one or the other entered the room. It wasn't discussed or counted right away, but the IC made sure to take it into the bathroom to count it in private before clothes were removed. No refunds after the clothes came off.

She entered the executive king room on the fifteenth floor, tossed her bag on the brown leather sofa, and turned on all the lights since the sun hadn't quite finished hiding, but also because she knew her visitor liked it that way. Bright.

She went into the bedroom and pulled back the rust cov-ers, fluffing up the down pillows. The time on the clock read ten minutes to six. She sent a text to her booker. Here.

Ten minutes later on the dot, she was stripped down to

her black cotton bra and panties, stockings, and garter, curly hair flowing down her back. There was a single knock at the door. She looked through the peephole, seeing her three-thousand-dollar, one-hour client, Mr. 31, and then forwarded the text a second time. That meant he'd arrived. The reply text sounded. She put her phone down and opened the door.

She smiled, but it wouldn't last long. "Good to see you, Pretty in Pink."

He stepped inside and closed the door without saying a word. He liked to be called pretty, so he smiled.

She looked down at his crotch. His hard-on was on. She frowned, and her voice turned bossy. "You came to my door excited. Make your dick go down, now!"

He looked at her with eyes that asked for permission to speak.

"Talk."

"I'm sorry, Mistress."

She nodded. "My slave."

He was white, portly, with graying hair that was slicked back, and he carried his usual gym bag as he stepped into the bedroom. Inside was a red wig, makeup, handcuffs, pink lingerie, nipple clips, and a paddle.

By 6:15 he lay across the bed all dolled up, when Money the master demanded, "Turn the fuck over."

He obliged with puppy dog eyes, replying "Yes, Mistress" in a soft, high-pitched, passive feminine tone. He lay in a fetal position, looking scared out of his girlie wits, yet his expression said he would have it no other way. "Am I your bitch?" he asked, and then he squirmed, peeking at Money like maybe trouble awaited him. Or perhaps hoping it did.

"Shut the fuck up. You talk when I tell you to talk, dammit."

The more shit Money talked, the harder his dick got under the lace fabric of his panties.

He never tried to please Money. Never made a move to put his mouth on the skin of her pussy, or his dick inside of her. Not even his fingers.

"And yes, you're my nasty little bitch, all right. Now kiss my feet. And let me hear your lips smack."

He moved from the bed and crawled onto the floor as Money raised her high-heeled foot onto his shoulder. He took her foot into his hands and removed her shoe, kissing the top of her foot loudly.

"I can't hear it."

He smacked louder.

"Now suck my toes, one by one, starting with my baby toe."

He brought his lips to her toes and worked them, smacking, licking, and sucking.

"Punk. You're just a sissy. A man in drag who's a cross-dressing-ass sissy. And you love it."

He sucked harder.

"Yeah, suck my big toe like I might suck your dick if you beg me, like a good little submissive."

He sucked it with vigor and looked up at her with wide blue eyes of pleasure.

She was a notch below yelling. "Don't look at me."

He looked down and continued his foot job.

"One day, I'm gonna walk you around New York City like a dog, with a cord tied to your scrawny little penis that I'll yank every time I want you to stop and sit and shake my hand like I tell you to. Take you to Central Park and make you piss on the grass. You piece of shit."

Being dominated was Pretty in Pink's only escape. It was

what he lived for. It served a purpose. It was his refuge from his life of being in control. His life of telling people what to do. His life of making decisions and being respected. His way of letting it all go, being free, freaky, and feminine as opposed to masculine and dominating.

He liked to be controlled without judgment while he lived out his urges and secret desires. From time to time, he had to have the opposite of what the world demanded of him. The same demands he knew awaited him as soon as he left the hotel room.

She jerked her foot away. "Pretty in Pink, get your ass back on the bed, up on all fours so I can fuck you in the ass, doggie style." She removed her other shoe and took the big black dildo from the dresser. "I'm gonna punish you for not kissing my feet the minute you walked into this damn room."

"Yes, Mistress Queens." Even his voice was pink. He stood, looking guilty of a crime while wearing silver clips on his nipples, pulled down his lace panties and stepped out of them all ladylike, and made his way to the corner of the bed—on all fours, as instructed.

"Now open up."

His hairy ass was propped up and ready. He buried his face into the pillow and took a peek back, seeming to anxiously await her next move after she secured the black leather strap along her hips. Prostate pleasure and rimming were his thing.

He was Tyler Copeland, Mr. 31, New York City's police commissioner.

In his mind, some things could be done only in private, in another world of no judgments and no rules, no hassles and no gossip.

Just as he squealed upon her full penetration, she popped him on his pale cheek. "Dirty girl." His cheek flushed dark red.

He grabbed hold of his excited dick as she fucked him into submission.

"Let go. I didn't say you could please yourself." She popped him on his dick.

He wept with pleasure at her control and did as she said. But even with him removing his hand, he still spilled his seed, reeling from his thrill. Just as he came, Money's phone sounded.

He glanced at it with teary, ecstasy-filled eyes.

She told him, "Keep your ass right where it is" and headed to her phone, picked it up, and read the text from Jamie.

Where are you and what are you doing?

Money shook her head. As if he didn't know she was at work.

Making grown men cry like little bitches, she thought but never typed.

Republican candidate former California governor Robert Sally has performed well in the polls, becoming a strong contender. Sally says he's trying to win over his party's conservative vote. Thus far, his tax plan does not fare well with low-income consumers, who prefer Senator Darrell Ellington's proposal to cut income tax rates across the board.

Two

Midori

Tuesday—May 17, 2011

Midori thought about what she and her sister Money had talked about. She hoped Virgil really wasn't dumb enough to set up the mayor of Philly in order to get his stepfather, Senator Darrell Ellington, elected as President. She hadn't been able to see Virgil since she had to go out of town so quickly. Knowing when she was to have returned, he was blowing up her phone unlike any other time before, trying to come by and see her from the moment she got back.

She'd had appointments seven nights straight and couldn't see him as much as she wanted to, making excuses as if she had evening real estate showings and was too exhausted.

Her trip the previous weekend with the Long Island doctor to the Florida Keys was spectacular. She wasn't even mad at her sister for assigning the booking to her. Turns out the client wanted the GFE, or girlfriend experience, as opposed to what most of the men who paid for her services wanted—the PSE, or porn star experience.

The PSE was usually freakier and definitely more expensive because it involved hard-core sex. Most of it was deep throat or anal, and ejaculations outside of the body, outside of the condom, mainly for visual effect, like in a porn movie. For the client, PSE with an escort was less about feelings and more about the performance.

The Long Island doctor, Mr. 81, who was in his fifties, paid top dollar for someone to simply be the girl next door, doing what some girlfriends do. Be his willing, feminine, sexy trophy. No drama allowed.

For a moment, while with him, Midori had actually forgotten she was a working girl and fell victim to the allure of the imaginary romance he was trying to portray for his own reasons. No one on the island knew who he was, unlike in the city. The two of them were incognito, holding hands, pretending to be a couple though having just met. While she fulfilled his fantasy, she felt cherished and got lost in the allure of the white sugar-sand beaches and spiraling coconut palm trees, under powder-blue skies in mid-eighty-degree weather. He fulfilled her heart's fantasy without even knowing it.

The first evening was like a true date. They met at the restaurant in a hotel called Shor. After dinner, he walked her to her own two-bedroom suite, and he went to his. They exchanged nothing more than a good-night peck on the lips.

The next day after breakfast, he took her shopping at the local boutiques and bought her formal evening wear, a sapphire bustier with a matching thong, skimpy lingerie, and a tangerine bikini. And then they went parasailing and scuba diving on the private beach. That evening they enjoyed a cozy dinner cruise at sunset and danced the night away like newlyweds.

Later, in his hotel suite, after sipping expensive champagne and feeding each other chocolate-dipped strawberries, she allowed him to live out his desires: French kissing, expert cunnilingus, her riding him until she had an orgasm, or three, and then him mounting her until he got his, all to the sounds of smooth, baby-making jazz. Then, after about an hour's worth of pillow talk, she went to her hotel room, floating on cloud nine.

He was the head of thoracic surgery at the University Hospital of Brooklyn, and if Taye Diggs had an older brother, he would be it. Dark skin, white teeth, bald head, sexy but he acted like he didn't know it. He was a leading, esteemed surgeon who mended hearts for a living. But it became obvious to Midori that he was trying to survive after having his heart broken.

After the throes of deep sex, while holding "Brooklyn" in his arms, he shared with her: "My wife is cheating on me. I don't want to give her half, since we didn't sign a prenup. After twenty-two years, we're in a sexless marriage. It all comes down to the fact that it's cheaper to keep her. So instead of having a chick on the side who wants more, I hire an escort every now and then. But I'm never with the same girl twice."

Midori gave a smile but frowned inside. In her mind she snapped her fingers, *Damn.*

The final day they rented scooters to get in some last-minute sightseeing, had lunch, then simply checked out of the hotel and headed off to the airport in separate town cars like it was all a dream. They never even spent one night together.

During the first-class flight back to New York after the trip, she couldn't stop thinking about Dr. Feelgood, even though he was old enough to be her father—which, she admitted to herself, added to the attraction. He was the exact type of person who could be the one. More than anything, more than money, she wanted a man who could do all of that to her and for her, and more, and save her from the life of using her vagina for a stranger's lust. In her mind, it was all just a pipedream.

But for the moment, back to reality, there she was, flat on her back, mind returning from its travels, starting to feel the tightening of rough, oversized hands around her slender brown throat. The hands of the one her sister warned her about: Bailey Brenner.

The white envelope was on the dresser. A well-earned twenty-five hundred dollars in cash for the hour was inside it, same as his normal fee, but this time she wasn't sharing it with the agency. With him, the hour always involved something that pushed the limits. It had been that way for a year now.

He was a forty-something Navy veteran who made a run for a New York congressional seat but lost. He was dark and tall and solid, well over two hundred fifty pounds with a low Afro. He was breathing hard, inhaling and exhaling loudly, as if it were her hands around his burly neck.

The kinky goings-on happened in the sixth floor suite at the Roosevelt Hotel on East Forty-Fifth and Madison in midtown Manhattan. Midori had hailed a cab from her Upper East Side apartment to meet him at 8:30 p.m., even though she had a 9:30 scheduled through Lip Service. She had already picked up the key to the room for that appointment, which was two floors up. The understanding was that he expected her to be waiting upon his arrival, dressed like a naughty librarian.

Though it was in the forties outside, to her it felt like a sauna in the room. The blades of the overhead fan spun in overdrive to subdue Midori's sweat, but failed. She'd put a menstrual cup deep inside of her pussy to stop the flow of her period. Being that time of the month didn't make it any better, but she couldn't let her menstruation get in the way of her money. This wasn't about her pussy, anyway. She tried to stay cool, playing along, thinking if she sped up the thrill, he'd speed up his happy ending and she could be done. "Tighter," she said with a fake grunt, trying to make it seem as though his grip was more of a strain than it actually was. It was her attempt to take his bondage fetish into high gear.

"Look at you. You like that shit. Being choked." He looked wildly excited.

She lay there on her back with a wildflower tattoo on her big toe, totally nude upon the sheets of the queen bed, smack-dab in the middle of a client's choking fantasy. Her freshly shaven landing strip went to waste. Her full breasts and oversized nipples were ignored. Tonight, he needed to scare her. Push the limits.

Midori breathed harder and deeper, in through her nose and out through her mouth. Just as her heart began to accelerate, she forced the secret word from her lips. "When."

He kept on.

She clenched her teeth and grabbed his thick wrists. Her eyes bugged. "When, dammit."

He stared at her like he was deaf.

"Bailey. Let go." Her elongated words were smashed by her tightening mouth. Her nerves were elevated.

He moved his gargantuan hands from around her throat and grabbed his stiff penis, choking it quickly and frantically. Her fear was his turn-on. "I'm about to shoot this on your belly. And then lick it off."

She rubbed her aching neck and watched him prepare for his jack-off.

His grunts sounded like a surefire heart attack awaited him, and his breathing sounded like a full-blown asthma attack would join in. He was a sight for sore eyes.

Midori braced herself as he adjusted the tip of his penis to her stomach. She watched his spill, feeling the warmth upon her skin. He released the last drop and leaned down to her, placing his mouth at her stomach, lapping up his own sperm.

The money made her ask, "You like that, don't you?" cheering him on. But she wondered what happened to him to make him enjoy the taste of his own salty seed.

He licked his lips.

Her stomach growled. She morphed herself into sitting back against the headboard. And then she watched him as he made his way to the bathroom. In her mind she was shaking her head. He was odd and she wasn't totally shocked. She'd seen his fetish side too many times before. But what amazed her most was why she returned, even after he pushed the limits time and time again.

She asked louder so he could hear her, "Why'd you tell my boss that I tore up the room because you wouldn't give me more money?"

"Because you did."

"I did not, Bailey, and you know it."

"You did."

"Whatever." She again soothed her neck with her hand.

"She already won't book you. Don't push your luck," she warned him.

"You know you wanna see me. You know you like me."

"Oh really?"

"Really."

Walking back in toward the bed, he handed her a warm washcloth.

"Thanks." She took it and began wiping his remnants of sperm off of her flat stomach.

He took the cloth back as she stood from the bed, taking the few steps to the chair where her clothes were draped. "You can't stay longer?" He set the cloth down on the table.

"No." She stepped into her red panties.

"Why not?"

"Because you came. You know the rules. Once you come, no matter how long you're booked, your time ends."

"Well, I say rules don't apply anymore."

"Oh yes they do. They're new rules. My rules. Besides, you were late."

He shrugged. "No big deal. I'll just pay for more time."

"No thanks. I'll just leave early to make it up."

"Another thousand?"

She shook her head. She thought twice, *Hmmm*, but still shook her head some more. She needed to leave before she crossed into Lip Service time. That was a no-no, especially since her sister was already pissed at her.

He said, "You must have another John lined up." He sat on the bed, breathing now back to normal.

She zipped up her pants and put on her bra.

"I have something to ask you."

"Bailey, I've got to get going." She carefully slipped her top over her head.

"Baby, why do you treat me like this?"

"Why do you call me baby?" Her confused face accented her inquiry.

"Because you are."

She adjusted her clothes and stepped into her black heels. "I'm not. It's not what you think it is. It's just an illusion. I'm not even real. I'm just a figment of your imagination."

"Not true. When can I see you again?"

"Not sure." She walked into the living room area and took the envelope, folding it up and stuffing it into her bag.

He stood, still naked, and followed her. "I guess I'll let Money know," he threatened.

"No you won't. Then I'll never see you again for sure." She placed the strap of the bag over her shoulder. "Bailey, I've gotta run."

"I love you."

She gave a weak smile, having heard it from him before, opened the door, and walked out without looking back, making her way down the hall and into the elevator.

By 9:25 she was in the next hotel room upstairs, showered. She'd worn a new menstrual cup and was dressed in her skirt and blouse, nude pumps, wearing reading glasses. Her hair was pinned up. She'd added concealer to the small bruise on the front of her neck. Tired, she texted her booker, Here, then lay down on the white sheet. She got a reply text, 10:00. Thrilled that he'd be a half hour late, she stretched out and dialed her boyfriend, Virgil.

He answered his phone, speaking without any level of hip or swag to his voice whatsoever. He was a very good-looking black man, toffee colored, with a fit body and curly hair.

She said in low gear, "I got your messages. I told you I was going out of town."

"You did. And you only called once the entire time."

"I was busy. But I'm back now. Just tired. About to go to bed."

"I've been really wanting to see you. Did you get my text about meeting me?"

She could hear the excitement in his voice. "I did."

"I left something in your purse."

"In my purse? Why would you have anything in my purse?"

"It was the last time I saw you, the night before you had your breakfast meeting at the Algonquin with Money. While we were at the movies I put my ink pen in your purse when you went to the bathroom. It was in my pants pocket and I didn't have a shirt pocket. I forgot about it. I need it."

"Okay. Well, I'll give it to you when I see you."

"Can I come by tonight?"

"Virgil, you'd come by this late to get a freakin' ink pen?"

"I'd come by this late to see you. I've missed you."

"Sounds like you miss your pen more than me." She tried to put him off for one more night. "You can get it tomorrow. I don't know what my schedule will be like, but I'm sure we can do something."

"Well then, how about lunch?"

"I'll try."

"Try? I guess the real estate market is picking up. You have more showings again?"

"Yes."

"Okay." He paused. "So, the trip to Key West was successful, I guess."

"Very."

"Next time we'll have to go together."

She glanced at the clock. "Okay."

"Midori, the debates are about to start soon. My stepfather

is getting ready. Things have been changing a lot around here. A lot of media. My mom is getting bombarded with interview requests. Things are about to get crazy."

"That's good. I'm really happy for you guys." She took a moment to wonder how a presidential hopeful's stepson would fare with the public if he was discovered dating a high-class hooker. To her, "about to get crazy" was an understatement.

"Listen, you know the e-mail thing with Mayor Graves I was telling you about?"

"Yes."

"I've just about got it figured out."

"Virgil, I still don't understand why you'd do that anyway. You need to let your dad win on his own. The risk of you getting caught isn't worth it."

"Caught? If you only knew how many people do that all the time. People who know the system like I do."

"Maybe, but what makes you think he has anything to hide anyway? It could just be a waste of time. And then if you do find something, how are you gonna make it an issue without anyone knowing it was you? It's just a bad idea all around."

"Well, I heard he's a racist."

"A racist? With a black wife?"

"Having a black wife doesn't mean anything."

"Yes it does. Who's going to marry someone of a race they hate? And if he is a racist, you thinking you can find e-mails to prove it is just dumb."

"It's not what I'll find in his e-mail account. It's what will be sent from his account."

She turned from her side to her back, her forearm of one arm on her forehead. "Virgil, I'm really surprised at you. Where does this come from? You need to stop. Let it go."

"Okay, you know what? I'll just make sure to keep it to myself."

"No. I want you to confide in me, but I also want you to let this go."

Virgil kept at it. "I could also just send him a racist cartoon, and then log in and see if he forwards it from his account as a joke."

"That'll be easily tracked."

"It won't. Believe me."

She exaggerated her yawn, making it sound twice as intense. "Virgil, look, I'm really tired. And by the way, yes, I'll have lunch with you. How about Japanese at Nobu? At noon."

"I'll be there. And can you please check your purse to make sure my pen is in it?"

"I'm in bed. I'm sure it is. I haven't worn that purse since I packed up to fly to Key West. I'll bring it tomorrow."

"Thanks."

"And slow down. Enjoy this. Don't blow it. Love you."

"See you tomorrow."

Fifteen minutes later, Brooklyn was fucking Mr. 91, a famous black male comedian who had a penchant for portraying the teenaged male student being seduced by the older vixen.

The game of fulfilling fantasies for money continued.

And she had a boyfriend who was none the wiser.

At least for another day.

The Republican candidates for president participated in the first presidential debate in Greenville, South Carolina, yesterday, with Kalin Graves and Darrell Ellington coming out on top. Ellington returned to New York this morning and is expected to appear on CNN tonight to discuss the direction of his campaign.

Three

∞

Leilani

Friday—June 3, 2011

Leilani "Manhattan" Sutton had already popped her birth control pill for the day, having gotten a new prescription after going in to see her regular gynecologist for her annual exam. All was clear. She was responsible and easy-breezy.

Leilani never gave Lip Service any lip about her workload, the pay, or the location, and she never complained about the clients. She was Money's number one and she knew it.

About a year after Money moved from Los Angeles to New York City to be with the husband who ended up leaving her, she brought Leilani into the Lip Service mix. Leilani, half Hawaiian and half who knew, was born and raised in Henderson, Nevada, just outside of Las Vegas. She moved to L.A. to get away from her boyfriend after she caught him cheating on her with a fellow showgirl where she worked at the Flamingo Hotel.

As soon as exotic-looking Leilani hit L.A., she got caught up in the groupie scene, and she liked the glamour and glitz of Hollywood. After being chased by A-list athletes, going out to every trendy club in town, and rarely coming home alone, she often gave up the goodies on the first night, never valuing her worth. She couldn't help but turn heads because of the way she was drawn, like a cartoon, and built like Jessica Rabbit. She had a Sofia Vergara–type body, and a face like Nicole Scherzinger. Word quickly got out among the athletes that she wasn't wife material. They traded their fuck stories of how they'd hit it and quit it, and how stellar her dick-sucking skills were. None of them took her seriously, and no one believed she could ever become famous for any talent besides her good head, even though she chased her goal of fame and fortune by any means necessary.

When Money was first dating the well-known sportscaster whom she later married then divorced, she met Leilani in L.A. at a Lakers game that Money's man was announcing. Leilani was a guest of the top player on the Lakers. She had street smarts and had been on her own since she was fourteen. She was very bright and often joked with Money that she had an I.Q. of 137, which matched her weight. She even made fun of herself to the point of saying she was so smart, she had figured out how to make room in her throat for a Volvo if she needed to. Money told her that was both funny and impressive, and made Leilani an offer years later that she didn't refuse. She moved to New York City to be Money's IC.

Leilani was excited about the Big Apple, the city that never slept. To her, it was more exhilarating than even Las

Vegas. She enjoyed the fact that the men she would service would no longer be athletes, and she'd get paid for it. At the time Leilani came into the fold, it was only Money and Midori. The three together made money hand over fist, and they were booking more hobbyists than they could handle.

Turned out, Leilani's Hawaiian mother was also in the sex-for-money business. She'd take her young daughter along on jobs and make her wait in the car alone until she was done. Leilani's dad was a John. Being pregnant hadn't stopped her mother from screwing men for money, even at seven months. Leilani was born in prison, delivered while her mom served three months for prostitution. Her mother got her back after completing rehab, but she relapsed, and instead of having sex just for the money, she started having sex for drugs.

Her mother overdosed right in front of Leilani when she was fourteen. Leilani was adopted, and after her adoptive father forced her to perform oral sex on him, she ran away at the age of sixteen.

She met a white man named Shawn, her first boyfriend, at a fast food restaurant where she worked. He got her a fake ID, and she was hired first as a waitress in the casinos and then as a showgirl. She told him all about her past life, and he accepted her and promised to be there for her, and be her one and only. He sort of got that right. He was her one and only, but she wasn't his one and only. He was unfaithful.

Ever since she left him and moved to L.A. and then New York, they still communicated over the phone. He felt Leilani needed to come home, back to Vegas, so they could make it work. She kept him at a distance to punish him for cheating. And the more she ignored him, the more he wanted her. Her fear was once he got her back, he'd go right back to wanting what he didn't have, known as the never-enough syndrome.

"I miss you, baby," she told him, talking on the phone just minutes before her appointment with Mr. 51. She would talk to Shawn in certain ways just to string him along on purpose.

"You too, babycakes. When are you coming out?"

"Soon." She sat on the taupe duvet in the bedroom of a chic, apartment-like suite at the Court Hotel on East Thirty-Ninth, applying pink baby lotion onto her legs. She kept an eye on the digital clock along the top of the huge plasma television.

He said, "This time I'm telling you, there's no going back to New York. You come here and that's it."

"I don't know about that. It's like, I've got connections here. The services I offer here as a caterer, well, they pay better. Plus, like I told you, we're not officially back together anyway. You know I still don't trust you, Shawn."

"Babycakes, I guaranteed you, you come back and that'll be it. It'll be you and me."

"You say that, but you can't stop cheating. Like, you'll never be a one-woman man."

"I can. You know I want to be. You come home and I'll prove it. I'm never risking losing you again. I promise."

One loud knock sounded.

Shawn asked immediately, "What was that? Where are you?"

"I'm at home. I was just closing the drawer, trying to get dressed. Look, I'm totally gonna have to run. I have an event I need to supervise in an hour. Gotta get out of here and get across town. I'll, um, call you back later, okay?" She jumped up and headed into the front room.

"Okay. If you say so." He sounded perturbed.

"Bye, Shawn," she said quietly.

He said nothing.

She waited two seconds for his good-bye or the sound of him disconnecting. Hearing nothing, she hung up. She stood before the door and said, "Just one minute." The last syllable of her last word lingered. Then she sent her text. Here.

"Hey," she said, opening the door and smiling brightly just as her phone chimed, signaling her reply text was received.

Mr. 51 said, in his baritone voice, "Good evening, Manhattan." He stepped inside quick. His wheat-colored suit and brown tie looked expensive. His dover-split brown shoes had fine English detailing.

She wore a short white robe and fluffy, white high-heeled slippers. "Oh, look at you. You look nice," she told him, closing the door.

He was six-four, with a politician's charm. "Thanks. Just coming from a meeting not far away from here." He wore wire-rimmed eyeglasses and had a wide nose and faint moustache. His hair was a close fade, slightly graying. He was dapper looking and walked with a youthful swagger, considering he was born in 1954.

"I see."

He eyed her from her head to her toes. "I still don't know why you don't get an agent and make some money with your looks."

"Thanks." She blushed and gave a giggle. "I was going to ask you something. I know you usually book an hour but they said it would be three hours. Is that right?"

He smiled, as if turned on by the sweetness in her tone. "Maybe. It depends." He stepped over to the olive sofa and removed his shoes and suit jacket. "I'm waiting on a call. It could come in fifteen minutes, it could come in three hours, but no longer than that. On standby for an interview."

"Okay. Whatever works for you, I'm totally fine with. Can I get you something to drink, maybe?"

"Just bottled water."

"Okay."

He went straight into the bedroom.

She told him, "I'll be right in. Make yourself comfortable." In escort language that meant *Take off your clothes*.

And he did. Butt-naked comfortable.

When she stepped back in with his chilled bottle of water, Darrell Ellington, New York state senator for the 17th District, current black Republican candidate, wealthy heir to a cosmetics fortune, was nude. He'd pulled back the duvet and his long, strong dick was at full attention.

"Well. Look at you," she said with energy, grinning.

"What I want to do is look at you." His hungry eyes agreed.

"Okay." She blinked fast.

"You need to take that robe off. My wife never undresses in front of me. I hate that." His expression exuded lust. "Let me watch you undress."

"No problem," she said, setting his water down on the nightstand on his side of the bed.

She kicked off one of her shoes and gave a flirty pout, flinging her long, wavy, dark hair. "You're happy to see me, aren't you?" she asked, looking at his dick.

He palmed his penis with his large right hand. "Oh, you know it."

She gave a happy-go-lucky laugh as she kicked off the other shoe and slowly untied the silk belt from around her waist. Her robe opened, and her white crotch-less teddy was revealed. The nipples were cut out, exposing her cinnamon areolas. She let the robe slide from her shoulder, onto the floor, and turned around, showing him a full view of her round ass cheeks, patting her right cheek and looking back at him. Her left cheek had a starburst tattoo.

"Holy ass cleavage. Damn, you're sexy as hell. I wouldn't know how to act if I had you every day. I'd never get any work done."

She looked back at him. "I bet you wouldn't. Considering what you're working with there, we'd be like, totally getting it on for sure."

"You're telling me."

She turned back to face him and slipped off the thin straps of her teddy.

"No. Leave that much of it on. Come here. I want you to sit on my face."

And she did as she was asked. Still wearing her sexy teddy, she stepped to the side of the bed and took the dental dam from its package, unrolling the sheer, rectangular sheet of pink latex. He liked to please her with his mouth and make her come, using his skills that he told Leilani didn't work on his wife.

She climbed on the bed on top of him, straddling his long, lean body, supporting her weight by placing her legs on either side of his shoulders. He scooted down just a bit to allow her to get in the right position for her shaven pussy to meet his mouth. She took a moment to place the dam over her entire vagina as a barrier between his mouth and her pussy, and he brought his hands to her juiced-up vulva to hold the sides of the rubber sheet in place.

He said, while looking up at her with lustful eyes, "Manhattan, I'm gonna work that pussy just the way you like it." He removed his eyeglasses so he could get serious.

"I know you will. You totally do it right every time."

She grabbed her own soft breasts and began to roll her nipples between her index fingers and thumbs, and he went to work, pointing his tongue to her lips and kissing her opening, adding pressure by darting his tongue from side to side, fast. She rubbed her nipples to help the cause, because unbeknownst to him, trying to make her come with his mouth never worked for her, either.

"Oh, yeah. Uh-huh." She reached back with one hand to grab his stiff penis, and stroked it at the same speed he licked her down.

He moved his oral work upward, to her tender pearl, and flattened his tongue, licking back and forth.

She ground into his face and looked down at him, then up at the ceiling. "You're supposed to be the one having fun."

She heard him moan, as if it was more his pleasure than hers.

After a few minutes, Leilani squeezed her nipple tighter and felt it was time to give him her fake orgasm. He slipped his tongue in and out with rapid-fire motions as if trying to make her nature hit its peak. She ceased rubbing his penis and moaned, grinding her pussy clockwise into his giving face. "Uuuhhh, uuuhhh. Yeah. Yeah. Oh. Oh." She pretended the sensation was too much to take, then acted like she was busting a nut against the senator's lips. Her grinding paused but his mouth kept going. She jerked and pressed her hands to the headboard, and then backed away a bit, seeming as if it was all too much, as if she was fighting to remove herself from his mouth's wonders.

He grinned from beneath her as she fell over onto her back, right beside him, rubbing her forehead and panting. "Oh my gosh, that was good. You know I always look forward to seeing you." She reached down to grab the latex that covered her vagina, placing it on top of the empty foil packaging on the nightstand.

"I aim to please," he said, looking proud.

"And so do I." She then asked, as if raring to go, "How do you want it?"

"Blow me." He sounded X-rated certain.

"My pleasure." She came to a stance.

"I don't know how you do it, but damn, you sure do."

"The way I do it is only for you." She had a look on her face like she would never lie.

He looked as if he wished she was truthful. "It is?"

"Yes. Your wish is my command."

Leilani climbed onto the bed and positioned her backside toward the quilted headboard, got on her knees next to him, and instead of mounting his face in a 69, she kept her backside near his chest, approaching his hard penis while keeping her ass up in the air for his close inspection. Instead of taking in his penis from between his legs, she opened her mouth and began sucking the tip from his point of view as he watched closely. He kept one hand along his balls, and his right arm along her back, inspecting every inch of her ass. She caressed his thighs and licked his bulbous head while giving it her full lips.

She breathed in and out of her nose carefully, focusing on her breathing, among other things. She relaxed her jaw, relaxed her neck and shoulders, and opened her mouth as wide as she could, taking in his length and width, and then she used her whole mouth to swallow, letting go of all the constrictions along the way. Her tongue was strong from developing it after much practice with using her fingers, and then dildos to increase her level of tolerance. She'd learned how to use the tip, the blade, the middle, and the back of her tongue. The back of her tongue was what she focused on most when she went extra deep. It was the place where the roof of her mouth suddenly dropped to another level. She focused on allowing the shaft of his penis to rest upon the fall-away portion of her tongue, as opposed to the tip of his dick touching the part of her throat that housed the gagging reflex. Actually, Leilani's gagging reflex was weak. She didn't panic and the back of her tongue didn't react, either, because she'd trained it not to.

She could go down on a penis to the point where a man could actually feel her trying to swallow it. And Mr. 51 was hooked. She was unique, she knew it, and he could swear by it.

She closed her mouth around his penis and brought her lips back up to the head, then all the way back down again.

He stared and held his breath, looking as though he was holding back his ejaculation with all of his might. The veins of his forehead were pronounced; his eyes were wide, his lips were pursed, and his wide nostrils were even more flared. He was silent, like he was in shock, like he'd never seen it before, even though he'd received Manhattan's head many, many times. He still seemed amazed.

She gave short oral strokes of the corona of his head, the widest part of his tip, and then halfway down the outer skin of his shaft and back up to the tip. Then she took her hand and spit as much saliva as she could to ease her motions, keeping her hand on him while she repositioned herself from beside him to move over and in between his legs, laying before him, giving him her sultry, hungry eyes, saying, "This suck-off is totally for you."

He looked at her sexy gaze and his dick throbbed to expand another half-inch. He closed his eyes, going to another place as she continued the rhythm of expert attention that involved both her mouth and her hand on his shaft and base, and tip. All dick bases were covered.

Then he moaned a grandiose moan.

She could taste his pre-cum and she continued, positioning, sucking, going deep by opening wide, giving firm licks while tightening up the pressure with her hands like the tightness of a virgin vagina. She used more saliva and rolled the blade of her tongue to accompany the insides of her mouth while she went deep, and then swallowed again. She sucked the top half while her hands stroked the bottom half, giving pressure with her lips. She sandwiched his shaft with up and down motions and brought her hand to the tip, just under the frenulum, the underside of the head, and then his breaths grew shorter. She then used her hands only.

His eyes popped open. "Oh damn. Here it comes. I'm coming." He sounded like he was in a panic, either welcoming its arrival or dreading it.

She felt the vibrating of his sperm traveling up his shaft by the throbbing stream of pressure against her right hand. He shot his stream up and out and along her fingers in spurts. She watched his flow and so did he, and then he leaned back and closed his eyes as the final drops subsided. He jerked, sensitive to the touch as she still stroked him, massaging his melting spill along his hot shaft.

Unlike hers, there seemed to be nothing fake about his orgasm.

"Damn. Why in the hell can't I have that every day? Uh, uh, uh." With sweat along his forehead, he shook his head and looked at the mess he made.

A while later, after they showered together, they cuddled

in bed, under the covers, watching the local news on television. Just as he reached over to hug her, breaking news was announced by a blonde, female news anchor.

"A member of the U.S. House of Representatives, Eric Walters, has been accused of soliciting a transsexual on an adult website, e-mailing a shirtless photo from his iPhone and sending sex texts. The recipient allegedly discovered Mr. Walters was a married congressman and turned over the e-mail and photos to Channel 2 news. We are investigating further, and we'll have more information on this breaking news story at the top of the hour."

Mr. 51 looked amazed, moving his hand from around Leilani, saying, "Damn. That was stupid. What a dumbass mess." He scooted back to lean against the headboard. "Why would he take pictures and post them anywhere? Why would he take pictures at all?"

"I don't know," she replied, scooting back next to him. She looked at him as if waiting for him to say more.

He saw her face. "You're giving me a look."

She shook her head fast. "Oh, no. Not even. Believe me, I am not one to judge."

"And you think I shouldn't judge too, right?"

"No, not at all. I totally wasn't thinking that."

He took the remote and turned the volume down, speaking with a suddenly deeper voice. "I know my life has changed with this campaign. I know I can't do what most people do. My life is an open book now. I have a wife and stepson to think about, too. Things are getting scrutinized now more than ever. Soon, I won't be able to go anywhere. I've gotta keep my nose clean. Don't think I don't know all of that."

"Really. I've never thought that. You're fine."

Sounding more certain than he looked, he said, "I'm pretty sure this is my last time doing this."

"Okay. I understand. But are you sure?"

He reached over and grabbed his bottled water and took a swig. He swallowed and said, "I don't know. All I know is, my sex drive is too high for one woman. It always has been. I think I've toned it down, but it's funny, my wife doesn't think so."

"I totally think you have a healthy sex drive."

"She'd hardly call it healthy. She tries her best to satisfy me. Sometimes twice a day. Thing is, our schedules are so different, and I'm getting busier." He set the bottle back down.

"I'll bet."

He glanced at the TV again. "But anyway, this guy, this Eric Walters cat, he just was sloppy. Sloppy won't work in politics."

"Well, you can bet Lip Service is careful. You can trust us."

"I can imagine there'd be a lot at stake for you all." He folded his hands along his chest.

"True." She placed her hand on his.

He asked, "You still thinking about going back home? Being with your guy?"

"He's not my guy. He's my ex, for sure." She got a bit closer. "Not ready to leave New York. Working for Lip Service is fine. It's hard to walk away from."

"Would you ever do it on your own? Here or in Vegas. Actually, there might be even more money in Vegas. All of this is legal there, right?"

"I really think that it is legal in some areas, but it's less lucrative. There's not as much risk out there. I mean, there's an escort service flyer handed out to tourists every step they take. Not sure if I'd prefer to be on my own."

Suddenly, his phone rang and he grabbed it, sending the caller straight to voice mail. It rang again and he sent it to voice mail again. Just as he began to look back up he asked, as if it was routine, "You think maybe I can get some pussy now?"

She answered quickly, "That's why I'm here."

"Yes, it is." He pulled the sheets away from his body to expose his hard-on, and pressed 1 for his voice mail. He listened and then sent a text, before dialing his secretary. "Got your message. Thanks for telling me. Yeah. I'm good. Listen. Send a car to pick me up at the Court Hotel in thirty minutes to take me to Maxwell's Steakhouse on Forty-Eighth. Please make a reservation under my name for two. If my wife calls, let her know I got her message, please, that I sent her a text, and that I'll meet her for dinner at 7:30. Bye." He hung up and set the phone down on the bed between them.

"No meeting after all?" Leilani asked.

"No. CNN canceled my interview to cover the latest Eric Walters sex text madness. He's about to issue a statement of apology, and resign."

He stood from the bed and went to the bathroom, dick stiff like he could hang a towel on it.

Leilani glanced over as a new text came in on his phone.

> Got your text. Sorry you couldn't pick up the phone when I called. Glad you're enjoying your Mom. Tell her I said hi. Love you, my Mr. President.

He said from the bathroom, "If my dick would go down I could pee and then get that pussy before I leave. If not, I'll be at home in the shower tonight choking my dick in your name, wishing I did."

She smiled and put the phone on the nightstand, and adjusted herself so that when he came out, he could see her on all fours.

Moments later, after he flushed the toilet and washed his hands, his penis saw her and bounced its way back into hard state. "Damn."

She saw his dick excitement. "Wow. You really are something. Like, totally amazing."

He took a condom and immediately penetrated her, fucking her deep like it was sexercise, bucking her by using repeated hip strength with such intense force it looked like he was riding a bull.

She ground her hips back at him in exact measure.

He said, as if on a wild high, "This is the fucking life."

MSNBC reports the governor of New Mexico, Clinton Ware, contemplated throwing his hat in the ring for president. However, recent accusations of sexual harassment during his term have swayed his decision. Senator Darrell Ellington and his campaign have blasted the governor, stating that such accusations against him would cause his entry into the race to be short lived.

Four

Kemba

Friday—June 17, 2011

Kemba Price's story was a little different from the others. His Protestant mother disapproved of her one and only son's questionable lifestyle. Price was the name he gave himself when he came to the states. He was born Kemba Abais, in a town called Mombasa, off the coast of Kenya.

When he was a teen, he'd sneak out of their apartment late at night to play gigolo, meeting the wealthy American tourist women at the Indian Ocean Beach Club resort. They were mainly lonely, wealthy, adventurous, older women who traveled for vacation sex. Usually white women. They'd come to town looking for a good time with African men, even though prostitution was illegal. He knew for a fact that one in five single women who visited from rich countries were looking to hook up. The sex tourism industry there was booming, much like it was for men who looked for vacation sex in Brazil.

His Kenyan mother couldn't quite put her finger on what her tall, dark, and mature-looking son was doing with his time. But one thing was for sure, whatever it was, he wasn't stopping. She threatened to lock him out of their one-bedroom apartment, where he slept on the living room sofa, if he didn't come home at a decent hour. One night she found the stash of cash he'd hidden under one of the cushions, but she couldn't get an answer out of him as to where it came from. But by the next night when he arrived back home, his mother was gone. And inside of a brown paper bag was all of his money, along with a gold and white Bible. He was devastated. Christian or not, she left her son and moved on with her life. He wasn't just a child abandoned by his Egyptian father, whom he'd only met once when he was twelve, but he was also abandoned by his mother when he was nineteen—abandoned because she couldn't deal with her suspicions of him being a prostitute.

Beryl Thomas was one of the white women he serviced. Twenty years his senior, she was trying to get her groove back in Kenya. She changed everything for him and made him her studly, six-foot-six, dread-wearing sex king. Then she made him an offer he couldn't refuse: one summer, five years after his mother left, she brought him back to New York City with her.

Months later, Money spotted him at the Mark Hotel on the East Side and added him as her one and only male employee, after so many requests had come in to Lip Service from females looking for straight men. And of course Money had to taste-test Kemba for herself. She approved big time and put him on the payroll immediately, naming him Harlem.

He quickly became a paid call guy, actually living in Harlem, the heart of Manhattan, in a grand condo. It was a penthouse suite for which his sugar momma, Beryl, paid five thousand per month out of her advertising agency executive money, in a nineteen-unit luxury building called the Lenox Grand, complete with hardwood floors, a chef's kitchen, and vanilla marble tile throughout. Her style was all white with silver accents. The only spot of color was a huge, orange shag rug in the sunken living room.

They were in an open relationship, and all he had to do was service her and be available when she needed him. She accepted the fact that he was an escort. Though they did manage to do what needed to be done to please each other, and say what needed to be said to each other, they made sure to get along, knowing it was hard enough to deal with the straight-laced societal standards of fidelity. Their standards were anything but straight-laced.

The rules they had were mainly hers and he obliged.

Both benefitted greatly.

She got her boy-toy stud who was hung like a horse.

And he got to live like a king and not even have to spend his own money.

It was ten in the morning when Beryl greeted him as he stepped into the kitchen area from their master bedroom. Their sprawling condo smelled like maple bacon and coffee.

"Hi, there," she said to him.

"Hey." His voice was deep.

"What do you have going on today?" Sitting at the bar on a white leather stool, Beryl split her focus between her iPhone and Kemba as he adjusted the strap on his gym bag, standing tall before her, looking like the hunk that he was.

"Not much. A client at midnight." Kemba's words were drizzled with a hint of Swahili.

"Why so late?" She took a crisp strip of bacon from the white saucer before her and bit it.

"Somebody's sneaking out, I guess. A married woman, ya know."

She chewed, swallowed, and smirked. "Oh, really? She's going to sneak out of bed to get dicked down and then slip back into bed before her man wakes up, huh?" She sipped hazelnut coffee from her ceramic cup and crossed her healthy legs. She wore white silk pajamas, and her jet black hair was draped along her wide shoulders.

"I don't ask. All I know is, it'll be quick."

"Okay." She nodded. "You're not having breakfast this morning?" She smiled.

"Nope. Plus you know I don't eat swine."

"There's oatmeal in there. I could make you a smoothie if you want."

"I'll grab some juice at the gym. I've gotta catch this Insanity class. It starts in ten minutes."

"Okay." She watched him switch his bag to his other shoulder and asked, "Will I see you later on?"

"Maybe so. You don't have anything going on yourself, hey?"

"No. Not today. I might get away for the weekend with Ryan, though."

"I see" was all he said.

"Yes, that's what I might do." She bounced her leg and looked at him.

He shrugged. "Okay."

"So, don't you even want to know where?"

"Nope."

"You know, it would be nice if you'd ask every now and then, Kemba. At least act like you care." She took another sip. Her happy level decreased.

"I do care. I know who Ryan is. You're safe. I know what he does for you. I know you're going away. No secrets. Done deal."

"Yep. Done deal." She nodded and gave him a sarcastic wink.

He smiled. "Good. You have a good day, now."

"You too."

"Love you."

"Love you, too." Her words were weak and she gave her focus to her phone.

Kemba placed his hand on the vanilla skin of Beryl's arm as he leaned in to kiss her on the lips.

She puckered and acted lazy until his lips met hers. He gave her a smack and her eyes showed she could possibly warm up. She placed her hand between his legs, taking hold of his heavy penis beneath his sweatsuit. He was at half attention.

Kemba was very large, just the way Beryl liked her men. She claimed she couldn't feel anything that wasn't a donkey dick that required a double-extra large-sized condom. She liked the Mandingo type, and she had one in Kemba.

He grinned as he moved her hand.

She told him, "It's okay. I'll get mine later. Maybe I'll stop by after your class and pick you up so we can go have a healthy lunch somewhere. What about the Uptown Juice Bar? Then we can come back here and relax before your appointment with Ms. Sneaky-Ass Wife."

"That's fine. Give me a couple of hours."

"Okay. Call me when you're just about done and I'll swing by."

"Done deal."

With a Roman nose, and skin as dark as Wesley Snipes's, Kemba stood in his black and white Nikes, wearing a black bandana over his head. His dreads hung down his wide back.

He took a step toward the door, then looked back toward her again, giving her a look as though he was thinking twice. "Naw. You'll get yours now."

Her eyes smiled.

He headed back her way and she instantly opened her robe, showing that she was braless, wearing only white panties.

Kemba put his bag down and gripped her breasts with his large, dark hands, brought his chiseled face to her cleavage, then squeezed them together. She gave a look of approval and placed her hands along the side of his face. He put his mouth to her left nipple and spread his generous lips around it, meeting the tawny peak with his long tongue, licking her as her tip hardened against his lips. He kissed her nipple like it was her clit, and began sucking it, flicking it, in and out of his mouth while massaging her right breast. He brought both breasts together and aligned both nipples, placing his mouth on the right nipple, then the left, the right, then the left, back and forth quickly. He began sucking the right one, when she said, "You are so damn hot."

Beryl rubbed her waxed pussy beneath the lace fabric of her underwear.

Kemba sucked harder and nursed on her breast, suckling it as though it was nourishment, and teasing it.

She leaned her head back and said, "Oh, baby, shit. You're about to make Momma come." Her self-pleasing hand movement sped up.

At that second, he ceased his mouth and hand grip, leaned

over to pick up his bag, and headed to the door, smiling a teasing good-bye. She gave him a look as if to say they'd definitely finish it off later.

He closed the door, and readjusted his pants to make room for his long member, now three-quarters hard. He took the elevator, nodded to the doorman, and walked down the street the short distance to his sanctuary, Planet Fitness, on the corner of 126th and Lenox.

Just as he approached the popular gym he glanced across the street at a restaurant, and his eyes zeroed in on a woman as she exited from a shiny, black stretch limousine. Her driver held the door open. She was tall, slender, and just as dark as he was, dressed in all black.

She was very conservative.

Very regal.

And very sexy.

She didn't turn in his direction, yet he examined her backside and made a mental note of her figure as she headed into the soul food restaurant called Sylvia's. Then she was gone.

He slowed his pace, kept looking for a lingering moment, even after her visual disappeared.

He shook his head and went inside, but not before he turned back around for a last glance of where she was.

And then he heard, "Oh excuse me, dude." This from a red-boned man, who looked startled as he jumped back a quarter inch to keep from bumping Kemba with his arm.

"Hey man, no problem. That was on me." Kemba froze in place. He knew the man's face. He'd seen him before. And he knew his name. "I wasn't looking where I was going."

"No problem." They sidestepped each other for about three seconds, and the man laughed. "Sorry, dude."

"Naw. It's cool. I'll go first," Kemba said.

"You do that." The man gestured with his hand.

"Thanks," Kemba said, as the man held open the glass door.

"My pleasure." The man watched Kemba.

Kemba looked back again, saw him looking, smiled, and headed inside. *Damn*, he said to himself. *Shit*. He couldn't figure out what it was that caused him to be full-on, 100 percent rigid in his pants. Was it the woman across the street, or the man he knew as Romeo?

About two hours later, Beryl waited outside in a taxi just as Kemba came out, white towel around his neck, gym bag slung over his shoulder. He stepped toward the cab just as he noticed the big black limousine across the street start to slowly pull away from the curb. He kept his eyes on the person in the backseat and made his way into the taxi and took a deep breath as that person's eyes found their way to him.

Their eyes locked.

He sat in the backseat next to Beryl and adjusted his bag just as the limo pulled down the street.

Then he realized both he and his woman had noticed the long black car with the tall, black woman dressed in black.

He said, "Hey."

Beryl, wearing all white, turned to him in silence after watching the car disappear, saying nothing.

Mrs. Ursula Ellington, political wife, had the attention of the both of them.

Libertarian candidate Dean Winters, who entered the race for president last month, has dropped out due to news that his wife has a terminal illness. He and his family are requesting privacy at this time. Winters's exit could propel Darrell Ellington ahead as both candidates are from the state of New York.

Five

∞

Money

Sunday—June 19, 2011

Money sat on her terrace under the covered gazebo behind her elegant home. She leaned back against the forest green wrought-iron patio chair and admired the fabulous garden setting.

Her backyard was framed by blooming violet crabapple and white dogwood trees, along with an emerald lawn, and yellow and lavender tulips that lined the S-shaped brick walkway. A pair of gray European Starling birds flew from tree to tree and then flew away, chirping with carefree splendor. Melodic.

The summer air was warm and still, and the sky was azure. Cloudless.

Her Pinot Grigio was chilled and she was in momentary heaven, just like a regular person. Just as it should've been before necessity became the motherhood of her wealth.

She was a madam, she reminded herself constantly.

She was taking money from financially privileged people and setting them up to have undercover sex with her employees, promising to never tell on them. And one of her employees was her very own sister. *Shit.*

She hadn't yet spoken to Midori since their conversation at the Algonquin. She knew her to be a pouter, and she expected Midori not to be the one to call first. But she'd need to check up on her before too long, just to let her know she was watching her. Even though her sister claimed to be willing and able to keep her boyfriend, Virgil Daye, in line, Money doubted it. He was a problem, but a small-time problem, much like Bailey Brenner, who'd been quiet. Money's big-time concern was the one person she really didn't want around her sister, and that was Romeo.

Romeo had been a sticky thorn in Money's side ever since she moved to New York.

Midori had a major argument with her parents and left home after their mom and dad moved to Atlanta. New York City was where she landed. At eighteen years old, with no connections and no money, Midori was quickly recruited onto the streets by Romeo. He kept her there for about a year, until Money's divorce and the creation of Lip Service. That was when Money began looking for her. After a text message from Midori to Money from a pay-as-you-go number in the 212 area code, Money tracked her down by enlisting a favor from one of her clients. Cell phone tower records led to the address of a seedy motel on the Lower East Side.

One hot summer evening, Money went looking for her sister and spotted her not far away from the motel. Money recognized her from behind. Midori was sturdy and bow-legged, and had a plump backside just like their mother's.

Midori stood next to a lamppost on the corner of Forsyth and Houston Streets, at the side of a hotel called the Gem.

She stood next to a short women with pink hair that was teased up into a beehive. Both were dressed in miniskirts and corsets, looking very obvious.

Money approached her sister and the woman. "Midori."

The other woman spoke first. "Who's asking?"

Money gave her no eye contact whatsoever. "Will you excuse us, please?"

The woman said with a high-pitched edge, "Excuse me dot com."

"No. Excuse you right on away from me. I was not talking to you."

The woman's voice dropped to baritone. "Well, I'm talking to you, okay?" She stepped closer and put her hand up, rolled her neck, popped her lip and her tongue. "What?" She gave two snaps up.

Money realized it was a man in drag. "Look, Shenaynay. Back off. This is none of your damn concern, so go ahead and make your money. But back the fuck off. Now"

She aimed her finger between Money's eyes like she was pulling the trigger. "Bang."

Money took a step back and looked her up and down.

Midori looked at her friend, "It's cool. I'm good."

The man in drag cut his eyes at them both. "Okay. Whatever's clever. But this chick better watch herself. Bitch-ass, high-society, no-lip-having, bug-eyed, corny-ass-earring-wearing, bucktooth, stanky-ass ho better recognize. Bang." He used a nod of his head for an exclamation point.

Money asked, "What the hell?"

Midori looked only at Money. "What do you want?"

The man-woman slowly headed to the front of the hotel, turned around and again pointed his finger as though pulling the trigger, then disappeared around the corner.

Money looked at her sister and immediately asked, "Where've you been?"

Her reply was snappy. "In my skin. Why?"

"Well, we've missed you."

Midori gave a chuckle. She wore red lipstick and long lashes. Her short blonde hair needed to be dyed as her brown roots were taking over. She was showing cleavage for days. "You have got to be kidding me."

Money put her hand on her sister's upper arm. "Come with me. I'm here to take you home."

Midori snatched it back. "No."

"Midori, you really don't need to do this."

"I don't need to do what? Make money like this? Well, I'll be damned. Look who the hell's talking."

Money asked, "What do you mean?" confirming that her sister had heard about her new line of work.

"I know what you do. Don't come around here like you're gonna save the day, when your ass needs to be saved, too. You're no better than me. Maybe you've got some fancy setup and I'm on the streets, but there's no difference, Money. None."

"You're right. I'm sure you've heard about my life."

"I have. Big city, small circles."

"Okay. Fair. But you can do better than this."

"This is just fine."

Money nodded. "Okay. So, tell me why you didn't return my text messages. You sent a message from a number that doesn't even have voice mail setup. "

"That's just the way I like it."

Money took half a step and said, "Come on. Come with me."

Midori stayed in place. "No."

Money faced her sister and folded her arms. "Look. Okay. I'm sorry for what happened."

"What are you talking about?"

"For Mom. For Dad. What Dad did. What Mom did. What Jimmy did."

Midori looked away. "I don't know what you mean."

Money got closer. "Oh, you know. But that's not what matters. What matters right now is that you come with me."

A male voice suddenly asked, "Can I help you?"

Money replied before she even turned around. "No." And then she faced him.

A bald-headed man with a tinge of Puerto Rico in his face stood before her and said firmly, "Back off. As a matter of fact, get lost." He wore a black dress shirt and black jeans. Very non-pimpish.

"It's a free country."

"No. It's not. It'll cost you."

Midori made her way over to stand behind him.

His look let Money know her sister feared him.

Money asked, "Romeo, right?"

"Queens, right? Oh, my bad. Midori here says it's Money Watts."

"Very good. And as far as what it'll cost me. You tell me."

"Oh, you want her for an hour. You want some pussy from your own sister?" He grinned big, as if he amused himself.

"Very funny. You know good and damn well what I'm talking about."

"I'm not hearing it. We've got to get back to work. Leave."

Money gave Midori a smile, then looked at him and

frowned. "Listen, I'll be in this hotel. This one right here." She pointed to the building. "I'll be here for two days and you can call and ask for me. When you do, just let me know how much. I'll get it to you. I promise."

He laughed. "Oh? You must not know this is my family." He looked back at Midori and then at Money. "Midori is mine."

"Everything has its price." Money again smiled at her sister. "Midori, I love you," she said, walking away toward the front door of the hotel. The hooker in drag was half a block down, giving Money the finger, and Money returned the gesture.

Turned out the next morning, twenty thousand in hundreds was all it took to get Romeo off their backs. Midori and Money caught a cab to Money's place in Queens. By the next week, Midori was making her own money. Three months later she had moved into her own place on the Upper East Side, where she met Senator Ellington's son, Virgil Daye, at a function she attended where she was supposed to escort an IT executive who was a no-show. Midori was off the streets, had met a man, but couldn't come clean to him about how she was making ends meet.

Since then, Midori knew Romeo had been keeping his eye on her. He made it known when he left the hotel with his cash that he would one day get her back.

And upon that reflection, Money's cell phone rang, shifting her mind to the present. "Yes," she answered, now having moved from her backyard to the exercise room in her home. She was beginning a three-mile walk on her elliptical machine, a towel around her neck.

"Hi," her booker said.

"What's up?"

"You just had a call come in on the booking line. Romeo wants you to call him. He said you changed your number. Said it's very important."

Money slowed her pace. "Are you kidding me?"

"No."

"The nerve."

"He said he needs to hear from you today."

"What's the number?"

"212-555-5212."

Money filed it away in her head. "Lord. Thanks. Text me the rundown for today."

"I just did."

"Oh, okay. Thanks." Money hung up. "Speaking of the devil." She gave a deep sigh and kept at her workout, focusing on her phone while she dialed the number, making sure to block her number.

"Talk to me." He answered fast, halfway through the first ring, sounding like a DJ.

"What?"

"What, what?"

"This is Money. What do you want?" She wiped her sweaty brow with her towel.

"Oh. There ya go. Okay. Good, girl."

"Romeo. Cut it. This is not good and you know it. Phone calls between us are stupid and very unnecessary. Please don't call my booker again."

He got straight to the point. "What's it gonna take to get Kemba over here?"

"Kemba?" She downshifted her pace even more.

"Yeah. Your boy. Oh, excuse me, Harlem."

She gave a sigh and a laugh. "Not up for discussion. Besides, why would he wanna go from me to you, with your ghetto-ass dime-store operation when he can live the Bergdorf Goodman lifestyle? That's just plain crazy."

"Call it what you want. I want you to know we're getting upscale over here. Riding up on your ass."

"Well, at least you know you're behind me."

"Ha. I could ride your ass from the front, too."

"I doubt that. The answer is no."

"How much? Your twenty thousand back. Or maybe thirty. I know he's pulling it in, making you a very rich bitch."

"I'm not your bitch, nigga. And Kemba is not a damn car. No trading, no discussing value, nothing. None of your damn business."

"Okay, but, honestly, I gave you one, now it's time for you to give me one. Or, I can just take him."

"If you believe that, then why in the hell are you calling me?" She sped up her pace again.

"To let you know I've got my eyes on him. And honestly, I really haven't taken my eyes off your little sister either. But, I would if—"

"Stop. You're telling me you'll give up on Midori if you get Kemba. They are people, dumbass, not trading cards. Neither one is up for any negotiating so just fuck off."

"You don't want me to—" The line disconnected after Money slid her finger over the screen.

"That is one stupid thug if he thinks he can come in on Lip Service and start stealing away my employees. He cannot play that recruiting game on Kemba like this is the NCAA. Kemba has proven himself," she said aloud.

She thought back to when Kemba was involved in an altercation with a love-starved woman whose husband was left impotent due to diabetes. The man had noticed a new pep in his wife's step and read the messages in her BlackBerry.

He found out about a hotel location she had scheduled in her calendar for the following night, so he showed up and waited. When his wife pulled up, he checked into the room next door and listened to his woman get run through. After he couldn't take it any longer, he banged on the adjoining door, shaking the knob and fighting to unlatch it. "Bitch, get your slutty ass up and open this door, now."

He damn near knocked down the wall, stormed from his room to their room door, and banged, cursed, kicked, and screamed. "Open this motherfucking door, now. I will kill you and that fool you're fuckin'. Open this goddamn door. Now!"

A hotel guest called the police, but hotel security showed up first. The woman never admitted to paying Kemba, never said anything about calling a booker first. And Kemba said nothing, either, only that he'd met her at the store, they'd talked on the phone, and, after having a drink, ended up in the hotel room. *To this day, I still book her and Kemba. And the woman is still married to the same impotent man.*

Money came back to the present and spoke to herself again. "Romeo's ass is the thorn in my side. Offering thirty thousand for Kemba. Please. I'm a millionaire."

The Republican candidates gear up for tonight's debate in Manchester, New Hampshire, where Kalin Graves, the mayor of Philadelphia, was born. CNN will cover the debate. The Republican presidential hopeful does not support same-sex marriage, which is expected to be a hot topic. Same-sex marriage is illegal in Pennsylvania, but became legal in his home state of New Hampshire in 2010.

Six

Money

Monday—July 11, 2011

Money was dressed and ready for her expected guest. She sat on the sofa in the living room when her doorbell rang. Stepping toward the door, she yelled, "Who is it?"

"It's me," her man, Jamie, yelled back.

Jamie Bitters, a bigwig with the sheriff's department before he got sticky fingers, would come by maybe once a week and hang out with Money. He was the only person she really chilled with who wasn't shocked by what she did. They could talk about miscellaneous bullshit, like stock market rates or sports, or watch the latest episode of *Love & Hip-Hop* together. It was less than a love affair but more than a friendship.

"What's up?" she asked after letting him in.

"Not much. You?"

"Oh, nothing much either."

He placed a plastic bag on dining room table.

"Chinese?"

"You know it."

She nodded. "That's what's up."

They enjoyed their meal, sipped on wine, and sat in her living room watching TV. She didn't bring up Romeo. She just lived like an everyday woman who had a man that came by. Average stuff.

After a few hours went by, his attention went from the television to her body. He began kissing her neck, rubbing her bare legs, and playing with her breasts. Before long, they got up from the couch and headed to her bedroom. For her, it was private dick time because she wanted to fuck, not because she had to.

He stood at attention next to her canopy bed, which had ivory sheers draped from the top to the floor. She lay on her back with her legs over the edge, a pillow under her hips.

The room was dimly lit. The iPod speakers shared the smooth sounds of the tail end of D'Angelo's "Brown Sugar."

Jamie hummed along as he worked at choreographing their sex session.

Money followed his lead, just enjoying the escape from reality.

Upon the side of her bed, he lifted her brown legs and held them straight up in front of him, moving himself so that his dickhead was lined up with her pussy. He gave a deep thrust with a jerk of his hips to plunge his entire penis inside of her. Her legs rested along his chest. He stroked them and licked the heels of her bare feet, sucking on her toes while fucking her pussy.

Then they got up and he arranged their bodies so that
they were on the settee at the foot of the bed, him on his
back with his legs on each side. She sat on top of him, facing
his feet. She looked down and rubbed his balls, squeezing
them together. He massaged her firm ass cheeks while she
rubbed her clit. She released her creamy white femininity
on his dick, masturbating while fucking him at the same
time.

The song was now "How Does It Feel?"

"Fucking good," she said from out of nowhere, as if replying to D'Angelo directly and not speaking to Jamie.

They ended up standing, with her leaning over the bed,
him spreading her legs as far apart as he could, guiding his
penis to penetrate her again. She pushed her hips backward
toward him in reply to the sensation his entry brought. He
was deep and he pulled out, yanking off his condom as he
spewed cum on her ass cheeks.

"You're the best," she told him.

His reply was "No, you are."

And as much as they were in sync in the bedroom, their
after-sex time in the bedroom never came. As usual, he left
right after they finished. They never did the cuddle, spooning, and pillow talk bonding. It was understood and it was
all good. She knew he just wasn't that into her. And she just
wasn't that into him, either.

Besides, she had anticipated it and had made an appointment for Mr. 11 to call at three in the morning from Manchester, New Hampshire.

Jamie had left at 3:02.

"Hi." Mr. 11 whispered as usual, careful not to wake up his
wife.

"You ready?"

"I am."

"You got that pretty dick in your hand?" Money asked, sounding phone-sex-operator erotic.

"I do."

"Good boy. You know I wish I was there with you, licking your balls with a tongue scrub while you stroke that pretty dick. Watching you watch me suck your ball sac and teabag you, bringing my tongue down to the part where your balls end and your asshole begins. Inserting my finger in your ass and finding your spot while you feel your blood racing and your dick filling up faster and faster, looking at me like I'm a dream. Like it can't be real that you could feel so damn good."

"Uh-huh. Uh-huh." He sounded anxious and horny.

"Don't say anything. I know you can't talk. Just listen to me get you off like you like it. I don't get to do this much anymore now that things have changed for you. But baby, you are my favorite and if I was your woman, I'd put you to bed by swallowing you every night, and you'd wake up with me between your legs, sucking you off with a good-morning hello, giving you my wet, warm mouth to swallow you down. I'd leave the covers over my head so you wouldn't even see me, you'd just look down and see someone going to work to please you, then you could lay back and fantasize about who it is in your mind. I want you to grip that cock in your hand and imagine me sitting my juicy pussy on that cock bareback, grinding on your dick while you squeeze my ass tight and shove yourself as far up into me as you can. Imagine someone else in the room, maybe even a man, sucking your nipple and then kissing you while I ride you. I know you'd like that. I know you brought that shit up before. I know you'd like a dick in your mouth while I ride you. He'd straddle your face and he'd watch your lips stretch along his dick while you'd feel me behind him, jumping off of your dick and then taking it into my mouth, tasting my own juices. I'd hear you moan and I'd hear him moan and just as he would say he was about to come, your cum would ooze into my mouth."

Mr. 11 moaned and grunted, then moaned again. His next grunts were three small ones in a row, deep and fast. "Ugh, ugh, ugh."

"Yeah, that's it. That's how you like it. That's how we do it."

"Ahhh." He panted and gave a sigh. Then, as if he recovered that quickly, he simply said, keeping his low tone, "Nice. Gotta go."

"Ciao, baby. Be good."

He hung up.

Money sent a text to her booker. **Done.**

She said aloud, "Hell, I might just switch to phone sex. At fifteen hundred a pop, that's the quickest, easiest job around."

Two minutes later, the booker called Money.

"Yes."

"Mr. 11 just called. He'll be in town soon. He asked for an out-call, but with a guy this time."

"Okay." Money was not surprised.

"And he's asked for a black one. You think Kemba?"

Money replied right away, "Oh no."

"Not even gay for pay?"

"No." She paused. "I'll work on it. I might even bring in a bi guy. This isn't the first time we've had this request. I'll let you know. Bye."

Money had gotten her own tune-up, made some money, and had added a new item to her to-do list: Getting Mr. 11,

Kalin Graves, the mayor of Philly who was running for president, a bi guy.

But she hadn't forgotten about Romeo. Keeping him away from her employees, mainly Kemba, was now at the top of her list.

Senator Darrell Ellington continues to shine as a standout during the presidential debates. Some say his charisma and power of persuasion will serve him well in garnering votes. His position on faith and family values has gone over well among conservative voters.

Seven

∽

Midori

Thursday—July 21, 2011

Midori averaged one to two clients per day, which could add up to a minimum of fourteen thousand dollars per week if she averaged a thousand a pop. She'd wished for money before, having no choice but to depend on Romeo giving it to her whenever he got good and ready, but now that cash wasn't an issue, she seemed focused on what it would take to get past her demons and live a normal life with the white picket fence, husband, two kids, and dog.

If there was any prospect of who she felt would learn to love her, it would've been Virgil Daye—that is, if she hadn't been lying about what she did for a living, but even he had backed off lately. She knew in her heart of hearts that there would probably be no real future with him, that the stepson of a presidential candidate could never marry a hooker. Most men would judge her, but maybe there'd be someone who wouldn't, and they'd live happily ever after. Maybe the sex would bond them and blind them and they'd want more. Just maybe.

The thing with her and Virgil was they hadn't yet had sex. So the bonding theory was not in the mix, which to her signaled he must've genuinely cared about spending time with her, taking her out, laughing with her, and being her companion, for reasons beyond what everyone else wanted her for. Actually, Virgil was a twenty-eight-year-old virgin. He wanted to wait until he was married to have sex. Though deep down she knew that even though they hadn't consummated their relationship, the virgin and the hooker could never be a match made in heaven.

She ended up having lunch with Virgil and gave him his beloved ink pen. They'd talked a few times since then, though she felt he was unusually distant. They hadn't seen each other in over a month. But tonight he wanted to come by. She promised to call after her last real estate showing of the day. He was on standby. And he appeared to be very anxious to see her, which made her happy.

It was late afternoon, almost rush hour, and she took a taxi to Park Avenue South and Twenty-Ninth Street, for a 6:00 appointment in a luxurious room at the Gansevoort Hotel.

Mr. 21 lived there. She'd had regular appointments with him for the past year. He always insisted she come to him. He was a Homeland Security executive, single, and was the one she called the "bitch" man, because he had such a fascination with the word. He also had another fascination.

She'd arrived at his chic apartment and headed straight to his bed. She stretched her hands back toward the silver studded headboard, wearing nothing but a smile. He liked her to lay nude first.

He sat upon the silver leather sofa. The glowing embers
from the granite fireplace added to the allure. He wore boxer
shorts and his dark penis poked through the opening, aimed
straight at her. He looked at her and she just looked back.
She knew to say nothing.

Finally, he spoke with his regular kinkiness, always
smelling like he wore too much Armani Code cologne.
"Look at the pretty-ass bitch in my bed." The only sound
other than their voices was the sound of the shower running
in the bathroom.

"Yes, I am. And waiting for you."

"Oh, you know I'm gonna have to fuck that shit."

She tried her best to look excited. "Yes, you are."

He stood, grabbing a condom from the chrome table and
letting his dick wear it. He stepped along the wood floor of
the bedroom. She propped a purple pillow under her head.

"Turn over so I can see your fat ass."

She obliged.

"That is a pretty damn sight there. Bitch's ass is big and
round and young."

"I know you're an ass man."

He watched himself in the wall mirror while mounting her
as she lay on her stomach. As he inserted himself, she eased
him in by doing a circle grind, milking him with a tight grip.
She made sure to keep her legs straight while taking his dick
for a ride.

She ground and fucked, and felt his penetration wall to
wall. Though he was short, he had a wide dick. It always hit
just the right spot to put pressure on her G spot, causing more
of a sensation than she really wanted from him. She tended
to play off her sensations until she was ready for his finale,
but she was feeling it.

He said suddenly, "Okay, bitch. Get in the shower."

They both got up and stepped into the chocolate-tiled, open glass shower together.

His penis was at full attention. She faced the wall behind him. He stood behind her and rubbed his penis on her ass. He then took a step back and turned the water down, all the way to cold.

"Ahhh." He tightened his jaw and clenched his teeth, seeming to make sure the sprays of water hit his dick.

She knew what he was about to do. What he'd always do. What he paid double for. It was what made her dread seeing him.

It was his machismo water sports game that did something for him. Something that continued to prove to her that men rented women for sex not just because they couldn't get laid, but also so they could live out the fantasies that most women would judge them for. They paid so someone would play along.

He turned back toward her as his dick had become semi-flaccid and stood with his legs far apart.

She closed her eyes.

He released a stream of pee on her backside while she stood, wishing with all her might it was over.

The temperature of his pee was warm and the flow was strong.

"You like that shit, bitch?"

"Uh-huh." Lying was part of the game, as was resisting the urge to turn around and slap the shit out of him.

He didn't even ejaculate. She always figured he'd do that later. He then said what he always said after he did his business, "You can leave after your shower." He stepped out and she turned the water up to hot, wanting to wash off his cologne and his urine and his presence. She turned up the force of the spray, washing, wishing, wondering. *Why?*

Fifteen minutes later she was in the cab.

As if it wasn't bad enough that she had to put up with such disrespect for the money, she got a text from freaky Bailey Brenner, requesting an appointment with her directly at midnight.

Can't was her only reply.

Bailey replied, Why not?

She didn't respond. She texted Virgil, Be home in an hour. See you then.

Virgil replied, C u then.

She texted, Can't wait.

When she got home, she tried her best to get herself together in time for Virgil's arrival. Not only her body, again making sure to scrub herself clean from her client's degrading urine, but also her mind, getting the word *bitch* out of her head. Getting herself in the mood to act like she'd been selling houses, not pussy. And not her self-esteem.

By eight that evening, she sat in the living room of her one-bedroom Upper East Side apartment at the Lucerne.

Wearing a shorts set, she stepped barefoot along the butterscotch carpet of her living room and headed to the limestone entryway at the front door.

"What's up?" Virgil asked, as she opened the door.

"Hi." She gave a half smile and hugged him.

He hugged her back, walking in as she closed the door. He made his way to her sectional, looking normal, but as soon as he sat his face went serious.

She noticed the change as she sat beside him. "What?"

He said, flat out, "I need to say something important. I've

wondered what was up with you. I've wondered about you for a while now. And I can't believe you put me and my family in the position we're in." It was like every word was rehearsed.

She angled her stare. "Virgil. What are you talking about?"

"Midori, I'm done. With us."

"Why?"

"Just know that."

"You came over here to break up with me?"

He sat forward with his elbows along his knees. "We were never together really. Just dating. I never told you I wanted a relationship."

She looked as though she begged to differ. "We both know the deal. We're a couple. You wouldn't come here using the term *done* if in your opinion nothing was ever started. That's game playing."

"Game playing?" He put his hand toward his chest. "Me. Okay. Where were you today?"

"Working. I told you I had a showing." She kept her sights on him, rarely even blinking.

"What were you showing, your nasty-ass pussy?" His face wore a snarl.

Her eyebrows raised and she gasped. "What?"

He began to speak louder. "Don't sit there like you're an angel. I know you went to the Florida Keys to fuck a doctor for money. You're a damn ho." He looked away and then back at her. "And your sister is your fucking pimp. This is some bullshit."

She felt her heart racing. "I don't know what you're talking about."

"Give it up. Stop with the bullshit."

"What is wrong with you?" Midori asked, then waited, knowing she was 100 percent busted. "My gosh."

He continued his rant. "Oh please. And to top it all off, there really is some shit going on with Mayor Graves, but not the racist crap I was talking about. Even my stepfather is mixed up in your little service you have going on. This shit can blow up in my face and screw up my family. You knew, and still you kept me in the dark just to have me in your life while playing this shit off. The question is, what is *your* problem?"

She fought to focus on how he was adding up all of the information correctly, wondering how he came up with the truth. "Okay. Wait. Obviously you did something to find that all out. Question is, what have you been up to? You're pointing the finger at me, but you're the one talking about breaking into e-mail accounts." She looked as though a light bulb had been turned on. "Hold up. That damn ink pen. Was that some kind of bugging device? Did you record me that day I talked to my sister? Did you put that pen in my purse on purpose?" She looked at him differently. "Why, you sneaky asshole."

"First of all, why would you worry about whether or not I'm recording something if nothing I say is true?" He came to a stance, reaching in his pocket for his keys. "Whatever. Bottom line is, I can't see you anymore."

She stood and pointed to the door. "Then get the hell out." In her heart she wanted to beg him to understand, but couldn't get past his deceit. She couldn't believe he'd been recording her.

He walked toward the door.

She added, her eyes beginning to water, "You're trying to start something between us out of something that's really no big deal."

"Oh, it *is* a big deal. You and your sister will be arrested."

"And you and your family will be ruined. Like you're going

to say something anyway. Can't believe you have the nerve to blame me when your stepfather has the problem. He's the one who feels the need to go outside of his marriage and cheat on your mom with rented pussy. You need to be at home talking to him."

He looked back at her as she followed behind him, and cut his eyes. "Thanks for admitting that all I said was right. I needed you to say just what you said."

"Whatever. You could've told me all of this over the phone. You're wasting my damn time." She felt a tear fall and wiped her cheek.

He stood at the door, his hand on the knob. "I told you in person out of respect. Respect is something you never showed me. And yeah, your time is worth about what, five hundred dollars an hour? I'll send you a check."

She wanted to say fifteen hundred, but instead she asked sarcastically, "Are you recording this, too?"

He yanked the door open. "Maybe."

She put her hand on the door, waiting for him to cross the threshold, still playing off her feelings. "Get the hell out of here. You are a straight-up mess. Who the hell do you think you are?"

"Who am I? I'm a man who wanted to get to know you but doesn't want to take a chance on turning a ho into a housewife. But maybe that's the very question you need to ask yourself. What would make you think I'd want a whore as my woman? That was a fantasy on your part that will never, ever come true." He looked like he was trying hard to nail her to the wall with his words.

All she could say was "Fuck you."

"Glad that never happened. With your nasty ass." He stepped away and was down the hall in a flash.

She yelled at his back, "Don't act like I'm the only problem, Virgil the virgin. You and your family can do a good enough job of fucking up without me. You wiretapping fool." She slammed the door and began to cry, voice still raised. "I can't believe he recorded me. If Money ever found out she'd kill me *and* him. Shit."

Midori grabbed her purse and took out her phone, sending a text to Bailey. **When and where?**

He replied back immediately. **2 hours. The Roosevelt. I'll send you the room number later. Love you.**

She didn't respond. Instead, she prepared herself to leave in an hour. Her tears came in full force from her feeling the loss of her only chance at being in a normal relationship with a companion, someone who would check on her and care about her well-being, who was interested in her, and who until recently would take her to dinner and dancing, making her laugh. It was over now, all because she lied about who she really was.

So she did the only thing she knew how to do, which was show up and spend time with somebody who unconditionally wanted her body for the hooker she was, since she couldn't have anyone who wanted her for her heart.

Other than maybe Bailey Brenner.

In a recent interview on NBC's Today *show, Mayor Kalin Graves challenged Senator Darrell Ellington, saying Ellington sponsored a controversial "sex education in schools" measure. Ellington replied in a statement saying he was not a sponsor, but he did vote in favor of sending the bill to the Senate. However, the bill was never voted on.*

Eight

Virgil

Friday—July 22, 2011

The six-thousand-square-foot, natural stone estate home that Ursula and Darrell Ellington lived in was in affluent Scarsdale, in Westchester Country. It was the very district that Senator Ellington served.

The senator's home office was large—so large, in fact, that it was only a tad bit smaller than the actual Oval Office at the White House.

Darrell Ellington had just hung up his cell phone as Virgil walked inside his office.

"Hey there, Virgil," Darrell said.

"I know you're not fond of me."

He looked at Virgil as if to say, *What the hell?* "Why would you say something like that? Have I ever given you that impression?"

"I know that you really don't like me."

"Of course I do. You're my son. Where is all of this coming from?"

The topic changed, sort of. "How's the race going?"

"It's going." Darrell Ellington began writing on a pad of paper.

"Everybody keeping their noses clean?"

"I guess so. Keeping clean is not something you focus on. You just live clean and the rest is spent on the campaign."

"I see. You think Mayor Graves keeps it clean?"

"I don't know."

Virgil took one step closer. "You think the world would trip if they knew that you cheat on my mother?"

He shook his head like he was hearing things. "Virgil. What? That's not true."

"Okay. I guess what I really want to know is, why do you cheat on her?"

"Excuse me?"

"Lip Service."

"What?"

"Oh no. You play dumb just about as terribly as someone else I know. Small world, huh?"

"Virgil, I have no idea what you're talking about." He looked down at his work.

Virgil approached and stopped within a few feet. "You do. I often wondered about you. I always thought you were just a little too good to be true. I should've known you were a freak."

"What are you talking about?"

Virgil was amazed by his stepfather's act of innocence. "Wow. You'd make a really great president. You're in the right line of work. Denial, denial, denial. You try your best to find out what the other person knows and then you see how weak the information is, and keep playing stupid. Very good."

Darrell shook his head again and put the pen down, gathering his papers. He arranged them by page number and sorted through them. "You know what? This conversation is over. I'm lost as to what you're referring to. You can have this conversation by yourself." He came to a stance and took hold of his cell.

"Actually, the best thing for you to do would be to save that dumb line of responses for my mom. I'm not the one you're fucking around on with hookers. But I will tell you one thing: my mother's well-being and happiness is my concern. You let this shit come back to bite her in the ass, and I will tell everything I know. You can bet on that."

He passed by Virgil, almost grazing his shoulder, saying, "Good-bye, son."

"Stop," Virgil demanded.

Darrell Ellington turned to face him.

"I am not your son. I'm your wife's son. And your wife wants the White House. You will give her that. And what I get out of it is two million dollars. Find it where you can. Money laundering or whatever. Call it a loan if need be. I'm starting a site. My own business. Better than where I work at Google. You'll tell Mom you offered it to me to help out and I took it. Yep, two million will help me lose my memory for sure."

"A loan?"

"Good listener."

"For silence?"

"A loan that I will never fucking pay your sorry cheating ass back."

Darrell turned and walked toward the door. "You have lost your mind. I have no idea what you're talking about."

"Will three million help you remember?"

He stopped but kept his back to Virgil. "You wouldn't."

"I would. In case you never noticed, I care about as much about you as the shit I flush down the toilet. I care about my mom. What she wants is what I want. And you hurting her is not gonna happen."

"Exactly. I would never hurt her. And I'm not loaning you a dime." Darrell exited swiftly, looking certain.

"Try me." Virgil's voice was loud and sure.

That evening, Virgil sat in his bedroom on the upstairs level of their home. He had a large bedroom and private bath, and an office for all of his computer gadgets, desktops, laptops, printers, and devices.

He was proud of himself for coming up with a way to make his stepfather pay for cheating on his mother by way of funding the establishment of Virgil's new business venture. For now, it seemed like the right thing to do. He knew his stepfather, who had inherited millions, could definitely afford it.

He lay back upon his bed, coming to grips with what started it all…his naiveté upon first meeting Midori that evening at an event where someone stood her up. And how he bonded to her, all the while thinking she was selling homes for a living. And now discovering she was an escort, running a line so close to his personal life. Out of all the escort agencies in the world, his stepfather—who was campaigning to be the next president of the United States—had to be patronizing Lip Service.

Sex was not something Virgil was familiar with, and he had a hard time understanding why people felt the need to go to such great lengths to get it, paying someone to lay them even when the person who paid was married.

Sex was, after all, overrated. It shouldn't be difficult for someone to wait for their ordained mate, their last love, their significant other. To save their bodies for that person shouldn't be so difficult. "Horny-ass mothafucka," he said aloud about his stepfather. "What is this world coming to?"

He then wondered who he was fooling. He wasn't born again. He and his mom went to church before, but not often since she married his stepfather. Virgil had no church home. *Ordained* to him meant someone saved who was destined to be with someone else who was saved. Saved wasn't what he was. Yes, he was saving himself, but not for the right one. He was saving himself from himself. From having to feel what he felt before. He was afraid.

Virgil's mind wandered back to that time, so long ago. It was the night of his high school prom. The night in a hotel room that was paid for by his mom. There was nothing uncommon about a teenaged boy and girl spending the night out. But the girl he'd been seeing, who promised to give it to him good that night, took one look at what he was packing or wasn't packing and laughed hysterically when she saw the size of his penis.

He hadn't played sports, so he never did the locker room thing. When he went to the bathroom and used the urinal, he never looked over at someone else's penis. He kept his eyes on himself. He just assumed other boys had done the same thing. He hadn't watched dirty movies as a teen. He'd only read a few *Playboy* magazines and had seen the women's vaginas on the pages. He jacked off to a centerfold model here and there. He really didn't know what to compare his own size to.

The technical term for what he had was a micropenis. Fully erect, his penis was about the size of his thumb. Compared to the average-size penis, he had a small shaft that was flanked by the pubis skin of his uncircumcised gland. The only other person who knew before his prom date was his mother. When he was young, she took him to the doctor because he was overweight. The doctor mentioned it and suggested waiting to see if he further developed after losing weight and after puberty, and that sometimes the hormonal process is delayed and the testosterone can take longer to do its thing.

Well, he did lose weight, but his mother never saw Virgil nude after that moment.

Now in his late twenties, nearly six feet tall and 190 pounds, it was obvious to Virgil that his penis wasn't going to grow on its own. And his mother just never brought it up again. Neither did he. Especially after what happened on prom night.

Though sex was something Virgil was able to live without for now, he did find self-stimulation to be a calming way of relieving stress. And this day had been a ten on the stress Richter scale.

He had pulled down his pants, taking his foot out of one leg of his sweats, and began massaging his penis. He'd usually find a way to stimulate himself, erecting it to its full two and one half inches. His library of dirty movies usually helped.

He used his index finger and thumb and twisted it, rubbed it, twirled it while watching a volumeless girl-on-girl movie. In his mind, he compared himself to the clit the way he would tease his dick. He assumed that he'd need to eventually use artificial ways of penetrating his last love, thinking in terms of doing what lesbians do, using his mouth to please her.

The movie he watched was of an Asian woman with a black woman, one extra slim, one extra curvy. He imagined what the sensation would feel like, as he leaned over and took the small pocket pussy, a hand masturbator shaped like a vagina, from his nightstand. He'd always kept it deep inside of a shoe box.

He barely got himself an inch inside of the nude-colored flexible stimulator when he began to moan, watching the vision of the Asian woman between the black woman's legs, prodding her with a tiny blue dildo. As the tip of the blue dildo went in, he focused on his tip going in the fake vagina he used, squeezing the rubberlike texture of the pussy as tight as he could to grip his penis. Before, he'd think of Midori, imagining her taking the time to let him stick his dick inside of her. Thinking of her always got him off. He thought he'd be too mad for that fantasy in his head, considering the argument they had, but he surprised himself, still feeling the turn-on of her in his mind.

Just as he was about to try to get another inch deeper, he reached over again and took the small bottle of lube, and squeezed a couple of drops inside, bringing the pussy to his head again, squeezing it with all of his might, giving a few good pumps while he watched the blue dildo push past the soft, bald lips of the dark, porcelain-skinned black girl, and he thought of Midori, naked, watching him.

He geared himself up to come just as the Asian woman got a good oral grip on the girl's clit, sucking like she was sucking her own finger, and to Virgil, that was the sensation he dreamed of feeling upon his tip. It brought him to a tenseness that caused his ass cheeks and thighs to flex. His toes pointed and his hand went to work, gripping the vagina around his tiny tip and then stopping as he felt himself giving off his orgasm, squirting his semen inside of the pocket pussy while he tightened his eyes to shut out the movie and focus only on

the vision in his head of Midori, turned on by him masturbating.

"Oooo, yesss. Ahhhh, yesssss." He sucked his teeth and
then heard a knock at his door, and someone turning the
doorknob, but it was locked. His eyes popped open and his
voice traveled from porn to norm. "Yes. Just a minute."

"You okay, son?" his mother, Ursula Ellington, asked.

He froze as he answered, "Yes. I am."

"Okay. Didn't want anything. Just checking."

He knew she knew.

He said nothing in reply but heard her footsteps slowly
fade down the hallway.

She was the one who bought him the pocket pussy and all
the other items in the shoe box. She had figured out what her
son needed. For now the sex toys, but eventually a woman to
love him as he was.

And he knew what his mother needed for herself. To be
the next First Lady. Period.

In the meantime, he washed off his soft, dependable, no-
hassle girlfriend and put her back in the drawer.

Back to the other issue at hand.

How to deal with his now ex-girlfriend, the escort, and his
political stepfather, the John.

Republican candidate Darrell Ellington has been criticized for being pro-choice. Robert Sally, a pro-life candidate who just entered the race, says he plans to zero in on Ellington to debate abortion, which is sure to be one of the most controversial and emotional debates to date.

Nine

∞

Leilani

Monday—July 25, 2011

Manhattan was booked to meet Mr. 51, Senator Darrell Ellington, at the Library Hotel on Madison Avenue, a boutique hotel known for its artsy rooms with collections of artwork and books. The particular room they were scheduled to meet in was called the Erotica Deluxe Room, complete with chocolates and champagne.

As soon as Mr. 51 walked into the room, Leilani noticed a different look upon his face. His charm was absent. He stood there in his dark blue suit, and she stood dressed in her fuchsia bra and panties. He looked unfazed, then immediately said, "Maybe I should be asking Money this, but I'm going to ask you."

"What? What's wrong?"

He looked only at her face. "Who knows?"

"Who knows what?"

"Who knows I'm here?"

"Knows you're here right now?" she asked.

"Now, then, whenever. Who knows?" He was no-nonsense.

"Outside of the company, no one. Why? Did, like, something happen?"

He walked toward the window, looked out, and turned back to face Leilani. "Just making sure no one's been talking. I mean that is why I spend all this money. If I wanted to be indiscreet, I could have a mistress on the side who'd backstab me when things didn't go her way. I'm not into that. I just wanted it clean. No mess-ups. No talking."

"No. I would totally never do that. Why would I? Why would *we*, meaning the company? Talking gets everyone in trouble. For sure, none of us want that."

He nodded. "Well, I'll just say this. Someone said something. I know they did."

"What makes you say that?"

He took heavy steps to the door. "Look. That's it. I only came here to ask you that. I'm not here to...have you. This will be my last time. Period."

"Okay. But you won't tell me what happened?" She stood close to him.

He turned toward her, then walked back to the window, reached in his pocket for his cell, and sent a text. "No. I can't. It's best that you don't know. Besides, I can handle it."

"I'm sure you can."

He kept his phone in his hand. "One thing I do want to know, though. Do you all use my name, or is there some sort of code for me?"

She looked sincere and concerned. "You know I can't tell you that. They tell us very little, anyway."

"Okay. Let's leave it where it is. From this moment on, I need to work out whatever it is that I need and look to my wife to fulfill it." He sounded like he was trying to convince himself. "This is way too much of a risk. Too much at stake. Every time I look up, someone in Washington or the political arena here in New York has us on the news for doing something stupid, some indiscretion."

She turned to face him. "True, but don't get nervous about it. That's when things happen. Just relax and follow your gut. If you think you need to stop, then stop."

"Makes me wonder how you stay so cool."

Leilani stepped closer to him again. "I don't. Each and every day I wake up, I just, like, realize it could be my last day of freedom. I have a hard time trusting new clients, you know, wondering if I'm being set up or if I'll get beat up or robbed. And I always hope my regulars won't get sloppy. But that's totally the risk. That's why it's so lucrative. Like you said, that's why you pay so much, and you're totally right. You're one of the good clients. You respect boundaries and don't drink or smoke or get rough." She touched his shoulder. "I want you to rest assured and know that what we do goes absolutely no further than this hotel room. Yes, there's a company I work for and all, but I was thinking about breaking away and doing this on my own, you know, like we discussed. I mean, why give half to someone else, when I'm the one doing all the work, you know what I mean?"

His expression showed his worry, but he still said, "I do. You need to do what you think is best."

"Actually, like tonight I was going to ask you if you'd think about, you know, like maybe trying me on the side. But, I see that you're done."

His voice gentled. "No. Can't do that."

"I totally understand, especially not after you have this feeling like someone is talking. I get it."

He stepped away and she had no choice but to remove her hand. He said, "Anyway, you take care."

A faint smile lifted the corner of her mouth. "You too. Do what you have to do."

"I will." He turned back to her, looking dissatisfied. "Honestly, I still need to know how this got out."

She gazed at him as he stood before the door. "I don't know what's going on. All I know is, since you've vowed to stop, then we'll stop. Do you want me to tell Money you won't be needing our services anymore?"

"No. She'll find out. Let this be the last we speak of it, and each other." He turned, opened the door, and stepped out.

"Bye." She leaned out of the door and wanted to wish him luck with his bid for the White House, but she didn't. She simply closed the door.

Leilani stayed in the room and logged on to her computer. She returned some e-mails, paid a bill or two, and spent the remaining time the senator had paid for just piddling around. Then she sent her usual text to the booker. **Done.**

A female candidate has entered the race: three-term Illinois congresswoman Marla Goins spoke at a rally today announcing her declaration. Goins was propelled into the race with support from the Tea Party movement. Civil unions were legalized in her state earlier in the year. She's angered some voters for pushing to give same-sex couples the right to marry in Illinois.

Ten

∞

Leilani

Monday—July 25, 2011

Leilani's next appointment was nearly three hours later at the W New York on Lexington Avenue. It was a woman, Ms. 101, who'd spent time with Kemba before. This time, it was Leilani's turn.

The female athlete's name was Temeka Palmer, and she was one of the top female basketball players in the world. She was also as bisexual as they came. She wanted men and women at different times. This time, it was time for new pussy.

Leilani had been with women many times and could take it or leave it, never interested in exploring girl-on-girl in her personal life, but for the money she knew just what to do. She wasn't just talented at giving men head, she could also give women head, too.

She and Temeka were in the bedroom lying atop a queen-sized bed. Temeka's brown hair flowed along the butter-yellow pillowcase. She was the type to wear makeup and heels and long fingernails. She was six foot three and flat-chested, and she had a big, strong rear end. She was also very sexy.

Pale pink begonias resting upon the nightstand gave off the smell of fresh apricots. An ebony bookcase stood to the left, a brown leather chair to the right. In the middle of red-boned Temeka's legs was Leilani. She didn't use a condomlike barrier. She had a look on her face as if she was pleased to be the pleaser. They were both nude. Both wet. Both able, only Leilani was the one getting paid for it.

Leilani nibbled and licked, and moved the baby-oil-scented labia skin of Temeka's neatly trimmed vagina to the side to expose her large, wide, reddish-brown clit.

Temeka gave a soft moan as more subtle tongue strokes were given.

Leilani used a broad-tongued motion and introduced the roughness of the upperside of her tongue to the top of Te-meka's clit. Once Leilani heard her sigh, she pointed her tongue and became more aggressive, closing her lips around the clit and sucking it entirely into her mouth. Temeka jerked and bucked her hips.

Leilani squeezed her lips around the tender jewel and gave it a lashing, using rolling motions of her tongue and lips. She used a twirl and vacuumed it up, still teasing Temeka by using the edge of her tongue to circle around the en-tire clit, first clockwise and then counterclockwise. It was like a butterfly's wings, and it made Temeka shiver. Her legs, which Leilani held back toward the headboard, involuntarily quaked. The rumble of the quaking matched the sound of Temeka's revved-up groans. "Oh yes. You sure the hell know what you're doing. Damn, woman."

Temeka looked down at Leilani as if she couldn't figure out how Leilani was managing to hit the right spots, as if Leilani knew her body well, as though they'd slept together before. Leilani was simply good with her mouth, and she took pride in it, aiming to please.

She went from a light flicking to heavier and faster flicks, and held steady as she heard Temeka give a deep, long moan, while her thick clitoris swelled in Leilani's mouth.

Leilani added a side-to-side sucking action and rode Temeka through her orgasm, staying with it, riding the waves that subsided and returned, subsided and returned, subsided and returned. She oscillated her tongue. As Temeka reached her height, she put her hand on Leilani's head and tried to push her away, signaling that the multiples were too much for her to bear, and Leilani acquiesced, backing off and smiling sexily.

Temeka spoke a breathy two words. "Good job."

"Pretty pussy."

"Now that is what I call some good head. Come here." Temeka used a come-hither motion with her finger that matched her eyes.

Leilani adjusted herself to lay on top of Temeka and they ground, kissing each other's necks, cheeks, and ears, running their hands through each other's long hair. Leilani rested her head along Temeka's defined shoulder.

"You're so soft," Temeka said.

"You are too. I like this."

Temeka admitted, "I wish I could feel like this with my girlfriend. She's a stud. Walks around wearing a cock under her clothes all day. People think she's just a friend. My son calls her Auntie. But no one can know she's my lover. Well, maybe they think it, but I'd never admit it. I'm a fem athlete. Everyone tries to put us all in the same box. I won't let them have the satisfaction of labeling me at all, let alone as some-one who only likes girls. I made a choice, after being with men, and chose to love a woman. But I crave both. And so, here I am."

Leilani waited until Temeka was done, making sure not to interrupt her time to share what she more than likely didn't tell most people. "And so, she's the dominate? Plays the mas-culine?"

"Yes."

"I see." Leilani smiled.

"Actually, I wanted to be the one who does that. The manly sex. That's one of the reasons why I asked for a woman." She then said, "I brought something I want to use."

Leilani giggled. "A strap-on?"

"Yes." Temeka giggled, too.

"I'm ready when you are."

"You sure?"

"Very sure." Leilani climbed off of her.

Temeka stood and reached inside her purse, taking out a clear, big-veined dildo attached to a white leather strap. She put it on, placing the harness around her waist and hips, and secured the hooks. She held the long penis in her hand, ready to use her man-weapon, and said, "Turn onto your back."

Leilani quickly laid on her back and opened her legs wide. Temeka climbed onto the bed, got up on her knees, and pushed Leilani's legs back, then kept one hand on Leilani's thigh and the other on her silicone dick, and introduced it to Leilani's pussy. Leilani stuck her own finger inside of herself, feeling the river of lust between her legs. "Oh, yes," she told Temeka. "She's good and ready."

Temeka rubbed the tip of the dildo around Leilani's juiced-up hole, teasing it and patting it along her pussy skin, and then she inserted herself, just a bit at first, and then more, pushing her big dick all the way inside.

Leilani moaned while saying, "Yeah. Get that."

Temeka said, lusty-eyed, "Look at that. It slipped right in." She dug in further and then in and out like a man, pumping, tightening her ass muscles as she fucked Leilani.

Leilani brought her legs back even more and reached up to play with Temeka's hard left nipple, watching the clear dick press in and out. She took in the sights of a chick with a dick fucking her insides.

Temeka looked like a pro, holding the base of the fake cock while fucking the fully accommodating, warm and wet vagina.

Leilani found herself surprised by the feeling. The whole idea of being screwed by a woman was doing it for her, and good. "Yeah. Fuck me like that. Ohhhh, shit. That's what the hell I'm talking about. Dominate that pussy, girl." She watched the muscles of Temeka's chest and arms flex, the strength of her toned hips plummeting inside of her. The power of her forearms and developed thighs adding to her strength. Yet Temeka's long hair bounced and flowed over her shoulders, and her long royal-blue nails pressed into Leilani's soft skin.

Temeka asked strongly, "You like that big dick in you, don't you?"

"Oh yeah. Hard as a damn rock."

"Who's the man, now?" she asked, seemingly doing what her girlfriend wouldn't let her do.

"You're the man, baby. Give it to me good, like that dick was growing out of you. Like you need to have your balls sucked while you're inside this pussy."

Temeka sounded extra turned on. "Yeah. Tear that pussy up and have you suck my dick, sucking all the fucking cum out of me." She used the word *fucking* like she'd never used the F word before in her entire life.

Leilani felt herself getting wetter and wetter. In her head she heard the song "Freak Like Me" by Adina Howard. She started grinding like she was working it on the dance floor. "Boom, boom. You've got that dick now. Damn, you're totally gonna make me come."

"Oh, no, you can't come on this dick already. Not just yet. Turn the fuck over. Now!"

Leilani changed positions, and Temeka was right behind her. Leilani got on all fours, ass propped up high, submissive. Temeka was totally in control, adjusting herself so that she could get close, and then she moved Leilani's ass cheeks upward and away from her opening so she could get past the girth of her ass to the opening of her anxious pussy.

She slipped her dick inside and Leilani grunted, "Oh fuck. Damn that feels good. Ahhh. Yeah."

"Uh-huh. Sweet-ass pussy getting taken by this big-ass dick. I'm on top now. I'm the stud now. I'm the one punishing that pussy now. Look at that."

Leilani was in a fog. "Oh yeah. Oooo shit, yeah."

"You want it deeper? Make you feel like I'm standing up in it. Laying that pipe in that pussy?"

"Oh yeah. Fuck me harder. Yeah."

Temeka began pumping faster and deeper, on one knee, the other leg bent so that she leveled herself with her foot. She had both hands along Leilani's upper ass cheeks, bracing her weight while leaning along her lower back, hitting that pussy from behind.

Leilani bounced back toward it to urge her on. The sounds of her creamy vagina soaking up the big dick were audible.

Temeka said, sounding sexy, with a suddenly deeper voice, "You know I'm about to come inside of you."

Leilani gave a look like she believed she really could. "Yes. I know. Give it to me. Come with me."

"Spit that juice when I spit my sperm."

"Aww, fuck, yes." It sounded as if they were making a movie.

"When I shoot this cum in you, I want you to lick every damn bit of creamy pussy juices from my dick to my balls. Lick me clean. You hear me?"

"Yes."

Temeka's voice reached its max. "You'd better. Now take this cum, dammit." She dug in further and screamed out loud from the rush of it all, the turn-on of being in control, of being the masculine one getting the pussy for once. "Yeah, I'm shootin' that cum inside that pussy. You feel it? Huh?" Temeka's orgasm shot from deep inside her pussy, squirting all over Leilani.

Though showered with Temeka's liquid, Leilani felt evidence of her own secreted excitement. "Yeah. I feel it. Oh, yeah. I'm coming hard. Damn that dick feels good." Leilani tightened her eyes and flexed her muscles and let her orgasm roll. "Awwwwwwwwwwwwwww, yessssssssssssss."

Temeka gave Leilani and herself a moment to recover, and then demanded, "Now get up and lick my dick clean."

In five seconds Temeka lay on her back with her hard dick that was soaked from Leilani's strong orgasm. Leilani took the dick down her throat deep, to the very back, slurping her way

back up to the tip, licking every bit of juice from it. Then she
undid the side hooks to the harness that Temeka wore and
pressed Temeka's legs back, licking up the flowing juices that
had oozed from her pussy past the hairs of her vagina. She
even ventured to suck the wetness from her perineum, the
space between her ass and her opening.

Temeka quivered with her eyes closed, lost somewhere in
her head.

Leilani continued to suck and slurp and lick her clean.
Then she sat up a bit, onto her knees, and allowed Temeka's
strong legs to rest along her shoulders. She kissed Temeka's
ankle where her WNBA tattoo lived and rubbed her thighs,
looking down at her.

Temeka opened her eyes and gave a shy smile. "Thank
you," she said, as if she had to be forgiven for fucking so hard,
imagining so much, expecting such freakiness, switching gen-
der roles. She was back to reality. Fantasy accomplished.

Leilani told her, looking serious as a heart attack, "You're
good at that girl, being in control. You should let your woman
enjoy that."

Temeka rubbed the smudged mascara from under her eyes
and nodded. "She's the boyish one. I'm the prissy one. I suck
her pussy and her dick. She's never had a dick in her life. She
hates being penetrated with a sex toy. She just wants me to
come from her eating my pussy and me getting fucked with
her strap-on. That's how she gets off. She can't *not* be in control. She'd never have it."

"Well, I will say this: if you ever feel the need to live out
that fantasy again, you ask for me. Hell, I'd pay for that. You
can totally fuck, girl. With your sexy ass."

"That's sweet of you to say." Temeka was indeed back to
being the femme.

"Like, maybe one day she'll go for it. You think?"

"I doubt it, but thanks."

Leilani didn't judge, knowing it was all about a sinner sharing her feelings with another sinner.

Temeka left, happy.

Leilani texted, Done, and went home, alone.

For the first time in her entire escort career, she masturbated to the repeated vision of Temeka fucking her and being the man. She fell asleep after her orgasm and was awakened by a text from her ex, Shawn, asking if he could come out to New York and see her.

Her reply was one word. No.

Republicans in the House blocked the president's jobs plan today. Republican candidates will weigh in on the topic of unemployment tonight in Wisconsin on a special panel which airs on Headline News. Also, candidate Kalin Graves, who previously endorsed state rights to legalize prostitution but has since changed his views, will discuss the hot topic with host Vinnie Tan.

Eleven

∞

Kemba

Friday—August 5, 2011

I t won't fit," Ms. 111 said, sounding frustrated, as she lay on her back in a king suite at the Marriott hotel in downtown Manhattan.

"Relax, baby. Let's go slow."

Kemba was about five inches of his ten into the seventy-year-old widowed woman who usually went out of the country to find a sex stud. She had no qualms about paying for some dick.

She did well financially with her retirement, as she had held a very high-level position in the judicial system up until ten years ago.

"Just use the tip, maybe. You're so wide. So long. I still have my insides but I'll need a hysterectomy if I let more of your cock in," she told him. She sounded like she was joking. She wore a frown.

He showed understanding. "Maybe we can do it from behind. Sometimes that's easier."

"Okay. If you say so." He climbed off of her, his hard-on sheathed in a condom. She glanced down at his grand entirety. "Wow, how did your mom handle your father? Whose side of the family does that run on, anyway?"

He held the weight of his penis in his hand. "I'm not sure. It just takes some getting used to."

"I don't know. I thought I'd seen them all. But you are really something else, Mr. Big Stuff."

"That's what I've heard."

"Can you give yourself a blow job? I've heard of that. All you'd need to do is lean forward and there it would be, knocking on your chin." She looked absolutely serious.

"I'm afraid not. Not that limber."

"Well, okay, let's try this 'from behind' thing." She lay on her side along the bold-colored lime-green-and-white-striped sheets. He moved in behind her. She scooted her pale, wrinkled body back toward him and lifted her leg just a bit, taking her hand to separate the skin of her deflated butt cheeks. "Let me move my muffins and try to squeeze you in. Can you get to it that way?" she asked, trying to look back at him.

"I'm sure I can. I'm going in." Kemba was amused but fought not to show it. He instead went ahead and inserted his very tip to her opening and pressed a bit.

She gave a slow moan like she was wounded.

"Are you okay?"

"I am. You can go in some more, big boy." She still kept her sense of humor.

"Hold on." He realized she was extra-dry due to her age, so he reached over to his side of the bed to get his water-based lubricant and rubbed it over his dick. He'd sexed up a lot of older women before, and had trained his dick to stay ready when those he fucked weren't his type. He called up various images in his mind, his mental Viagra. Images of a hot porno scene or his favorite sexual experience, the ones that kept him hard when he needed to be. He had worked out a system. Performing was his bread and butter; he had to get it up and stay up, so whatever it took, he did it.

For now, his dick was more curious than anything else. He met the woman's gray-haired pussy again with his penis, sliding it in just about an inch, and when he felt it was safe he went another inch, and then another, and managed to get half of it in without her scooting away.

It was like she was holding her breath, so he asked, "Are you okay?"

Her reply was, "Who's your dad, anyway? King Kong?"

He smiled and pushed some more.

She said, sounding alarmed, "That's enough. That's enough."

He grinned behind her and asked, "What gets you off?"

She said right away. "Having my nipples sucked. And sucking dick."

He nodded, saying, "Okay." He pulled out and she immediately took her dentures out and set them on the side table.

He gasped inside and thought, *Humph. This could be interesting.*

She lay on her back while he removed the condom and got on his knees to just the right spot to meet her mouth with his dick, inserting himself. She said, "I'll take you places you ain't never been before. I'm gonna rock your world." He laughed inside and wondered if she watched BET or what. She was trying to sound hip. But her face spelled *grandma*. Her mouth was wide open, accommodating every inch of the dick her pussy couldn't.

He looked down at her, impressed that she was able to take in his entirety. The feeling of a toothless woman had him going.

She used her right hand to guide him further. His width filled the circumference of her mouth.

Kemba said, "I'll suck your nipples in a minute, but right now, this feels so good. You've got all that dick in there."

She moaned against his skin while she worked.

She gagged, allowing the saliva to assist in keeping her hand slippery. He could feel the sensation of her stroke, her tongue, and her lips. She was gumming him down, old-school style.

He asked, looking pleased, "You trying to make me come?"

She looked up at him and her eyes watered so much from his size that it looked like she was crying. But she tried even more to suck him down.

He pulled himself back, trying not to ejaculate, remembering who it was that had paid whom. "You're very good, but this is all about you."

She let go of his dick, giving a grin that was all gums, and reached over to pop her teeth back in her mouth. "My husband used to love that." She looked proud of herself. "I had a lover in the Bahamas who would make me squirt. Gotta get back to see him. He's black like you, but nowhere near as big. You're a beautiful man."

"Thanks. And you're a beautiful woman. Now let me suck those pretty titties of yours. Maybe it'll remind you of him."

She inserted her middle finger inside her pussy, and then two more, and Kemba caressed her sagging breasts, taking one into his mouth, giving back-and-forth licks to her nipple, which hardened instantly. Then he did the other one. He sucked her while she finger-fucked herself faster and faster. He kept at her right nipple, watching her watch him. She buried another finger inside of herself and said, "I found my spot. It's right there. Oh yes. Suck me."

He did as she liked.

She gave a final digging around with her fingers and bucked when she yanked her fingers out, releasing a liquid trickle that made Kemba's eyes bug out of his head. She growled and another trickle expelled. It leaked onto the sheets. He stopped sucking her nipple just as she said, "That was just what I needed. I've still got it." She got up, walking slowly, and began putting her clothes back on. "You made me squirt that squirt, boy!"

"Oh yes. You still got it, indeed," he said, almost in shock. "I'm about half your age and I've never seen anything like that. You're doing okay." He lied. Beryl got her squirt on regularly. But the liquid Ms. 111 expelled smelled like urine, though he didn't dare bust her bubble.

"Thanks. I've got to go," she told him, looking fully charged.

"I understand."

She gave a wink as she grabbed her purse. "Whoever your sweetheart is, she'll need some vaginal rejuvenation after working that for a spell. That's a full-time job."

He laughed.

She slowly walked to the door. "Don't you bruise that pretty banana now."

"Not even."

Ten seconds later, she was gone. Kemba had made his money.

His mental Viagra kept him up again.

It never let him down even when it was the GILFs who needed some dick, too.

Just like when he was back in Kenya.

Senator Darrell Ellington's wife, Ursula Jackson Ellington, who comes from a long line of politicians as her deceased father was the former mayor of Atlanta, will host a political fund-raiser this evening at the offices of her former employer, Paine Webber, which is where she met her husband while he worked in government affairs and she was a senior consultant.

Twelve

∞

Kemba

Friday—August 5, 2011

By two that afternoon, after his late checkout from the hotel, Kemba called Beryl as he headed out of the room, but she didn't answer. He headed through the busy lobby of the Marriott wearing a tight blue sweater and blue jeans. Faces and movement were all around him, but he instantly froze in place upon seeing her. She was the beautiful, tall black woman he'd seen almost two months ago in the long black limo.

Almost as if in slow motion, while everything else around him sped by, she walked toward him in a black cashmere sweater and knit pants, and then passed him. He spun around in wonder. Her hair was dark and shiny. Her face was brown and flawless. His mouth was wide open.

She stopped on a dime and looked back at him, asking, "Don't I know you?" pointing her slender finger his way.

Her young assistant paused.

Kemba said to himself, *Yes.* He gave a huge nod and extended his hand. "Yes. You were getting into your limo and I was coming out of the gym. It's good to see you again. I'm Kemba."

"You too. I'm Ursula."

"Small world," he said. He could smell her citrus scent. Her lips were full and painted a shimmery bronze.

"Yes, it is. A beautiful small world." She looked at her assistant while adjusting her black Coach shoulder bag to her other arm. "Nona, I'll be right with you. You can head upstairs to your room."

Nona nodded and walked away, looking back to give her boss a hurry-up look before heading to the elevator.

Ursula asked, "So, do you live in Harlem?"

"Yes."

"I see. What brings you here? I mean to this hotel?"

He sped right over her inquiry. "Let me ask you. Do you drink?" He pointed to the bar across the lobby.

"I do, but not this time of day."

"I understand." He kept staring at her. "You're even more beautiful close up."

"Thank you." She gave a flirtatious scan of him, from his dreads to his feet. "Do you know my last name?"

"No. Would I?"

Her reply was "We'd make some beautiful babies." She stared at his full lips.

He smiled, exposing every single tooth in his mouth. "I agree."

"You from here?"

"Kenya."

"Nice." She paused as if her mind was spinning. "Are

you waiting for someone? You didn't tell me why you're here."

Kemba got creative. "I'm a trainer. I worked someone out earlier." He cleared his throat.

"Oh. I can see your calling card." She looked straight at his defined arms and even licked her lips. "Very nice."

He dipped his head. "Thanks."

"So, can you meet me upstairs in about twenty minutes?"

He said right away, looking at her like he was unsure, "Oh, I don't know, this is all moving kinda fast...hell yeah." He grinned big and laughed.

"Funny man. Okay. I like that." She reached in her bag and handed him her room key. "Twelve-twelve."

He put the key in his pants pocket, nodding. "See you in twenty."

Her phone rang and she answered it. "Nona, I'm coming right up to your room. Open the door for me." She winked at him and walked away.

He watched the design of her figure again, almost in a trance, and shook himself out of it, heading to the bar. *Damn.*

As Kemba sat down and ordered a Corona, the young male bartender asked, "Isn't that Senator Darrell Ellington's wife?"

"Is it?" Kemba asked.

The bartender reached down into the under fridge. "Is her name Ursula?"

"Sure is." He looked back toward where she'd gone.

"She's a very beautiful woman. *Very* beautiful." He opened the bottle and set it before Kemba.

"Yes. Very." Kemba looked intrigued. "Thanks." He reached into his pocket and looked at the key card. Then he looked at his wristwatch, counting down the minutes, praying time would hurry up and pass.

Thirty minutes later, Kemba slid his thick tongue in and out of Ursula's dark brown pussy, tongue-fucking her into another world.

She held her breath with every plunge of his long, scooping mouth-muscle that invaded her cavity. She kept her sights on him as his bottom lip scooped her labia into position and his top lip acted as an accomplice to his tongue action, both assisting him by keeping her erect clitoris in just the right place for him to truly eat as if she were a sugar cane.

He toyed with her lips and opening, and then found her sweet spot. It was larger than most and a dark shade of pink. It swelled beyond its foreskin, exposing itself on its own. The protective hood had retracted just from the excitement, exposing the sensitive glans that lay beneath. It looked like the head of a penis. It was the extra-long love button that her husband had probably ignored, but Kemba knew better.

The shaft of it lay vertically, just above her opening, where at its divide, it looked like an upside down letter Y. That was how up close and personal he was. He took its pretty axis into his mouth and sucked it like it was a crooked finger. His technique was impressive and cannibalistic. He gave her hungry eyes like he was there for a meal, not an appetizer.

The nerve endings of her organ were going haywire. The tension was at its height. He backed away from it for a second and blew on it lightly. It pointed outward toward him as though begging for more, seeming to open like a blooming daffodil. He housed it again with his spiraling tongue and mouth.

Ursula ceased watching him. Her thrill seemed too much to handle, and she looked like she could burst. He inserted his long middle finger inside her while sucking. Her pleasure had reached its max. Her Y was ready for the big O.

He rubbed his tongue back and forth upon her organ. She screamed one loud scream and pressed her own hand to her mouth, fighting to keep herself from yelling bloody murder. "Ooooo, ooooo, I've never, noooo, ahhh, nooo. Yesssss!" Her body squirmed as if it were wondering who the hell she was.

Ursula came so hard, she squeezed Kemba's head between her legs like he was in a WWE headlock. He backed away as her thighs released him, and he wiped his mouth. "Your clit is perfect. I love it."

She sounded winded. "No, I love it. Where in the hell did you learn that?"

"Just trying to please."

"Shit."

He said not another word but moved himself over to put on a rubber, then climbed on top of her. He lay upon her and opened her legs wide, sliding his penis inside with ease.

She gave one long "Uuunghh" upon his entry, seeming to take in the feeling of having his girth inside of her. "Oh my Lord."

His ten inches fit like a glove, and the deeper he went, the more she ground against him to assist his penetration.

He asked, bringing his face close to hers. "You wanna work this dick, huh?"

"Yes," she said without hesitation.

He said calmly, "I'm adding pressure to your clit when I grind. What I need you to do is, move your hips downward as I enter, and upward at the end of my stroke, giving downward and then outward rolls of your hips, just roll your pelvis with mine, and follow my lead. Move it downward as I go inward, and then roll outward as I pull outward, ready to stroke again. You'll get the upward friction from me against your pretty clit. And with the size of your clit, this can be amazing."

"Okay." She seemed in a trance.

"Relax." He began.

She took a deep breath as his chest pressed against hers. He pushed his hips toward her, going deep while she rolled her hips downward. She followed his lead and did as she was told.

"Breathe with me. That's it." He moaned in approval.

She eyed his black skin and hugged him tightly as they fucked missionary. He could feel her heartbeat, her breaths, her movements, as he worked to please her. They were in sync after having just met. It felt wrong but so right.

He said in her ear while fucking her, "I know you're Senator Ellington's wife. He's one lucky man."

She replied by opening her mouth and finding his tongue with hers, French-kissing him. Their DNA exchanged. Their hormones mixed.

He began kissing her forehead, caressing her face with his lips, giving passionate kisses upon her eyelids, tracing her nose, her cheeks, and her lips with his. "You're so beautiful. My God."

She took him in while moving as one. He savored the feeling of his fingers running through her hair. He looked her in the eyes and stayed with her until she came to her clitoral excursion peak, releasing the feeling of a new, rolling orgasm. She shed her thrill, and he shed his fifteen minutes later.

After making it into the bathroom to toss the condom, he came back to lie beside her. They faced each other, her leg resting upon his as if they'd lain like that a million times.

He said, "I never expected to see you again. I'm still shocked."

She said, looking sated, "I never thought I'd do this, asking a stranger to be alone with me. I'm a married woman."

"You're a sexy woman, is what you are."

She gave a blushing smile. "There's just something about you. I can't explain it. All I can think about is seeing you again. Can we?"

"We can." He nodded, looking like she'd just read his mind.

She explained, "If we exchange numbers, I'll call you from a phone number where the ID says Dallas. It's my side number."

"Okay. I get it." He didn't ask why.

She stared at him and rubbed her hand along his hairline. "I love your dreads." Her gaze did not waver.

"Thanks. I love your hair," he told her, pleased that her hair was natural, unlike Beryl, who wore a weave.

"Thanks." She then said, "Kemba. I'm bit older than you."

"You're perfect."

Looking extra flattered, she closed her eyes and then opened them quickly. "I'm sorry but I realize, well, you'd better go. My assistant will need me to go over some things with her soon. I'm doing a fund-raiser tonight and need to prepare." She moved her leg from his.

"I understand." He kissed her again along her forehead and then got up from the bed. He walked to the desk and wrote his number on a notepad.

He turned to see her staring at his body. She said, "You're built like a Greek god. Your name should be Apollo."

He laughed, stepping into his pants and putting on his shirt.

"By the way, just so you know, I have never done this before. I don't know what's gotten into me."

"I'm glad you did." He put on his shoes.

"Thanks for the workout," she said teasingly. "Have a good day, Kemba."

"You do the same, beautiful." He walked back to her and kissed her on the lips, and then he exited.

He headed home to his woman. He had just given away for free the very same dick that women paid thousands for. But in his mind, his woman Beryl gave her pussy away for free to men other than him, so what was the difference? He knew this was not a part of their agreement, but it was his way of passively getting even in their open relationship.

He was trying out new things, and he hoped that this was only the beginning with pretty clit Ursula.

The youngest Republican candidate, Seth Taylor, was a guest on Jimmy Kimmel Live, where he discussed being a former professional skier and talked about his love of flying airplanes. He is said to be a favorite among younger voters. He also admitted that Darrell Ellington is his strongest opponent and that their views are similar, but said Ellington was out of touch with the new generation of voters, ages 18–29, something Ellington denied while giving a speech in Illinois.

Thirteen

Virgil

Monday—August 22, 2011

How'd you talk him into that?" Ursula Ellington asked her son after taking a seat at his desk in his home office.

He typed away on the keyboard, looking back and forth between his two computer monitors. "I pitched a business plan to him."

"You did? For a search engine?" she asked.

"Yep."

"Interesting." She looked conflicted. "Virgil, why didn't you tell me about it?"

"It popped into my head one day when I was in class, and then when I went to work I started doing some research on what it would take to get it started."

"I see. How far along have you gotten on it? What does it do?"

He spoke fast. "Mom, I'll show it to you once I get it launched. It's a website."

"Okay. You think maybe I can see the business plan?" She crossed her arms.

"Ask your husband for it," he said, still not looking at her.

"He said he deleted the e-mail."

"He did, huh? Oh well." He shrugged.

She arched her brow. "At least tell me what it's called. He said it's a like a search engine. Maybe I can start spreading the word."

"Don't. It'll jinx things."

"Virgil, I really wish you weren't so secretive. This is good. You should share it."

"Darrell gave me what I needed."

"Two million dollars is what you needed? That much?" She looked unnerved.

"It's part of the money it'll take to get it registered and designed and off the ground. Marketing and promotion is a whole other cost."

She gave a deep exhale and uncrossed her arms. "My goodness, my son the inventor." She looked around. "All of these gadgets and diagrams. I guess it's good. Just make sure you can pay him back. That's a lot of money."

"You married a man with a lot of money. He's good."

"Good or not, it was a loan. Stick to the terms, Virgil. Make this work, please. Besides, there's a lot of money and attention going into this campaign right now. We need to be careful with our finances."

"I know."

She persisted. "At least tell me the name of it."

He sighed like he'd rather not, but did to get it over with. He finally took her into his sights. "It's called HackAttack dot com. And it's not a search engine. It's a website that tracks hackers and shuts them down. It'll identify them and undo the damage they've done. It's one of a kind. But I don't want anyone getting the idea yet. Even in the proposal, I didn't disclose the name of it. And I'd appreciate it if you didn't either."

She smiled. "Oh, my. That's amazing. How do you go about that? I mean, how would you get one step ahead of them?"

"High-tech sensor devices that identify hackers based on keystrokes. Mom, I can't talk about it anymore."

"Okay. My goodness. Son, that's great. Congratulations." She stood and headed for the door.

"Thanks." He returned his attention to the computer monitors.

She turned. "Oh, and another thing. Your stepfather and I had a conversation over the phone this morning about, well, your new job at Google is coming together and things are gearing up with the campaign and all. We thought maybe the timing might be right for you to start looking for your own place. I can help you look, of course, but if you've got some stable income now, plus your father's death benefit from the insurance policy payoff when you turned twenty-five, it just might be a good time for you to move out. If, of course, you think you can afford it."

Virgil looked right at her. "Mom, can we talk about that later, please? I've got to prepare a PowerPoint presentation for tomorrow. Trying to get this done."

"Sure we can. When?"

"Later." He glanced down at his work. "This house is a monstrosity. Six bedrooms and six thousand square feet, and you make it sound like I'm in the way."

She replied with a soothing voice. "Of course not. It's not about us having room."

"Like I said. Let's talk about it later."

"Okay." She was quiet and then seemed to press Virgil again for an answer. "I really want to let Darrell know what you and I agreed to the next time I talk to him. He's out of town until the weekend."

"Oh really?"

"Yes."

Virgil shook his head, knowing his stepfather was behind his mother's insistence. "Nothing yet. Tell him I don't know. I just need a little bit more time here."

She nodded but looked conflicted. "Okay. But really, you should think about it. I mean, you're twenty-eight and we've never lived apart. I'll miss you, but maybe you can get some place close by. I'll let him know we talked."

"Yeah. You do that. Tell him I'll talk to him about it later."

"Will I see you for dinner, son?"

"I doubt it." He clicked the mouse.

"Okay fine. Bye."

"Uh-huh."

Virgil was braced and ready for his stepfather's passive antics.

Game on.

MSNBC reports that the remaining Republican candidates will debate in Columbia, South Carolina, tomorrow in place of the previous debate, which was canceled due to weather. Senator Ellington was on WISTV News 10 in Columbia this morning, saying he looks forward to a heated debate.

Fourteen

Kemba

Friday—August 26, 2011

Beryl was out on a Friday night and it was almost midnight.

Kemba lay nude along the black sheets in their bed with only the light of the television. He was exhausted after two appointments that day, but he couldn't manage to doze off. He tossed and turned and channel-surfed, praying for sleep, knowing he had another appointment at nine o'clock in the morning.

His phone signaled a text. He knew it was Beryl saying she was on her way home. He picked up his cell and saw that the text came from Dallas. Ursula.

Can you talk?

His immediate reply was, **Yes**. And one minute later, his phone rang.

"Hello."

Her voice was soft. "Hi there. Sorry it's so late. My husband is out of town and I'm alone. Couldn't sleep."

"It's cool. I couldn't sleep either."

"Oh, were you trying to? I'm sorry."

He assured her. "It's fine. Glad you called. How are you, beautiful?"

"Okay, I guess. Just have a lot on my mind. Some good, some not so good. But one of the good things is I can't stop thinking about us, about the time we got together. It was so good, so satisfying. I can't get it out of my head." She sounded sad.

He said, "I understand. I feel the same way."

Ursula sniffled and then was silent.

He waited and then asked, "Are you okay?"

"Yes." She sniffled some more, and her voice sounded weak. "I'm fine." Then she started breathing heavy and began to weep.

"Calm down." He turned onto his back.

"It's just…" She gave a loud sigh. "I have this life. It's turning out to be more and more public. I put on a happy face, but honestly, my sex life is the worst. My husband is a sex addict."

"Are you sure?" he asked. "I mean, maybe he just has a high sex drive."

She seemed apologetic. "No, I'm sorry. I shouldn't share these intimate details with you. This is wrong."

"Listen, it's okay if you need to get it out. You can talk to me. I'm a man and I know men."

She sounded congested. "He's gotta have it all the time. I can't satisfy him. I can't be with him every minute. He's out of town now and there's no telling what he's doing."

"Have you caught him cheating before?"

"No. But I just know he's up to something." She sniffled again. "Kemba, he wakes up jacking off. He was doing it four times a day. If I turn him down, I know he'll be even more apt to get satisfied elsewhere. And if I don't turn him down and agree to have sex, I pray that it's over each time. It's so mechanical. So about him. So non-tender."

"I'm sorry. You deserve better than that. Have you talked to him about how you want it?"

"We've been to couples' counseling where we discussed it. He wasn't completely honest with the counselor because he didn't want them to know the whole truth. I asked him recently about taming his sex drive."

"Was he open to it?"

"He was in denial. He says he's down to masturbating once or twice a day."

"That's gotta be tough on you both, I'm sure."

She said, "I've never cheated until now, and you've proven to me that just like I imagined, I can be with someone I'm compatible with in bed."

"Being compatible is about more than sex. If it's good in other areas, I'm sure you two can work this out. If you both want to, that is."

"That's the million-dollar question...do I want to?"

"True."

She was almost whispering. "He does these predictable things, and watches me when I get in bed, every step I take when I walk around, and then pulls out his penis and jerks it. I feel like an object. Then he directs me on the way he wants it, telling me to lay on the bed as he stands over me and demands a blow job, then eventually has fast and sweaty sex with me while he talks this corny sex talk. He doesn't even notice if I grind back or talk or have an orgasm."

"Does he try to please you, like eating you out?" he asked, feeling himself getting hard.

"Oh, that's just going through the motions. He does not know what he's doing, at all, and I just fake it to get it over with. It's awful. It's hell."

He took hold of his dick under the covers. "I would think he'd try and please you to get you ready first, or ask you to try new things. If I was your man, I would take care of your every need."

"If." She was quiet.

"I'd find your tender spot and work it out." He massaged his tip with his thumb.

"I know. You did. I was watching to see what you were doing. You must have gone to Pussy Eating University. Shit." She sucked her teeth and moaned.

"I did." He began stroking himself fully. "I keep thinking back to watching you come when my face was between your legs. How wet you got. Your pretty clit. Damn, girl." He gripped himself tighter.

She sounded turned on, too. "And you. Your dick is made for my pussy. I keep imagining what it felt like with you inside of me. I think about it even when I'm with him." Her tone shifted, like she was trying to get a grip. "I'm sorry."

"Don't apologize. I understand." Kemba didn't dare tell her that he thought about her while he was having sex with Beryl. He only said, "We were good together, you and me."

She cleared her throat and then said, "I've got to go. He's calling right now. I'll talk to you later."

He felt his stiffness subside. "Okay. Bye, beautiful."

"Bye."

Kemba hung up and removed his hand from himself. He thought about what could happen if Ursula wasn't married, and if he wasn't in his situation. Would he be ready for a regular, closed relationship? Not the type where the man has sex for money, brings his dick home to his woman, and the woman is out all night getting her freak on, then bringing her pussy home to her man.

He believed it had to get better and that regular was ahead of him.

He aimed the remote at the TV and pressed Off, turned to his side, his dick now completely soft, and within five minutes fell asleep.

Beryl came home after five in the morning, and he awoke to her sucking his dick.

He thought of Ursula, the politician's wife, and they fucked until well past seven.

Republican candidate Kalin Graves criticized the president for cutting veterans' benefits, saying it was disgusting how the president was cutting millions of military dollars, especially for those in need of medical help and particularly those who suffer from posttraumatic stress disorder.

Fifteen

Midori

Monday—September 12, 2011

Midori had seen Bailey quite a few times since she and Virgil had broken up. Bailey had been unveiling new ways to live out his fantasy scenarios, like having her dress and talk like Marilyn Monroe while he got on his knees before her, eating her underneath her dress and growling like a wild animal. Another time he blindfolded her and wanted her to pretend he broke into her room to rob her, then have her beg him to fuck her.

He did all of this while claiming to not be able to get enough of her. As freaky as he was, she kept taking his money anyway. Kept showing up in spite of him pushing the limits. She felt a mix of despising him for what he craved and a feeling of almost seeing it as her comfort zone.

The cash had been counted and Midori lay with Bailey in

the lavish hotel room. He had a look of paranoia in his eyes. Paranoia mixed with love.

He said to her, "I think you've been staying away from me on purpose."

She explained, "I haven't. I've just been busy."

"Well, you've been making me wait way too long to see you." He turned on his side to face her.

She looked up. "It's called setting an appointment. A date and time that works for us both, not just for you." She tried to catch a glimpse of the digital clock without Bailey noticing.

"I'm guessing you really don't need the money anyway."

"I haven't needed money in a while. *Need* is the wrong word. It's a want. I want money. I want to feel I have enough saved to make a decision. All of this will stop. So get all you can while you can."

He lifted his head. "What does that mean?"

She looked over at him, seeming impatient. His lips were chapped and she could smell his stale breath. "Bailey, what do you want today?"

"I'm confused. Why do you even keep seeing me? It's not like you give a damn."

"Because I want to. If I didn't want to, I wouldn't."

He reached over and propped a pillow under his head. "I think it's more. I think you're feeling me more than you admit."

She gave off a small chortle. "Bailey. Let me tell you something. I'm smart enough to know that the reality of any hooker, prostitute, escort, streetwalker, call girl, whatever you want to call it, getting snatched up by Captain Save-A-Ho and living happily ever is nil."

"I beg to differ. I've heard of porn stars who find the right one and get married. What do you want?"

She gave a sigh. "Bailey, the question is what do *you* want? Tonight. Now. What new and exciting kinky game do you want to play?"

He said, frowning, "You've got someone, don't you? I know you do."

"Actually, I don't. Now tell me what you want."

"Whoever he is, I hope he takes the time to look deeper than what you do for a living."

"Oh, and you do, huh? Bailey, I'm no last-resort woman. Let me tell you, I've been through some things, maybe not as bad as some people. But any man who doesn't understand me for my good and my bad sides, and love me through it instead of judging me for laying on my back for money and nothing more, can kiss my ass. It might be embarrassing to some, a sin, sick, perverted, whatever, but everybody has a story. It's usually the ones throwing the stones that have the most fragile houses of their own. Fuck them."

He nodded. "Uh-oh. I see I hit a nerve."

"Bailey, stop." She looked back up at the ceiling.

"I would love you. I do love you."

She sat up, scooting herself back. "I can't figure you out. First of all, you spend a lot of money and I understand why you do, but maybe one day you'll find someone who will love you through all of your stuff, too, and you'll trust someone enough to tell them about what kinky crap you like, and then you can stop having to pay, as much as I enjoy the cash. They say find someone just as fucked up as you are and live happily ever after. You've never told me if you ever had a girlfriend. That's on you. I don't usually take time to even go that deep with clients, but honestly, you are really hard to figure out. And, I still don't know why you told Money that I tore up that hotel room. Was it so she'd forbid me from seeing you again, so we could make arrangements like this on our own? Whatever." She popped her tongue. "Shoot. I try to be nice and still come back to be with you, but most women you pay would think twice—not that I haven't, mind you. And then you keep telling me you love me when you don't even know me, don't have the slightest idea about who I am. And I don't know about you either, other than you get your rocks off by having sex that feeds your fetishes." She looked away. "I have to ask you to please stop saying you love me. It's just the fantasy for you. But it isn't a fantasy for me. It doesn't flatter me or make me want to see you anymore. It actually makes me want to stay away from you."

"I love you." His words were sweet but his eyes were sour.

"Stop it." She stared right at the clock and turned her body to face him. "Look, I know one thing, it's getting deep into your hour. Is that what you want tonight, to talk?"

"I wanna play."

"Then get to it, please. Enough with the conversation. I can't take anymore. You want to spank me, choke me, make me bark, call me names, drop hot candle wax on my nipples, what?"

He pointed to the wooden slats of the headboard. "I want to handcuff you and pretend you're my prisoner."

She didn't blink, only asked, "Where are the cuffs? Let me see them."

He sat up and looked into a bag next to the bed. He handed them to her. "Here."

They were heavy metal with a lock, short chain links between them, semirusted like they'd been used before. "And where's the key?"

"Right here." He held the tiny key in his hand.

She looked at the key and again at the cuffs. She shook

her head. "Sex worker rule number three is, never get tied up or cuffed." She looked certain.

"I'll uncuff you."

"I can't take that risk." She handed them back to him.

"You don't trust me?"

"Honestly, I don't trust anyone."

"How about one hand?" he suggested.

"I could still be stuck here."

He put the key on the nightstand, and then suddenly looked up at the ceiling and in a flash, threw the handcuffs across the room, against the wall.

Midori jumped out of her skin.

He gave her an evil stare.

She hopped up and stood, backing away from the bed, keeping an eye on him.

He hurried to where she was, looking furious, and whacked her straight across the face with the palm of his hand.

Her head jerked to the left and she put her hand on her face. "Owww, shit! What the hell is wrong with you?"

His nose flared. "Why are you not following my orders?"

"Your orders?" Her eyes bulged. "Bailey. You just hit me."

He tightened his jaw and raised his hand and smacked her again along the same side of her face.

Her head jerked again and she took a step back, trying to focus through a dizzy, stinging haze. "What is your damn problem?"

He stood next to her. "Shut the hell up. If you'd like, I can call the police right now. What do you think would happen to you? You're a paid whore. If I want to fucking cuff you, I'll cuff you. Now get back on the bed."

She kept her hand to her cheek, looking pained and

stunned. "What is this about, Bailey? What is wrong with you?"

"What's wrong is that you told me no. You violated the rules." He looked unstable, raising his hand again.

She put up her arm up in defense. "Okay."

"You're here because you love me, and you know it."

"Bailey." Her voice begged him.

"Aren't you?" He seemed ready to swing again. "Lower your arm."

She retreated, putting her arm down. "Yes. Yes, I am."

"Tell me. I want to hear you say it. I've never heard you say it. Say you love me."

She spoke the three words slowly. "I love you."

"That's better." He put his hand down and gave a snarling gaze.

She tried to take a step around him toward the sofa where her clothes were, but he blocked her, bringing his body to bump hers. "Bailey, just let me go. Let me go and that'll be it. I'll never say another word about it."

"Hell no. I came here and paid you and I want what I paid you for. I want it rough. I want to take it. With force. Do you hear me?" His breath was again close enough for her to smell.

"Yes." She blinked fast. Her sad eyes were glassy.

He yanked her by the arm and dragged her to the foot of the bed. "Now bend over."

Midori braced herself and bent over, the side of her face along the mattress. Her cheek stung and her ear was sore. From behind, she could hear Bailey at least slap the latex from the condom onto his dick, like he could catch something from her more than she could catch something from him. She shut her eyes tight, which brought the release of her tears down her cheeks, and he plunged into the puckered skin of her anus like it was her vagina. She gritted her teeth and held her breath, heart thumping in panic against the mattress.

His rant was livid. "You don't tell me no, you hear? I'll take what I want. If I want to cuff you, I'll cuff you. You're talking about who you don't trust. You show up in hotel rooms with strange men who could end up taking your life and you have the nerve to suddenly have fucking boundaries. I've tried to be nice to you. I told you how I feel, but that's not enough." He kept pumping away.

She kept grimacing.

"You tell me it's my fantasy and then you reject me. I don't know how much more you think I can take. You got me this way. You made me have to take it. It's all your fault. It's your fault it has to be like this. This is what can happen when you're a dirty little whore who fucks strangers. You never know who the hell is gonna be inside of you, getting off because you are a dirty hooker."

Midori just listened and fought off her anxious screams. She stayed quiet and waited, hoping he'd finish and get it over with. Would he be done with her soon? If so, she vowed, it would be the very last time she'd ever see psycho Bailey Brenner again.

He continued his punishment. His words were irate and kinky. "Never been in an ass this tight. I like it in here. And I'll have to do it again. I like the feel of this grip. It's like my dick could blow up inside of you. You'd better be glad I didn't bring my nine-millimeter and stick it inside of you. I'm about to. Yeah. That's a good burst. Coming in that ass all because you told me no. See." He gave an angry grunt and shot his sperm inside of the condom, again grunting longer and deeper, sounding like he was in pain. And then he seemed to instantly snap out of it, yanking himself out, simply saying, "Yeah. I took that." He backed up like he was the man.

She slowly stood, feeling degraded and humiliated, just as he wanted her to feel. She looked over at him with hate.

His wild eyes shifted from her face to his dick to the bathroom door. He stepped to the door, cupping his hand under his dick.

When he was one foot past the bathroom door, Midori had her eyes on her purse and her dress along the sofa. As soon as he was two steps in, she dashed over to her bag, snatched it up, grabbed her dress, and bolted to the door, leaving her shoes, panties and bra there. She was gone before he could step from the bathroom to the living room, and to the room door.

Midori ran butt naked to the stairwell like she was doing a forty-yard dash, down the five flights of stairs, at the same time tossing her dress over her head, slipping into it before she darted out of the stairwell door that led to the lobby.

She hailed a cab back to her place, and from the moment she left the hotel room until the moment she got home, Bailey called. She turned her phone off, headed to her bathroom, and checked out her face in the mirror. Her cheek was scarlet red and her nose was scratched. Her mascara was smeared from burying her teary face in the mattress. She turned on the water to her shower and stepped inside, finally letting out her cries. She sobbed so heavily she could barely breathe. She rinsed herself with a bar of soap and washed her vagina. She inserted her middle finger and realized how wet she was. She smelled her finger, then inserted it once more, smelling it again, realizing it was her own juices. She'd had an orgasm. Her heart thumped in her chest and she gulped hard, wishing the evidence of her turn-on wasn't a reality.

She washed her achy face and sore body, making sure to clean every orifice over and over, and washing her hair. Then she repeated it.

Within a half hour, she lay on her sleigh bed naked, just staring at the walls, still crying. She curled up into a fetal position and cried herself to sleep on top of the covers, wet hair and wet eyes, until the sun brought on a new day.

She awoke and frowned at the rays of the sun, realizing it was not a dream. She was raped, but couldn't report it.

She finally turned on her phone and there were eleven messages from Bailey saying he was sorry, and she deleted them all.

The last one was a voice mail that she hadn't expected to hear. "Midori, something told me to call you. I couldn't sleep all night. Money gave me your number. We miss you. We're sorry. I'm sorry. And I just wanted you to know that above all else, I love you, wildflower. Mom."

Without hesitation, Midori pressed 7 and erased it as well. Her estranged mother's voice did nothing to soothe her abused soul.

Next there was a text from her booker. Midori had been requested back again to be with Mr. 81, Dr. Feelgood, for a weekend. She needed to fly out to Puerto Rico on September 23 for three days. She took in a long breath and then gave an equally long exhale.

And cried some more.

For the tragedies of her past.

And the fact that her mind was taught such sickness that still lived in her head.

She said out loud, "One day."

Praying that day would come sooner than later.

Two of the Republican candidates are African-Americans: Robert Sally and Darrell Ellington. If one of them wins, it will be the second time in U.S. history that our nation has elected an African-American president.

Sixteen

∞

Money

Tuesday—September 20, 2011

Pretty in Pink, aka Mr. 31, wore a pale pink, extra-thin Durex condom over his thrilled penis as Money went down on him at the Belvedere Hotel. Money was seated on a sea-foam-blue guest chair in the bedroom as he stood over her. She ceased her unfinished blow job and said firmly, "Move."

He took steps back and stood before her in his pink garter, black stockings, pink high heels, and black padded bra. He wore heavy makeup, including false lashes and hot pink lipstick, but this time he didn't wear his wig, which made him look even more confused.

"Come here," Money demanded, as she stood. She took the few steps to the bed and he followed.

He bent over, replying, "Yes, Ms. Queens."

"Good boy." She popped his cheeks with her hand, first his left cheek and then his right, until he began to turn red. He shook in anticipation as her hand met his skin. She continued.

He took off the condom and took hold of his penis, squealing like a girl while she spanked him down, even tapping near his testicles.

She said, "You want it harder, don't you?"

"Yes, Mistress."

She spanked him again with more force. The harder she spanked, the more he sped up his stroking motion.

"You had enough?"

"Yes, Mistress."

"You ready to come for me?"

"Yes, Mistress."

"Turn around now and do it. Come in your hand."

He turned and cupped his left hand, jacking himself with his right hand, and released his sperm squirt by squirt. He gave off a sound like he was fighting to bridle his high-pitched moans of pleasure. He sounded like a wounded animal. "Ohhhhh."

She instructed him, looking no-nonsense. "Hush. Don't say a word. Not a sound."

That only made him shoot a little bit more.

Money's cell rang just as Mr. 31 was in submissive heaven, but it seemed that the sound of the ringing phone was like an alarm, reminding him of the real world. He looked instantly ready to shift back into man-mode.

Money walked to her phone as he headed into the bathroom. She asked, "What is it?"

"It's me, Leilani."

"I know. What?"

Leilani spoke quickly. "I drove to my appointment. And, well, it was like only about ten minutes away and I was running late, so I didn't catch a cab. And well, after my appointment, I was in an accident."

"An accident."

"Yes. A cab just totally sideswiped me."

"Where are you?" Money turned to face the wall, placing her hand on her hip.

"I was arrested."

Money tapped her foot. "For what?"

"Driving while under the influence."

"Leilani. Were you alone?"

"Yes."

"You were drinking while working...Leilani, that's a total violation."

Leilani only said, "I need you to come and get me, please."

"Come and get you? You're kidding, right?"

"No. They won't let me drive." Leilani's voice was full of worry.

"Then hail a cab." Money rubbed her forehead. Her face showed her displeasure.

"They need bail money. Cash. I only have like maybe a hundred dollars on me. Plus, I need someone to take me to get my car, but they took my license so I can't drive."

Money gave a small laugh. "Oh well. That part is on you. Only a hundred dollars. Where are you?"

"Manhattan Central Booking."

Money said angrily and impatiently, "I'll get Jamie over there to take you home." *Click.*

She shook her head, still holding on to her phone as Mr. 31 exited the bathroom. He looked up at her while applying cold cream to his face to remove his makeup.

She said, "Tyler," calling him by his first name.

"Yes."

"One of my girls got in trouble. A DWI."

"I heard you talking. Where is she?"

"She's at Central in Manhattan."

"What's her name?"

"It's Leilani. Leilani Sutton."

"Done. And I agree. She should take a cab."

"I'll text her and let her know. Thanks."

He walked back in the bathroom and transformed from the feminine look he had for his play-date to the masculine look he arrived in. He left wearing a gray suit and tie, though his shoulder bag contained his other life.

It was not the first time the New York City police commissioner provided favors to Money in her time of need.

And more than likely it wouldn't be the last.

Money caught a cab to her home and got in a quick workout, and then sat on the sofa, making herself watch old movies. She was on her second movie, *Bridesmaids*, having eaten Ben & Jerry's red-velvet ice cream, trying to get a break in the action. She hadn't heard from Leilani and hadn't bothered to ask Jamie to help out just yet. He'd been fairly quiet, and she was okay with that. She'd gotten used to his distance, and his random spurts of attention.

One person she did want to talk to, just to clear the air and check in, was Midori. She knew if she didn't at least keep an eye on her sister, there was no telling what Romeo might do, or what Midori would let Bailey or Virgil do.

She shook out her shoulders and prepared herself to play nice, all in the name of keeping Lip Service afloat.

Money dialed Midori's number and paused her movie.

"Yes," Midori answered, sounding plain. "Hi, Money."

"Hi. What's been up with you?"

"Nothing."

"I hear you're going out of town again this Friday."

"I am."

"Good."

Instead of speaking, Midori cleared her throat. There was an awkward silence.

Money said, "I'm just checking in with you. You, Leilani, and Kemba really need to keep yourselves straight. Make sure we're in line at all times."

"I know that."

Money could still sense her distance. "Midori, we've got to get past this thing about Virgil. I'm assuming you've got him on your radar."

"I do. And I know you don't like him."

"It's not that I don't like him. I just, I don't want him playing Maxwell Smart and starting something we'll all regret."

"He's fine."

"Okay. And what about Bailey? What's up with him?"

Midori said, with fast-moving words, "Haven't seen him."

"Good." Money followed up with "You sure?"

"I said I haven't seen him. You really don't need to ask me things twice."

"Okay, fine. I do have to ask if you've heard from Romeo?"

"No. Why?"

"He called."

"Called you? Why?"

Money took the brown throw from the back of her sofa and laid it across her legs. "Just keep an eye out for him. You know, same old same old. Threatening to get you back."

"Oh, I don't think so. He's got some nerve." Midori showed a smidgen of energy.

"That he does. Said if not you, then Kemba."

"Kemba? He'd never be able to get Kemba to stoop that low. Kemba's got it made. There are a lot of women willing to pay for a man like him. No telling what Romeo would have him doing."

"I agree. I think Kemba has more sense than that." Money took a deep breath and went there, taking a trip into their past, feeling she needed to address it because of Midori's behavior. Money knew her sister's issues stemmed from problems with their parents—problems no one wanted to address. Money acted tough, but she truly loved her sister and was concerned for her well-being. Maybe talking things out would help Midori deal with things and let her know that if no one else cared, she did. "Listen, I want to tell you something. I keep thinking about all of the crap that happened the day you left home. About all that mess that made you leave. The day you left, Mom called and told me you stormed out, and then she told me why. I think that has a lot to do with you not being happy."

"I knew she would. Easy for her to tell you after forgetting to tell me. I am happy. I'm fine. I don't want you always telling me what I'd better do and not do. I've got enough sense to stay out of trouble."

"I can't help it. I'm your big sister before anything else. And I'm trying to keep this business afloat. As far as you being happy or not, I can hear it in your voice, and I saw it on your face. I'm really hoping, actually, I'm praying, you get past everything."

"It was no big deal."

"Midori, look, I found out what happened the day you left.

You overheard Mom yelling at Dad during their argument because they thought you weren't home. He brought up the day when she was eight months pregnant with you, and that he kicked her in the stomach hoping he would cause her to miscarry."

Midori's energy dipped again. "Whatever."

Money paused and took a deep breath. "I know how messed up it is for you to realize that all the years you thought Dad was your birth father, he wasn't. It was hard to hear him call Mom names for cheating on him back when she was modeling and to say that his best friend, Jimmy, was your father."

Midori was silent.

Money said, "Midori. Please talk to me."

Midori asked slowly, "You really didn't know all along?"

"No. Not until you left. Mom called me upset, not knowing where you were. That's when she told me everything."

Midori was again silent.

Money waited her out.

Midori asked, "Did Jimmy know he was my father? I have to know."

"Honestly, I don't know. I'm thinking he did and that's why Dad flipped out when he found out you and Jimmy slept together, that if he did it knowing he was your father, that was sick. That it would be bad enough if Jimmy didn't know, but if he did, that was heartbreaking."

Midori gave a loud exhale. "Heartbreaking for who?"

"For Dad. For you."

"Please stop saying 'Dad' like he's my father."

"I'm sorry."

Midori raised her voice, sounding frustrated. "Look, I slept with Jimmy on purpose to get back at *your* father. I felt he hated me. I wanted your father to hurt. All my life he showed me no attention. I didn't know that in trying to get the man I thought was my father to show some feelings for me, I'd end up sleeping with my real dad. It's just disgusting. It's all too much."

"It's tough. And I know it's hard to deal with. Hard to get over. I'm so sorry."

"You keep apologizing. You don't owe me an apology."

"I'm apologizing for them. I admit that Mom and my dad are a strange-ass couple. They've been through a lot, even though Dad cheated on her over and over, and got caught with hookers, and stepped out on her no telling how many times, not to mention her cheating, too. Since then, I think you and I learned that infidelity is a normal thing."

"You didn't get treated the way he treated me. You were his birth daughter. I was another man's child. You don't know what it's like. You'll never know." Midori's voice began to slow.

"No, I won't. You're right. He has always been like ice, though, very cold, even to me. I felt that and I lived with it. He just is who he is."

Midori was quiet yet again.

Money took a deep breath and felt her emotions rumble. She said, "Aside from that, I want you to know that what I'm sorry for is getting you into this business. Really regretting the day I asked you to work for me."

Midori seemed sincere. "You gave me a way out from Romeo and the streets. It was my choice. Not yours."

"Yeah, but I guess what I really did was take you from the frying pan to the skillet."

"You didn't. I'm fine."

"Maybe. Though sometimes, I feel like there's no difference between walking the streets and laying up in a hotel waiting for a client to show up." She paused. "But I'm in this too deep. Can't let it fall apart now. That's why I'm bringing this up about Mom. I want you to get better. Believe it or not, I want you to be happy."

"Yeah, well sometimes it seems Lip Service comes before everything and everyone."

Money waited in thought.

Midori waited longer.

Money wanted to tell her sister that it had to be that way. That there was no way she was going to jail. She couldn't tell her that she was only checking in to make sure Midori wasn't unraveling, and that she was reaching out to keep her sister from getting desperate just because of her past. Money finally said instead, "Well, listen, you enjoy yourself in Puerto Rico. And hey..."

"Yeah."

"You know, sex to an escort is an act, not love. Don't come back married now." She forced a big laugh.

Midori managed a small one. "That'd be the day."

"Yes."

"And Money?"

"Yes."

"You said Mom told you everything the day I left."

"Yes."

"Actually, she didn't tell you everything because she doesn't know everything."

Money asked quickly, "Really. What else is there?"

"One day you'll know. One day I'll tell you."

"Oh, Midori, you and your *one days*."

"One day."

"Okay. You promise?"

"I promise. Bye." She sounded plain again.

"Ciao, sis. Be safe."

Money hung up, rested her head back upon the sofa, and wept.

She had to survive, in spite of herself.

Seventeen

∞

Leilani

Friday—September 23, 2011

Leilani went to the arraignment, only to happily find that the DA had dropped the charges. For the last couple of days, she'd been dealing with her insurance company, trying to get the taxicab company to pay for damages to her car.

Jamie Bitters, Money's guy and the driver for Lip Service, took her to get her car. Turned out her license was not suspended. Jamie lectured her on the dangers of driving after drinking and on the dangers of taking a drink while on an appointment.

The day she appeared in court, the judge, a middle-aged black man, heard and dismissed the case.

Today, that very judge was in the throes of licking her pussy through a sheer dental dam. She sucked his condom-covered dick, in a 69 position in the Central Park View Suite at the luxurious Mandarin Oriental Tower. Leilani figured that Money must've pulled some strings, and that part of those strings probably meant the judge was getting the pussy hookup.

Their bare bodies were intertwined upon the king bed. The curtains were wide open, exposing the floor-to-ceiling views of the park and Manhattan skyline.

His expensive suit rested on the gold lounger and her dress was tossed on the carpeted floor, as he'd stripped her down with body kisses and carried her to bed.

Her head was along a black pillow as he lay above her in reverse. She knew he was trying to please her, but the latex between her skin and his lips always seemed to limit her pleasure. He, on the other hand, was having a hard time concentrating. It was obvious that the 69 he was receiving was distracting him from giving, mainly because he was being served up by the best head-giver in town, who was taking him deep.

He backed his face away from his pussy-eating duties, looked back, and said, "Wow. This is one helluva thank-you, here."

She kept working on him.

He started grinding his penis into her mouth like it was her vagina. "You can take all that. Damn." He was of course impressed.

He didn't have a large dick, but it was big enough to keep her focused on her technique of breathing and extending her tongue.

She began stroking him with her hand and he said, "No hands. Don't use your hands."

She moved her hand away so he could have it his way. But she knew, either way, he wouldn't last long.

He seemed to forget he was supposed to be the 9 and she was the 6. Being lazy, he asked while still looking back at her, "If I could just take that condom off..."

She shook her head in reply, with him still in her mouth, making sure to suck that magic tip, the part of the dick that makes it all happen. She knew what she was doing. She knew the male anatomy very well.

He resumed his pussy licking for a moment and then spoke again. "I've never done this before with the plastic. If I could take it off of you, I could really show you what I do."

Before she could reply, he bucked his hips in a fast motion and looked up at the ceiling, tightening up and giving off a sound like he was losing his ever-loving mind: "Awww, awww, ungh, nnnnnnooooo. Ughhhh." He pumped a final, deep pump while she tightened her lip grip and took him deep so he could feel her throat swallow against his shaft, and he filled up the condom inside her mouth, yelling, "Oh yeah. This is the shit, here. Hell, yeah." He stayed right where he was, even after she removed him from her mouth. It seemed he was fighting off come spasms. His crotch and behind were in her face. He said, as though in a trance, "Yeah. That was amazing."

He moved his left leg from beside her shoulder and adjusted himself to sit on the edge of the bed and catch his breath. He used his hand to keep the filled condom in place.

She sat up and said, "I'm totally glad you liked it."

"That's an understatement. We're gonna have to do this again."

"An escort newbie, huh?" she asked, seeing the obvious wonder on his face.

"You could say that."

She laughed. "I see."

He asked out of the blue. "You wanna have lunch with me sometime?"

She grinned. "Oh, no. But thank you."

"I understand. Sorry if I shouldn't have asked."

"No. It's totally fine. I'm flattered, actually."

He looked at her as if lust was playing tricks on his heart. "When I saw you in the courtroom, I was like, my, my, my. And now, wow. I'm just amazed that I'm here with you."

"That's very sweet of you to say." Leilani gave a soft grin and crossed her arms. She wondered if they were done.

He asked, "How much more time do I have?"

Looking at the clock across the room, she said, "Your time is just about up, actually."

He turned to face her. "Okay. So, how does this work? Can I pay for more?" He looked in awe.

She stood. "Next time. You can request me. As you know, my name is Manhattan."

"Okay." He stared at her fit, curvy body without blinking. He slowly stood and went into the bathroom, and disposed of his condom, then turned on the shower. "You want to take a quick shower with me?"

Before she could refuse, she heard: *Knock. Knock.*

"Who's that?" he asked loudly, stepping to the doorway of the bathroom.

She put her finger to her lips. "Shhhh," she said softly. "I don't know." She tiptoed to the door naked and looked through the peephole, hearing a voice that matched the face she saw.

"Leilani. It's me. Shawn. Open the door."

Her heart raced and she said in a whisper, tiptoeing back, "Oh shit."

He wrapped a towel around his waist, asking, "What's going on?"

"Umm. I'm sorry, but that's someone I know."

"Someone you know?"

She hurried to get dressed as she spoke. "Yes."

He whispered, too. "No one can know I'm here."

She nodded. "What I need to do is go out there and talk to him. I'll get him to go downstairs with me. You just make sure you lock the door as soon as I step out."

Knock. Knock. "Leilani."

"Are you sure that'll work?" he asked.

"Yes. I can handle him. You just leave as fast as you can."

He shook his head and dropped the towel, stepping into his pants and following her to the door.

She grabbed the key card and stepped close to the door. "Coming." She opened it and closed it in one split second. She could hear the judge securing the inside latch so she said loudly, "What in the hell are you doing here?" storming away so he would follow.

Shawn, a blond, handsome white man, six feet tall, said, "You tell me you got in an accident, then you don't return my calls. You tell me I can't come out and see you but you act like I'm really going to move on, just like that."

She only asked, "Why are you here?"

"I had a meeting out here. I wanted to surprise you at first, then I thought I'd ask if I could come out. You said no." He stood behind her as she pressed the elevator button, trying her best to ignore the sight of him. He continued, "But I came anyway and booked myself into this hotel, and bam. There you were going toward the elevators while I was heading to the business center." He pointed back to the room. "Who's in there, anyway?"

"The question is, how'd you get my room number?"

"The girl at the front desk told me."

She gave the sound of a single laugh. "Well, she's about to get fired. What's up with this elevator?" She looked up at the light and saw that it had stopped three floors above them.

He asked, "Leilani. What are you doing here? Catering?"

She still looked forward. "I live in New York. I have a right to be here. Plus. I'm single and available. But that's not the question. The question is, what are you doing sneaking up on me instead of calling me to say you're here? You totally should've called to say you saw me, instead of just coming up and knocking on the door, unannounced. I'm not having this. If this is, like, your way of getting me back, it's totally not working."

He looked at her from head to toe. "What is wrong with you? You look like you just woke up."

"Stop with the damn questions. Just leave." She looked toward the hotel room and then up at the light, seeing that the elevator car was one floor above.

"I can't leave. I'm staying here at this hotel. I already told you."

"Good. Well then, go to your room." She shooed him away with her eyes.

He took a deep breath. "Leilani. Wait. Have dinner with me. Please. I'll be here for a few days at the least."

"No."

"Just call me."

"Good-bye, Shawn." The elevator chimed. The door parted.

She stepped inside, and he followed.

He kept talking as she repeatedly pushed the button to the lobby. "You think I don't know you've got somebody in there?"

The doors closed.

"I don't care what you know."

He said nothing, looking forward.

She said nothing, looking down at her feet.

Then as the elevator door opened she said, "Good-bye."

He stepped off, but she stayed on and pressed the button to her floor. Shawn stood there and watched her, looking lost. Just as the doors joined together and shut him out of her sight, she saw a glimpse of the judge exiting the stairwell, walking fast, wearing his suit, without giving a second of eye contact. The elevator went back up.

She arrived at her floor and hurried from the elevator back into her room. She sat on the bed and said, "I'll be damned. He's got some nerve."

She took a moment, just thinking about how he showed up out of the blue.

She checked her phone but he hadn't called, so she turned on the TV. The shower was still running from when the judge had turned it on.

Just as she turned to go into the bathroom, she saw Senator Darrell Ellington with his wife on Headline News. He stood at a podium and she stood behind him, smiling lovingly. He addressed a group of supporters in Florida. He was now one of the five remaining Republican candidates.

She picked up the remote and turned up the volume. Senator Ellington spoke about family values and how his fellow candidate, Robert Sally, hadn't paid child support for ten years. He spoke of the importance of the sanctity of marriage, and how parents need to be devoted to their children.

She gave a smirk and took off her clothes, then picked up her phone, texted, Done, and stepped her high-class body into the shower to clean it up for the next stranger's pleasure.

A man who was having impotency problems. She'd need to work hard to get him up.

She said aloud, "Damn. If the world only understood the power of the pussy. It can make a man lose his ever-loving mind."

The debate at Dartmouth College turned ugly when Darrell Ellington and Kalin Graves again sparred on the topic of gay marriage. Candidate Marla Goins agreed with Senator Ellington, though they disagreed on the topic of health-care benefits for unmarried same-sex partners.

Eighteen

∞

Kemba

Wednesday—October 12, 2011

Kemba and Beryl's penthouse suite in Harlem had the ambiance of an erotic love nest. Juniper breeze candles burned along the fireplace in the bedroom. The flames of the black oak log threw off a romantic shimmer of light. And seductive music by Marvin Gaye serenaded their movements.

It was sexual healing time.

And Beryl howled.

Her head met the floor.

Her back was against the wall.

Her legs were wall-to-wall, similar to the off-white shag carpeting.

Her split was an upside-down equator.

Kemba was northbound, bending his legs to just the right height to hit it.

His ten-inch pole did some serious deep-sea fishing. He held onto her thick thighs, keeping her legs wide open.

He drilled his fullness and length and power and might as far inside of his woman as he could get, tightening his glutes and working his legs to get as deep as she wanted. He even wore his Air Jordans for traction.

Her years of gymnastics came in handy as she raised up a little higher, much like she was doing a handstand. The definition in her arms showed the strain of her weight, but the pleasure on her face said it was worth it.

She did a full split with glee, aiding his ability to cut her white bald vagina in half with his massive black dick.

She spoke upside down, sounding soulful. "Oh, yes. Fuck the shit out of me. Get that. Make it cry. Fuck that cunt like I slapped your momma. You Kenyan, Egyptian, Mandingo, Swahili, stud ass, sex king, tall, dark, hung Negro mothafucka, you."

He grinned at her thrill. "Look at you talking shit upside down. Got your ass prone."

"Yeah, I'll bet none of those bitches who pay for your big dick can handle all this pipe without being scared out of their minds."

He didn't dare answer her, for real for real, so he said, "Nope. They can't. Only you, babe."

"Yeah. I'm serving you a deep-ass pussy on a platter while standing on my head. Beat that. Freaking like this makes me wanna buy you that damn black Jag you want." She was a notch away from yelling, even upside down.

"Oh really?"

She was hella loud. "Really. Make me come. You know what to do."

He pulled out and she adjusted herself from up against the wall, flipping her legs over and coming to a stance from her position. Her face was flushed and her body was hot. He picked her up like it was nothing, even though she weighed over one-sixty, and placed her on her back at the very end of their poster bed.

He stood before her, moved her ass all the way to the edge, nearly hanging off the end, and pulled her legs toward him with his forearms. He aligned her just right and penetrated her again.

She followed his rhythm and at first, kept her hands along her chest, playing with her breasts, in full control of what she was doing and what she was saying.

She kept up her fuck talking. "Yeah, that's it. Do that. Standing there looking like a king. Fine-ass pussy killer you. Hit that spot. Work that spot. Make me squirt like a damn faucet, God damn it."

He said, "Oh, I hear you. I think you're ready."

"Oh yeah. I'm ready. Shit yeah."

He readjusted his grip on her legs, leaned forward a bit, and got his footing right so that his shoes were positioned along the white carpet, and he got a motion going so smooth, it was in the exact beat of the next song, "Let's Get It On," playing in the background.

Kemba sped up and bucked and fucked, while Beryl made a noise, a long moan that revved up to a deep groan, and then she spoke short, unrecognizable words, sounding like she was speaking in tongues. Her voice got shakier the more he poked a steady stream of friction at the right angle, over and over, dipping down to make sure he aimed upward, keeping his rhythm.

Her hand had moved from her breasts, to somewhere

above her head, one hand cupped and then relaxed, the other hand gripping the sheet and then letting go.

She sounded like she was losing her mind as he started to grind her into stupidity. She rambled on as her titties flopped every which-a-way, and the sound of his skin hitting her ass was loud. She closed her eyes, and then just as she said, "Uuuuuhhnn, uuuuhhnn, uuuuhhnn," Kemba reached down and yanked his dick out. She bore down, and he swatted her large clit with his long dick and beat it senseless. A stream of liquid expelled from her middle that shot so high it hit his chest and ran down his belly. She yelled like she was either dying or being born. It smelled of sweet clover and was semicloudy. It was nothing like his granny lover's spill. This was the real thing, female ejaculate.

He reinserted and she said, "No. Yes. No."

Mind-blowing.

He bucked again and she made those crazy sounds again. He pulled out and beat her clit and she released her stream again, first a short one, then a long one. He inserted again, but this time Beryl sounded like she was crying.

"Stop. I can't take it. Dammit."

He inserted again anyway and fucked her, feeling her pussy clench. Her groans were loud and nasty as her intermittent shudders vibrated along her spine. He shot his own orgasm deep inside of the woman who he turned out each and every time they fucked.

She was bonded from her orgasms, saying "I love you," while sniffling.

He was in Erotic City. "Ahhhhh, shit. Yeah. Uuuuhhh. I love your ass, too," he said, just as he waited for the stream of sperm to finish its journey through his lengthy dick. He pulled out and stood over the bed before her, as she scooted to lay flat on her back, panting.

Beryl and Kemba could fuck so pretty. It was award winning, deep, intense, and 100 percent mutually satisfying.

He knew Beryl felt it was the way it was because they kept it new and fresh, and because they had the freedom of an open relationship.

Kemba felt it was the way it was because he was the only one who was ever able to bring on the aerobic waterworks of his freaky sugar momma.

Her next sentence got his attention. "I want Ryan to join us."

"What the hell?" He stepped away from the wet spot on the carpet—even his Jordans were wet—and he rubbed her liquid from the skin of his abdomen.

She said again, wiping a tear that had fallen along her face, "Ryan. I want him to see what you do to me."

"You're kidding, right?"

"I'm dead serious. He's down if you are." She didn't even blink.

He asked, looking astonished, "You invited that dude to our relationship? To be with us?"

"Please, we fuck other people all the time. I thought it'd be cool to go to the next level. Have a threesome."

He looked at his dick as it went down. "Not with some dude. Oh hell no. Two hard dicks in a room is one too many."

"Kemba, you're acting like a prude."

"I'm not." He stepped over to the dresser, looking at his reflection in the mirror.

She stretched out the kinks in her legs and rubbed her thighs. "I thought you were more open-minded than that. I thought pleasing me was something you enjoyed doing."

"I do. But I can please you all by myself. I don't need any damn help."

She explained, "I'm saying let's spice it up. Not you and him touching. Both of you pleasing me." She looked excited by the thought. "I'll bet I can take it."

"I bet you can." He looked sure.

"He is black, but he's not as big as you." She offered a smile like she felt she needed to stroke his ego.

His expression stayed firm. "Beryl, please. I really don't wanna hear about Ryan's penis, black or white. Conversation ended." He headed toward the hallway. "I'll be right back. You want something to drink?"

"I'll have a sip of whatever you have."

He turned back, giving her a look. "Okay. While I'm gone, you get that freaky shit out of your head."

"Please. Most men are a drink away from it." She rubbed her eyes and adjusted the pillow under her head.

Kemba yelled back, "Well, this man is the exception to your silly-ass rule. Guaranteed."

Something in him wanted to agree to her threesome suggestion, but he was more worried about what she'd think if he went for it. That maybe he really was okay with two dicks in the room. That he liked men. So he said no. But in his head he remained curious.

Former governor Robert Sally criticized the president's budget in a campaign rally, knocking him for what he calls ignoring entitlement programs. Darrell Ellington agreed, calling the president's budget a gloomy reflection of his failed policies of the past.

Nineteen

∞

Virgil

Thursday—November 10, 2011

CNN's Political Ticker reported:

> Team Darrell Ellington continued to take on rival Kalin Graves over his fiscal record while serving in the Senate. Ellington's campaign is scheduled to hold a press conference on Thursday and issue a barrage of campaign statements criticizing Graves, the mayor of Philadelphia, for his past support of earmarks and "reckless spending." Republican candidate Ellington's popularity continues to soar, some say because of his conservative views on popular yet crucial topics like gay marriage and welfare reform.

Virgil looked disappointed as he sat in the family room of their home, watching his stepfather on television. "Ha!

What about his views on prostitution? I'd love it if someone would put a microphone in his face and ask him to address that topic. Hypocritical ass." He'd had an afternoon business meeting at the Google offices, then came home early to continue more research and development on the business side of his own anti-hacking venture.

Virgil switched channels but kept finding more political buzz about the presidential campaign. On nearly every channel he saw his stepfather, and most times his mom, Ursula, was by Darrell's side. He also saw a video of his stepfather's biggest opponent, Philadelphia mayor Kalin Graves, in a black suit with a red tie, and his lovely wife, Sasha Graves, in a red suit with pearls. They were both offering continuous Colgate smiles, looking conservative and energetic. And they had a beautiful biracial teenage daughter by their side dressed in pink. The media often addressed the fact that silver-haired Kalin Graves was white and his sophisticated wife was black, making mention of how it was a first in political history to have an interracial couple as candidate and wife. Virgil still wondered if the rumors that Kalin Graves was really a racist were true. But his gut told him that he knew enough, just knowing he patronized Lip Service. He decided to let it all go. For the time being.

Knowing the reality of both Kalin Graves's and his stepfather's infidelities turned his stomach. He wondered how both could be so careless. But still and all, his mother continued to be the priority. The absence of Midori had been more and more noticeable. It had been four months. She was very quiet. He did leave messages and sent a few e-mails, but no reply. He knew she was angry, but in his heart, with all that was going on, her absence was missed. In spite of it all, no matter what, she was someone he could talk to. And he needed to talk about everything right now, from the realities of his stepfather's infidelities, to the possibility of him having to move, to the excitement of his new business venture, to his feelings about what he and Midori had been through. The fact that he got so close to someone who could also be part of the demise of his family, and the demise of the business she worked for, had him conflicted.

With the house extra-quiet and the squeaky-clean expectations of the political life feeling like the enemy, he gave in and placed another call.

This time he got a "Hello." But Midori did not sound welcoming.

"Hi there. How are you?" Virgil sounded both surprised and elated that she answered.

"Fine."

"Where've you been? I called you a few times. Left messages."

She sounded edgy. "I was out of town a couple of times. But, honestly, I really don't know why it matters. Even if I was in town, I wouldn't have called you back, Virgil."

"Be nice."

She interjected, "Oh, be nice? You weren't being very nice when you cussed me out and stormed out of here."

"You're right. Just wanna be nice now."

"So, you wanna be friends? After all that, is that what you're saying?"

"What's wrong with that?"

"It was apparently all wrong for you to even be associated with me. I'm surprised you're risking the possibility of living in the White House by calling me. Besides, considering that you record people by using your little spy gadgets, why would I even want to talk to you?"

He wondered himself, saying, "I understand. I'd just hoped you would."

She said, sounding cautious, "You're not recording this call, are you?"

"I'm not."

She had much attitude. "Whatever, Virgil. I'll never trust you again."

He decided to say what he really thought. "I could be saying that, too. You lied to me yet you'll never trust me? Ms. Real Estate Agent."

"Oh please. Virgil, what do you want?"

"I don't know. I was just sitting here. My stepfather's face and name are everywhere I look. Things are getting crazy. Plus, my mother and I talked about me moving out. I'm thinking about it. I just needed to talk to you, that's all. I miss us."

All she said was, "Oh really? So they're mad at you? What'd you do to them? Spy on them, too?" Her sarcasm was clear.

He wasn't surprised. "No."

"And she doesn't know about him?"

"No."

"I'll bet she does."

"Believe me, she doesn't." He aimed the conversation in another direction. "But what I called for was just to say that I miss you. It's been a while. And I was wondering if we could see each other, you know, have a cup of coffee or something."

"Why?"

"Like I said, I miss you. Still can't believe how things went down. It's like something's missing, though. And seeing you would be good, you know?"

"Oh really?"

"Really."

She actually asked, "When, Virgil?"

He smiled so big that it could be heard in his reply. "Oh, I was thinking, today maybe. I'm gonna meet my real estate agent in SoHo this afternoon. Gonna look at some properties. Wondered if you could go with me."

She replied without hesitation. "To look at places? No thanks."

"Why not?"

"Because, I just can't. I have an appointment."

"Where?"

"Gramercy," she replied dryly.

"Good, then you can meet me."

"I can't go with you. I don't wanna do things like that. It just seems too couple-ish. I'm still coming to terms with everything. My whole life. Losing you. Lying to you. You recording me. It's too soon to be friends."

"Okay." He knew he deserved it, but he stayed insistent. "Well, maybe we can just meet for a minute. Maybe at the spot we went to the first day we went out. Little Cupcake Bakeshop on Prince Street."

"You want to meet for cupcakes?"

"I do. What time can you be there?"

She was quiet.

"Please." He wished for her heart to soften.

"I don't know about you." She thought for a minute. "Maybe 2:00. Just for a second. Then I have to leave."

He pumped his fist into the air. "Good. I'm meeting my Realtor at 3:30. Perfect."

Midori sounded anything but thrilled. "See you there."

"Bye."

∞

Midori wore her white linen dress, cropped leather jacket, and red heels while at the quaint bakery in trendy SoHo. She sat inside at the tiny round table for two. She was halfway through a cup of banana pudding, with a cup of strong black coffee to wash it down.

Virgil walked up and pulled out the other chair, in his gray pants and white shirt. He even wore a pocket protector with three pens inside. "I see you got a jump on it, huh, gorgeous?"

She said, after sipping her coffee, "I can't come here and pass this up. It's sinful." She looked at him as he sat down and leaned back.

He saw a small box. "I see you got some to go."

"The lemon and strawberry ones." She watched him carefully.

"Oh, okay." He stared at her, admiring her face.

She looked him up and down with caution, like she was reluctant to engage.

"What? You want to check my pockets? All I have is my cell and my wallet."

"No." She looked away and then asked, "So, you're not getting anything?"

"No."

She looked him up and down again. "Why come here and not order anything?"

"I didn't come here for cupcakes."

"So, you lied...again." She gave a frown.

"I deserve that. Bring it on."

"Are you on some guilt trip, Virgil?"

"Not even."

"You sure? Not sorry that you acted like an ass when you broke up with me?"

He asked, "Are you on a guilt trip for lying to me?"

"Not even. I'm just saying, with you being a man, I'd think you'd be hanging out, dating, going hog wild, hitting everything that walks by. You're free to do whatever you want to do."

"I want to be right here."

"Yeah, right. You've probably been out with someone."

"I haven't. You?"

"Me? Who'd want me? I'm a hooker, remember?" She sipped her coffee and smiled.

"So you went out of town for work?"

"Yes. Real estate."

He cleared his throat instead of laughing. "Did you like him?"

"Honestly, yes, I did. But why are you all up in my business?"

He leaned forward. "Just asking. Wondering if maybe we can talk every now and then. Be honest with each other. Be up front. Be real. No judgment. Especially now that we've got all of the crap out of the way."

She took a small bit of the pudding and spoke while eating. "Hard not to judge my life. Don't be so sure you've got my crap out of the way. And I won't be so sure I know about all of yours." She licked the spoon.

"My life is nothing to be proud of. I've got problems like everyone else."

"Oh, please. You've got it made. You're about to be the son of the next president of the United States. What's so bad about that?"

"Let's just say, I didn't live the type of life people would think. My birth dad treated me like crap. He cheated on my mom one time too many and then he died. After that she met my stepfather. It took me a minute, but I convinced myself that he treated her good. Though now that I know about his indiscretions, I can see more clearly. It's some bullshit. But hey, whose life doesn't have some shit going on?"

She eyed him down. "You really are a mama's boy, aren't you?"

"If she's happy, I'm happy."

"Virgil, she's your mom, not your woman."

His expression didn't change. He didn't even look offended. "I know that."

"Maybe it is a good idea that you're looking for your own place. Maybe you need to cut that cord. Be independent. Be on your own."

"I agree. Start my own family one day. There's nothing like family. Like blood."

"Humph. Sometimes, some make the cut and some don't."

"I get it." He smiled. "Talking to you reminds me. One thing we had going for us was that we could always talk. After all these months of not speaking, I want you to know, I hope we can still at least talk to each other."

She looked serious. "I trusted you."

"And I trusted *you*."

She said, holding her coffee in her hand, "We broke that."

"Yes, we did." He leaned his elbows on the table and said, "Listen, my Realtor asked me to come over to Brooklyn, to the Williamsburg area. I'm thinking about that area because I realized some of the listings he e-mailed me here in SoHo are too expensive. Like over two million. I'm paying cash but want to spend half that, or less."

"Half of that? Cash?" she asked.

"Yes."

She looked surprised and impressed. "Excuse me. I didn't

know you had it like that. Didn't know Google paid their engineering directors that kinda money."

He told her. "They don't. I have a little money saved up. So, anyway, there are a couple of condos. One is seven hundred thousand in an area that's like a mini SoHo, and one is over nine hundred thousand. I think it's a two-bedroom waterfront condo, view of the skyline beyond the East River. I'm pretty sure it has panoramic views. I want you to go with me. Please. Just help me decide."

She replied, setting her coffee mug down. "Virgil, I think the East River condo sounds nice. But I can't come with you. I have that appointment near Gramercy soon. I'm sorry." She sounded like she was trying to let him down easy. "The waterfront would be great, though. It sounds beautiful. You'll make the right decision." She then pushed her chair away, stood, and took hold of her purse and to-go box.

He stood. "Okay. Well, thanks for coming. I really appreciate it."

"Yeah. I'm gonna run. It was good seeing you. If you need any real estate tips, let me know."

He laughed. "I'll do that," he said, as she stepped away. "I missed you."

She turned and waved, saying only, "Good-bye. Good luck."

And just like that, she was gone.

Twenty

Virgil

Thursday—November 10, 2011

Virgil had only been in the taxi five minutes heading to meet his Realtor in Williamsburg when he got a text from Midori:

> My appointment canceled. Please stop by
> my place when you're done. I'll be wait-
> ing.

"Hot damn," he said aloud in the backseat. The fast-driving taxi driver glanced at him in the rearview mirror. Virgil kept looking down at his phone and typed, I'll be there. Thank u.

It was close to six in the evening when Virgil and Midori sat on the sectional in the living room of her Upper East Side apartment, the same room where he broke it off months earlier after finding out what she really did for living.

She sat on one end wearing leggings and a black tee. He sat on the other end, still in his dress pants and dress shirt.

She was the one who asked, "So, what is it? What's up with us?"

"You tell me."

"I don't know. I want to be with someone who accepts me, that's all. Not someone who holds my life against me like I'm some jezebel."

"I can understand that."

Her legs were crossed. "Could you ever get past the fact that I've slept with so many men? I mean, keep it real."

"I don't know."

She leaned forward and used her hands as she spoke. "Okay. Could you accept me if your stepdad ends up winning the election in November? The president's son dating the escort. That's tabloid material. You say you don't want to hurt your mom. That would hurt her. I don't want to be some woman you hide out because you have to keep it a secret. I think you made a decision to not be with me, and hurt me rather than hurt her."

He looked calm. "Being with you has nothing to do with her. You lied to me. Like we said, we have trust issues."

"Virgil, we have moral issues. We have salacious issues of secrets and escorts. We have issues of politics and infidelity."

He leaned forward, too. "I'm talking about no one other than the two of us in this room. If we tried again, honestly, I wouldn't want you to keep doing what you're doing. I'd want you to stop. I need to make a decision about you without basing it on them. Their lives are their lives. They make choices they have to live with, just like I do."

She shook her head. "That sounds great, but it's not realistic. I know how you feel about your mom."

"What's real is that I don't want to live this life alone. I've got a good job, I'm continuing my education, and I want a family."

She asked, "Is it okay for me to want the same? I dream of that, too, you know?"

"Okay. Let's work toward that. Let's try and see where things go."

She looked uncertain, leaning back against the cushions. "Virgil, I can't commit to that. I'm still doing what I'm doing and that won't fit. Not right now anyway."

"Then when? Do you see yourself ever stopping?"

"I do." She looked down at her lap.

"Then there's no time better than now."

"I can't. Not just yet. Just a little time."

"You're saying you need just a little more money in your pocket?"

"Maybe a year's worth, maybe less."

He asked, "So, it's about your bank balance? You're letting money determine when your heart can be fulfilled?"

She sighed and gave him her eyes. "My heart will be fine. Yes, it's odd what I do and why I've planned certain things the way I have. But let me ask you. I can't help but to keep wondering. If you care so much for me, and miss me, and would be willing to move forward, why is it we never made love?" She frowned.

He seemed to lapse into his own thoughts and replied, "You know why."

"I know what you said. You said you're saving yourself. But, you're almost thirty."

"True. But I've gone this long."

Her face lightened up and she suddenly stood and stepped up to him, right up against his leg. She took his hand. "Baby. Make love to me."

"Midori."

"Please." She leaned over to kiss him on his cheek.

He looked her dead in the eye and stood.

She led him down the long hallway to her bedroom where he'd spent the night in the past but never had sex.

She flipped a switch along the wall and the blinds lowered at the same time that the sounds of jazz played from the overhead speakers, and she headed to the bed.

He stopped as he got close. "Midori. I need to wait."

"Wait for what? I don't wanna wait anymore."

"I do."

"Virgil, let me show you how good it could feel. Even if we don't end up together, I just don't want someone else to be your first." She faced him, pulled down her leggings, took off her top, and showed him her braless, pantiless, nude self.

He looked longingly at her body and let out a loud sigh. He'd seen her naked before when she'd walk around the bedroom after taking a shower, but this time, every inch of her looked ripe and ready.

She lay back on the chocolate bedspread of her queen bed and opened her legs, playing with herself by rubbing her vulva, spreading her lips apart.

He aimed a direct stare at her opening. It was pink and moist looking. She stuck her middle finger inside then put her finger into her mouth. "Umm, good. You need to know what pussy tastes like. Or do you already?"

"I don't."

With seductive eyes, she told him, "I promise, if you're wondering about me, I've been tested. You can wear a condom if you want. And my latest results from last week are in my dresser drawer. Fuck me, Virgil. Let me feel you inside of me."

He shook his head and looked down at the floor. "I can't. I'm sorry." His eyes quickly raised to between her legs again. "You look amazing. I just...I'm not ready."

"When will you be? At least let me suck you. Let me make you come."

He still said, "I can't."

She tilted her head. "Are you into women?"

"Trust me. I am," he said, as if there was no doubt.

"I'm just wondering because I'm really trying here." She scooted back and closed her legs. Her energy downshifted. "They say the squarest-looking men are the biggest freaks. Hell, you're proving that wrong. Is it because of what I do? Would you have had sex with me today if you didn't know what I do for a living?"

"No. That's not it."

"I don't understand. Who saves themselves like that?" she asked, batting her eyes.

"Midori. Don't be mad."

"Forget it. Just forget it."

He approached the side of the bed. "Midori. Look at me."

She crossed her arms.

He began to unzip his pants, and he let them fall, then he pulled his white underwear down to his knees. He lifted up his shirt so she could see everything, and stood there. His heart pounded.

She slowly brought her eyes to him and lowered her sights to his penis.

He looked like he was holding his breath, waiting for her to laugh or for her to run out of the room.

What she said was, "You have a great body. I love your body."

Midori climbed from the bed and stood before Virgil, unbuttoning his shirt and removing it. He stepped out of his pants and underwear, naked in front of a woman for the second time in his life.

She was in front of him naked as though they were both the same when it all came down to it. And they kissed.

She took his hand and they sat on the edge of the bed. She lay back and patted the mattress. "I want you right here."

His penis was stiff. He lay on his back and she got on top of him, again kissing, and grinding on him. She kissed his neck, chest, nipples, pectorals, and went further until she met the boundary of his curly pubic hair. She scooted her body down between his legs, and lightly touched his penis with her fingertips, licking the foreskin that housed his tiny shaft as it peeked from the edge. She pointed her tongue to his tip and kissed his dick with full lips, looking up at him. "I love you. I love your penis, too."

He exhaled loudly, with a sigh.

He kept his arms still and his hands flat along the mattress on either side of his tense body, just watching the reality of Midori's mouth meeting his penis.

He struggled to process the fact that she had no reaction. No criticism. No fear. He couldn't take his eyes off her. He felt himself actually getting more stiff than ever before. He could see just a little more of his shaft the more she kissed it, licked it.

His legs made room for her journey, as he bent his knees and opened wider. She licked his testicles, and the seam that ran down the middle of his scrotum. His balls were actually very large. She squeezed them between her lips, taking her right hand to rub his dick back and forth.

Virgil felt a rush travel from his balls to his dick. He was hot and he was nervous, but he stayed in place for her to continue showing him what it was like to have a woman go down on him.

She rubbed his thigh and brought her lips to his dick again, taking it into her mouth and giving it a suck like she would a lollipop, offering tongue and wetness and warmth.

Virgil tensed up and his chest rose and fell according to his fast breathing. Instantly, he felt his ejaculate travel and escape from his tip. He clenched his hands to a fist and begged his body to slow its roll, but his sperm spilled right into Midori's mouth. She didn't back off; she stayed put and drank from him. It was a rush of semen like he'd never experienced. He gave continued grunts and kept watching her face as she offered big eyes until her last swallow. She looked at him as though she was supposed to swallow, like it would be rude not to.

"You taste good," she told him.

He just stared as she moved over to lay alongside him, resting her body up against his and placing her head along his chest.

"Thank you for letting me have you," she said, looking pleased.

"Thank *you*." He looked stunned.

She rubbed his arm and they lay still, listening to the music, saying nothing else, then fell asleep.

He awoke while she still slept, with groggy eyes, and he said, "I love you, too."

The beginning of a trust rebuilding.

Two people from two totally different worlds.

Trying.

Kalin Graves and Seth Taylor disagreed this morning as they appeared on the Today *show, discussing the sensitive topic of homosexuality. Graves called it a sin and a choice, while Taylor, who is the only Republican candidate who supports same-sex marriage, said it is not a choice and that being gay starts in the womb.*

Twenty-One

Midori

Friday—November 18, 2011

I t was a cold Friday night and after all that had happened between them, Money and Midori agreed to take time out for some sisterly bonding over dinner in the theater district. Even after the phone call that seemed to break the ice, Money invited her sister out for a meal, just to make sure.

First they walked around, all bundled up in coats and scarves, and took in the vitality of the bustling, neon electric blocks of Times Square, hitting Sephora and M&M's World specifically, admiring the glitter and glitz of the holiday window displays.

An hour later, in the trendy Oceana Restaurant, they sat near the bar under the blue overheard, aquariumlike lights. They sipped on Pinot Noir and enjoyed steamed oysters, awaiting their main courses of seared shrimp and grits for Money, and broiled mahi-mahi for Midori.

Midori reflected back to her wonderful weekend in Puerto Rico a while back with Dr. Feelgood. He was once again charming, attentive, generous, funny, and fine. And as before, he slept overnight alone and headed back to his life with a cheating wife, all just to keep from having to share his wealth with her, breaking his own rule by spending a second vacation weekend with the same escort whom he knew as Brooklyn. Midori broke it all down. "I thought Dr. Feelgood liked me, outside of all this," she told her sister.

They were both dressed in dark brown without having planned it. One in a knit, Viviana shoulder dress and one in a Dolce and Gabbana pantsuit.

Money asked, "Who?"

"Dr. Feelgood."

"Is that what you call him?"

"Yes. Okay, Mr. 81. He was so smooth and such a gentleman. Money, he really knows how to treat a woman."

"But like you said, he's married, right?"

"Yes."

"Then I beg to differ. He really doesn't know how to treat his wife."

Midori explained, "She's cheating."

"Yeah, well, just wait till she finds out he's spending tens of thousands to pay for sex. He'll wish he'd just gone ahead and filed for divorce. His records will be subpoenaed. That could mess us up."

"You're always thinking about the business."

"I am."

"What about looking at the side of him that's wonderful? Maybe he'd be a dream come true."

Money looked doubtful. "I told you about that. It doesn't happen."

"Well, that trip to Puerto Rico was just as amazing as the Florida Keys. His wife must've found a damn good man on the side if she'd risk losing him. He's a heart surgeon and he looks good as fuck."

"Good as fuck? Oh, well then. He must be handsome. 'Cause fucking is good." Money giggled.

Midori's face gave way to a smile. "Yes, he's very sexy."

"Well, all that glitters definitely ain't gold. That's just his side of the story. For all we know he could be kicking her ass."

"Money, stop. Anyway, I'm telling you, I needed that getaway. Sometimes getaways are the ticket."

"I guess so. It was Dr. Feelgood who asked for you. This time it wasn't us who decided."

"I know. But still, I was happy to go."

"Well good." Money sipped her wine and then asked, "Does it bother you that the majority of these men are married?"

"No. I understand. Sometimes it's the taken men who call. I get the big picture."

"Good."

Midori folded her arms along the table. "I was thinking, if someone I was with paid for sex on the side, I guess that would be my come-around, you think?"

Money explained, "No woman wants that. But in my opinion, I think a woman should be more worried about a man who'd end up finding a woman to sleep with him for free. That means she likes him. But if he pays, he's less likely to feel an attachment or desire. He'll head on back home to the wife like he got away with something. It's almost like that makes them even happier. Their ego is fluffed up. They're not gonna leave the wife for the hooker. I just don't see it. Maybe this business makes me look at men differently, but I think they're more likely to leave their woman for the girl they meet at the club." She scooted back in her chair. "Like my husband left me for that bitch in L.A. They both felt something. Something deeper than sex. But hey, sex can bond two people if they do it often enough. Sometimes these guys just want a pussy that's different from the one they have at home. It's too much for them to cut the good woman loose and take a chance that the pussy that felt good wouldn't drive them fucking crazy. Go figure."

"Yeah. True. I was gonna ask you, are you getting more calls from women who want men these days? Kemba must have a lot of repeat business."

"He does. Kemba, though, he's really large. Some women can't handle him."

Midori asked, looking amused, "And they're complaining? Big is a good thing."

"One or two have asked if we had someone else."

"Wow. That man is beautiful. A real chick magnet."

"He is. But you get a lot of requests, too. Is everything cool with that Homeland Security guy? The one who pays more for the waterworks."

Midori shook her head and picked up her wineglass. "That's hard to take. It's good money, but I think I told you before, I'll bet he's the type to beat his woman's ass. He doesn't like women one bit. No telling what happened to him when he was a kid." She sipped.

Money nodded. "Sometimes they're missing something in life, at home maybe. I believe you can have the best marriage in the world, and your man will fuck around if given the chance. I've lived it. I've seen it. I hear about it. I know the smell of it. I, for one, don't believe in fidelity. I don't think people are made to be with one person for the rest of their lives. Monogamy is not natural. I'm not the one to trip out if my man cheated. I didn't trip this last time. I just filed for divorce and kept it moving."

"I really do think fidelity is possible. I believe both people can be faithful."

"Well, when you see it, will you introduce me to it? Because it is one elusive sucker." Money grinned.

"I will." Midori smiled and looked around for the waiter.

"I will say, what you don't know won't hurt you. You gonna cheat, and I don't know about it, let's move forward. Just be smart about it."

"How can you use the words *smart* and *cheater* at the same time? Like we're supposed to be giving them credit for outsmarting the woman?" Midori asked, placing her glass on the table while blinking fast.

"No, I'm not saying that. Just like the guys who come to us. They need to be discreet. *Discreet* is the word I'm looking for."

"Good. That's better." She smiled.

"Look at you, getting all riled up."

"You know us. We always did have our little debates."

Money smiled, too. "True. I know it's been tough. But I'm glad Bailey seems to have disappeared. He hasn't called for service. And I really do hope things are cool with you and Virgil."

"Oh, him? We broke up."

"You did?" Money looked surprised.

Midori picked up her drink again. "Yeah. We argued about even the thought of him threatening to break into the mayor's e-mail. He later told me he would let all that go and see how his stepdad does on his own. He did want to see me again after we broke up, but I said no. It just wouldn't work. You know, him having a stepfather running for office. It was all a fantasy."

"Okay now. You sure you won't change your mind and check it out? See what happens."

"I do wonder at times, but no, I won't. Can I tell you something?"

Money nodded.

"I did fall for him. But I know it wouldn't work."

"I can understand that. Plus, with him still thinking you're in real estate, not knowing the truth. You'd need to deal with that. He does still think that, right?"

"He does." She hoped her face didn't show her lie.

"I see. Just keep him a little bit close, just so you know what he's up to. We haven't heard from Senator Ellington in a minute, either. And since he seems to be doing well in the polls, the more popular he gets, he won't be able to go anywhere without people recognizing him. So you're right. That's probably a done deal. I'm glad all of that 'spying on the opponent' crap has died down."

"Me too."

"Hi," Money said to a good-looking white guy who walked by, heading to the nearby bar. He smiled and took his seat upon a teal-blue bar stool. One minute later another man walked up to him, and the two of them talked.

Money and Midori chatted some more before Money leaned in. "I'll bet you he's an escort."

Midori looked over coyly. "Why?"

"Okay, well, maybe it's a first date, but it's definitely two men hooking up."

"Really. You think they're gay?"

"Look at them." They both checked them out harder as the bartender set two drinks in front of the men. "The touching of the forearm, blushing, giggling. They're flirting just like a man and a woman would. And look, a damn mai tai. What man drinks mai tais unless he's got a little fruit in his basket?"

"Fruit basket? Please. I don't see it, but, if you say so." Midori glanced away, shaking her head at her sister.

The second man patted the first man on the back, then got up and walked away, heading in the direction of the restroom.

Money placed her lap napkin on the table. "Midori, come with me. Don't want the guy to come back thinking I'm hitting on his friend. Plus, I want you to hear this." She scooted her chair back and got up.

"Okay." Midori put down her drink and got up, too.

Money led the way a few steps to where the man sat. "Ummm, hi. Excuse us. My name is Ms. Watts. This is my friend."

"Hi," he said, smiling at them both.

Midori nodded. "Hi."

Money said, "Can I ask you a question?"

"Sure."

"Have you ever thought about the business? You know—escorting people on dates?"

"No."

"Well, can you call me on your phone right now, just in case you ever think about it? It's a six-figure income. Maybe more."

He took his BlackBerry from the bar and handed it to her. "Okay. Here, you do it."

"Okay." Money dialed herself. Her phone rang from the

table where she and Midori had sat. She hung up his phone. "Your name?"

"They call me Bronx."

"Bronx. I like that. Okay. Well. Sorry to bother you. You have a good one."

"You too," he said to them both.

As they went back to their table Money said, "Maybe I'm wrong, but something's up with him."

"He is handsome."

"Fine as fuck."

"Maybe fine as shit. But not quite fine as fuck." Midori laughed, and they sat back down.

"Oh. Okay. Not as fine as your good doctor."

"Not even."

"Can't believe they call him Bronx. That fits right in." Her cell beeped. She looked at her phone and read the text, saying in a low tone, "Bronx is asking when he can start."

"Really?" Midori looked surprised.

Money didn't. She smiled and glanced over at him. His back was to her and he was still sitting alone. She said, "I'm telling him I'll have the booker call him. And I'm keying in here that it's both men and women." She typed and then put her phone down. It beeped right back. She looked at it. "Bingo," she said softly to Midori. "He said perfect. Told you."

"Wow. I never would've guessed."

"This is good. I'm convinced there's more money in closeted clients than straight ones. He's gonna be good for us. We'll get him tested and ready."

She called her booker and spoke in almost a whisper, looking around to see who might be nearby as she fingered the strands of her long hair. "Hey. I think I've got the match for Mr. 11. I'll text you his phone number. Hook them up as soon as Mr. 11 is in town. His name is Bronx. I know. Thanks." She hung up.

"Just like that?" Midori asked.

"Just like that."

"Well, aren't you the recruiter?"

"Of course I am. Besides, if I don't recruit, believe me, Romeo's ass will."

The waiter walked up and placed their main courses before them.

"There he is," Midori said, looking relieved. She inhaled the aroma of her seafood, then said, "You're also my sister."

"That I am." Money broke out into a full smile. She told the waiter, "Thanks."

He asked, "Can I get you ladies anything else?"

"No, we're good," replied Midori. He walked away and she said to Money, "One day, we'll get our happily-ever-after."

"If you say so, Midori. If you say so."

Republican candidate Seth Taylor said in a speech in Washington, D.C., that Darrell Ellington is not concerned about the poor, and he does not believe that wealthy Ellington will fight for the middle class if he wins the presidency.

Twenty-Two

Money

Friday—December 16, 2011

It had been an evening of drinks and laughter, like Money and Jamie were actually best friends. They were in her bed and he lay on his back after their second round of drinks. She lay on her stomach, leaning up so she could talk to him. The room smelled like her cherry blossom diffuser. "Did I ever thank you for taking Leilani to get her car that day?"

"Yes, you did. That's my job. I never get to do what you pay me for," he said.

Money's face was flushed from her buzz. "Believe me, I'd rather pay you and never need to use you, than actually need you." Her speech was slurred. She rubbed her forehead and scratched her head, fluffing up her already tussled hair.

"I understand. I still don't know why she used her own car to drive to an appointment anyway."

"She said she was running late."

He told Money, "You need to let her know, let all of them know, they should tell you when they need a ride to these appointments. I mean let you make the call about if I can get there in time or not. And for her to be drinking with a client? Not cool."

Her eyebrows dipped. "I know. I told her that. They just take taxis because it's easier. If we lived anyplace other than New York City, you'd have a lot of driving to do. But, Leilani's problem is, she's too nice. She probably didn't say no. I guess she learned her lesson."

"You think she'd ever be a problem?" he asked.

"Leilani? No. She's just a glamour-puss who's got my hobbyists going crazy." She struggled with the word *hobbyists*.

He looked like he noticed. "Okay, so she's pretty, and she can suck a dick. But can you trust her?"

"Jamie, I can't trust anybody. No one. Not even you. I trust no one."

"Thanks a lot," he said, shaking his head as if brushing off the comment. "I still say you should talk to her again."

Money looked at him like he was crazy. "Who the hell are *you* all of a sudden? You're never involved in anything, you rarely call, and now after one pickup to take my girl to the impound shop, you decide to care about the confidentiality methods and business operations of my company? Give me a break."

"What's your problem?"

"I've been doing this shit on my own for years and did damn good by myself. Now you want to tell me how to run my business? So, what? You know how to do this better than me?"

"You're kidding, right? I said two things about Leilani, and you came to that conclusion. Damn. Pardon me then."

"Oh, you're pardoned, all right." She snapped her fingers and rolled her neck.

"You're a trip."

"I am. And so are you."

"That's true, too." He nodded in agreement. "I wasn't gonna ask you, but now's as good a time as any, even though you're cranky as hell. I'm gonna need about fifty thousand. Just got some things to take care of. My family in Colorado. They got in some trouble."

Right away she said, "Jamie, fuck you. You always need money. My name is Money Watts, not Money Tree. Why don't you use the money you get for the job you never do?"

"That takes care of the basics. This is something extra."

"Don't you have credit? Can't you get a loan? Or better yet, get a real job, considering that all of your time is pretty much fucking free."

He said, keeping an eye on her angry expression, "I'm on call, remember? I need to be available. And I make sure I am, whether you call me or not. Working would mean I'd have to give this up."

"Oh, bullshit. You're trying to tell me if it wasn't for your devotion to this gig, you'd be free to get your finances in order? You'd be able to make enough money to help out your family in Colorado instead of begging me for money. Again."

"First of all, you know I have a record. If I get a job, the first thing they're going to do is run a background check."

"Right. Yeah, I do know that. That's why you work for me. But how many times are you gonna come asking me for more money? If you ask me, I say you're up to some illegal shit."

"Please. Like what?" he asked.

"Like you spend too much money to just be trying to live.

You're either doing something illegal, or you're smoking it up. Shit, you might be a fucking drug addict for all I know."

"I'm not."

"Yeah, like you'd tell me." She adjusted herself to sit up. "Jamie, sometimes I can't deal with the way we trip. You piss me off and go away, I piss you off and don't take your calls. Yet you always seem to come back and when you do, you're asking me for something. Fifty thousand is a lot of damn money. It's like I'm the one paying you for sex. You're the only dick I get and you get a salary every two weeks out of it. But you are not fucking me good enough for all this extra money you're asking for. Every time you get yourself in a mess, I'm supposed to bail you out. You need to cut that shit out. Ain't no bodyguard who never guards, and driver who never drives, as lucky as you." She kept blinking like there was a strong wind in the room. She reached over to the bottle of vodka.

He examined her flushed face. "You need to put that down."

"Hell no. This makes me forget." She poured the clear liquid into her glass.

"All this talking you're doing, you ain't forgot a damn thing. What it does is make you even more pissed at me."

"I am, shit." She put the bottle back down.

"Cool. So, let's fuck it out." He dared her. "Get in that reverse cowgirl position and see how much shit you talk then."

She reached for the glass and then stopped, leaving it where it was. "Don't talk about it, be about it."

He got up and took a black foil condom package from his wallet and went straight for the sofa in the corner of her room. He lay back along the couch, wrapped up his dick, and said, "Here. Get on it."

She headed straight to him with sultry but heavy eyes and climbed on top and straddled him, facing his feet. One leg was bent so that her foot was flat along the couch, and the other foot was along the pile carpeting. She took his dick from beneath her and slid it inside her pussy, sitting all the way down on it, giving soft moans for every inch it traveled.

He talked much shit. "Yeah, get you some good dick. Always making sure everybody else gets their fuck on. Hell, my girl needs to feel good, too."

He fucked her hard at the same time he caressed her lower back and ass. She reached down and grabbed his balls, rolling them between her fingers. She felt him stiffen even more, and with her other hand she played with her hardened clitoris, pausing only for a second to bring her fingers to her mouth, licking them, and again rubbing her clit as it throbbed upon her touch.

He kept up his pace. "That pussy is hungry tonight. Look at you ride that dick. Shit."

"Uh-huh," she said. And then she looked back at him and said, "Fuck you."

"Ya think?" His eyes were wide.

She sliced him with her eyes and leaned forward. She bucked her ass cheeks up and down, then reached down to touch the base of his penis, feeling the wetness that oozed from her. She rubbed her clit again and focused on tightening up her walls, using her pelvic floor exercise while he was inside.

"Grip that shit. Hell yeah."

She was trying to turn him on and turn him out, but it backfired on her, and she could tell she was the one losing the battle. The feeling of him working so hard to fuck her back, and her fingers along the tip of her clit, made her howl as her orgasm hit. She continued to stimulate herself with her hand.

He kept on fucking her. "Uh-huh."

She leaned back, flinging her hair and focusing on the roll of her orgasm. "Uhhh."

He became still and rubbed her back. "What next?" he asked, working up a way to continue in another position.

"I've got you," she said, rising up to face him, then sitting down and inserting him again. She was extra juiced up.

"Yeah, you want some more, huh?"

She cut her eyes again and rubbed her breasts, adjusted one to her mouth, and began sucking her own tittie.

"Hell yeah." He put his hands on each side on her waist and guided her movements, carefully easing her down as he pressed inside, carefully giving her the dick.

She stopped playing with her breasts and concentrated on the feeling, saying, "Uh-huh. You're just trying to get me to say yes to that money you need."

"No." He worked her with his stiffness.

"You'll have it tomorrow," she told him with lust on her flushed face.

He didn't say thank you verbally, but sped up his stroke as she bounced up and down upon him, looking like she could blame her buzz on the dick more than blaming it on the alcohol.

She asked out of nowhere, "If something ever happened to me, would you be there?"

"Hell yeah."

She closed her eyes. "Fuck you."

"Ya think?" he asked again.

"Hush. I like the noise you make when you shut the fuck

up," Money said from a place deep inside, as he buried himself inside her.

He managed a quick laugh and seemed to work extra hard to earn his money, fucking Money like she was his full-time woman.

Like it should have been if it could have been, love.

The only female candidate for president, Marla Goins is expected to withdraw upon admitting her addiction to prescription pills. Darrell Ellington, who celebrates his fifty-eighth birthday today, wished her well in her fight, and vowed to create a panel to investigate and prosecute prescription drug abuse, if he's elected president.

Twenty-Three

Leilani

Thursday—January 12, 2012

It was a new year. The holidays had come and gone, and the political race geared up with less than ten months until the primaries. The list of Republican candidates was down to four, with the only female having dropped out of the race. Campaign promises had been made and already broken, and another promise was broken, too. Darrell Ellington was back for more Lip Service on the side.

"I really didn't expect to hear from you," Leilani told Darrell. She closed the front door to her luxury condo on Twenty-Eighth Street in West Chelsea. They'd agreed to meet when he called from Cincinnati the previous day. "Haven't seen you in so long, but I'm glad you're here."

He was the same dapper politician she'd been watching on television, the senator who was now one of the top candidates. "Yeah. I was going to do the hotel thing, but I just decided to have my driver bring me here. He's waiting downstairs." He stood dressed for the cold weather in a trench coat, scarf, and suit. He talked fast and looked less relaxed than before. Yet, he was there nonetheless.

Leilani wore only a large white T-shirt. "Your driver? He's cool like that?"

He stood in the entryway. "He is."

"Where does he think you are?"

He looked down at her legs as he spoke. "Told him I needed to sign some financial papers so I can get ready to release my tax return information." He took off his coat and scarf and hung them on the wooden coat rack.

She said, "Okay. I guess that means you won't be here long."

"True."

"I keep seeing you on the TV and Internet. I'm glad your campaign is going well."

His reply was only, "You got anything on under there?"

"No."

Then he said, "I'm ready." He unbelted his dress pants and they fell to the floor, then he pulled down his underwear, stepping out of both. With his dick in hand, he stood before her. She got on her knees before him, smiling.

He looked down and the first thing he did was bang his dick on her lips, saying, "I saw that done in a movie and thought of you. Suck it."

"My pleasure."

"And by the way, it's my birthday. Make it extra special."

She kissed his dick and gave him bedroom eyes in her living room. She said in a sex-kitten voice, "Happy Birthday, Mr. President."

"Oh, yeah. Uh-huh." His ego was out of control.

Leilani began licking his upper thighs, wrapping her hand around the bottom of his shaft. She opened her mouth wide and bobbed her head, making sure to twirl her tongue, twisting her left hand and using her right hand to alternate directions like she was wringing out a towel.

"Yeah."

She continued to squeeze her hands before dropping them and taking his entire penis into her mouth. She looked up at him as he looked up at the ceiling, hands on hips, being served for his birthday just as he wanted it.

She licked upward to the head of his penis and made it wet, bringing him to the edge.

"Back up," he said in a panic, stopping the flow of sperm by squeezing his tip, just under the head.

She was prepared to drink him, but he quickly moved himself backward.

He asked fast, "Where's your bathroom?"

She pointed.

He hurried down the hall to her bathroom, holding his dick.

She heard him give a long moan as he ejaculated into the toilet water. Then there was the sound of the toilet flushing and the sound of running water in the sink. He walked back in, and stepped back into his underwear and pants, belting himself up, looking just like he did when he arrived five minutes earlier.

He asked, "You made the charge on the credit card?"

"I did," she said, standing by the door.

"Good." He opened the door and stepped out.

She said, quietly, "Happy Birthday," again.

He only smiled and left, not even offering a wave, thank-you, or parting glance.

She closed the door and leaned her body against it for a moment, then went on about her day. She got ready to head out to her weekly spa treatment of a massage, wax, and facial, having just had one of the top five most talked-about politicians in the country in her living room, receiving oral sex.

She knew that if it came down to it, she'd have to suddenly catch a case of amnesia about knowing the senator. He was cutting it close, and she had a feeling that day would come soon. Things would probably blow up and she'd be caught up in the sandstorm. But the thought of what type of spotlight the explosion might bring turned her on a bit, got her excited.

She knew she was living dangerously. She also knew the senator was just another man who couldn't help thinking with his dick and not his mind.

Men.

The president refused to pick a winner for the Super Bowl, but said he's expecting a good game. Two of the Republican candidates, Darrell Ellington and Robert Sally, attended the game in Indianapolis, making themselves available for photo opportunities with the press.

Twenty-Four

∞

Kemba

Super Bowl Sunday—February 5, 2012

It was Super Bowl Sunday, and the New York Giants played the New England Patriots in Indianapolis. New York was abuzz with pride. The energy was electric in the town and fans showed their New York Giants pride at every corner. The sports bars were packed and most TVs were tuned in to the game. Beryl and Kemba decided to skip the outside elements of the cold and stay inside for a cozy, warm Super Bowl party of their own with their fifty-five-inch plasma.

An empty pizza box delivered by Presidential Pizza rested on the glass coffee table.

They'd watched the first quarter, and the Giants were up by nine. "That's the way," Kemba said with certainty. He wore his GMEN T-shirt, representing, even though he'd known the city of New York for only a little while.

Beryl was barefoot, wearing a white tee and white workout pants. She had been bitten by the New York bug ten years prior. "We can't get too comfortable because Brady's known for getting hot. It ain't over 'til it's over."

She returned from the kitchen with more cold beer and popcorn, and laughed over a Coca-Cola commercial with polar bears. "That's wild. Get 'em," she said, as she set the bowl and cold bottles down on the coffee table.

Kemba laughed too, then headed to the bathroom and closed the door when Beryl yelled out, "Your phone is vibrating."

He replied loudly, "Okay," from the other side of the bathroom door as he heard Beryl actually answer his phone.

"Hello." He tried to hurry so he could hear the exchange. "Who are you calling?" he heard her ask. "Yes, this is Kemba's number. Dallas?"

Kemba listened intently, pissed off that she'd actually answered it.

"A friend? Oh my God." Her voice lowered. "I know this isn't who I think it is...Ursula?"

Kemba's panic showed itself and he pulled up his pants and hurried to exit the bathroom.

"You have got to be kidding me. Why are you calling this number? I know you're not returning my man's call."

Kemba stood right next to Beryl, nerves on high, and reached for his phone. "Give it to me."

She pushed Kemba away and spun around, turning her back to him, and continued talking. "You have to go? Oh, hell no. See, this shit is a trip. Sleeping with my husband wasn't enough all those years ago and now you're trying to take my new man? Fuck what you have to do. I want answers right now!"

She listened, frowning, and Kemba stepped closer to where she stood.

She began to yell. "It was a mistake, all right. Why in the hell do you go after my men? Because I know you're not just Kemba's friend. Kemba doesn't have female friends."

"Beryl, stop," said Kemba, sounding level-headed but his heart was pounding.

She ignored him and kept talking, getting even louder, flailing her hand around as she spoke. "You're a dirty whore. You're married, but that doesn't matter to you, does it?"

"Hang up," Kemba demanded.

Beryl gave him a look of evil, yelling at him while his phone was to her ear. "You stupid-ass fool. This is the woman I saw you eyeing down outside the gym that day. The one who came out of Sylvia's restaurant. The woman whose husband is running for president. You know her. The woman I'm 100 percent sure you've been fucking. The woman who shares blood with me."

His jaw dropped. He stood next to her and waited for what she'd said to sink in.

"Asshole. Your newest trick, Ursula, is my fucking sister!"

"Hold up." He waited, as if he needed her to repeat what she'd just said.

"No, you hold up."

He gave a confused, angled stare. "How can she be your sister when she's black and you're white?"

She yelled at the top of her lungs, still holding the phone, "We have the same white mother and different fathers, if you must know. Her father is black and mine is white. What fucking difference does it make? She's my damn sister, dummy! And I know she saw me in the taxi that day with you." Beryl then screamed as she heard what Ursula said over the phone. "What? No big deal? Oh, yes, it is a big-ass deal. Kemba is my man. We live together, bitch. It's not what I think, it's what I know. You of all people know that I am not dumb. Surely there's enough dick in New York City for you to cheat on your husband with, than to be cheating with my man, *again*."

Kemba stepped toward her. "Beryl, calm down."

Beryl backed away from him as she looked at the screen of the phone and bellowed, "Oh, I'm gonna call her ass back right now." She scrambled to press Call.

"No, you're not. Calm down."

"Fucking voice mail!" She tossed the phone onto the couch. "How long have you been fucking 'Dallas'? Dallas was her nickname from her favorite TV show when we were kids."

He gave her a careful stare, as if looking for a way to ease her anger. He put his hands up. "Why don't you just take a breath?"

"I don't need a breath. I need some damn answers!"

"Look. Okay. You and me, we have an open relationship. I don't answer your phone. And honestly, I don't appreciate you answering mine."

Her eyes popped out of her head, and a deep vertical line formed between them. "Oh no, you are not going to go there. I've got the right to do whatever the fuck I want. I pay that damn phone bill. I pay every goddamn bill around this motherfucker. Now I can either go back and check the bill to find out exactly how well the two of you know each other. Or, you can just tell me now."

"You can, but listen—"

"The only thing I want to hear is you telling me what the fuck is up. Or did you not hear me say that she is my fucking sister!" Her head shook like she was on the brink of losing it.

"I heard you." He looked down for a split second, as though hoping for the right words to come to mind, then looked back up at the face that had changed from the football-watching girlfriend to the green-eyed monster in no time flat.

"Bet you didn't count on this shit, huh? That she'd be my fucking relative, did you? But shit, why not? You've fucked every damn body in New York. This was bound to happen. Lusting over her when she came out of the restaurant. You think I didn't notice that. You weren't even cool about it. You looked like you were about to come in your damn pants."

"Beryl, it was all business with her."

"What? Lip Service business? So you're saying you did fuck her?"

"No and yes."

"No and yes what? Does the *yes* go with the question about you fucking her?"

"Yes. Don't ask me any more questions. I told you it was business."

"Fool, your clients who you fuck for business don't call you on your cell phone. They call Lip Service and then Lip Service sends you a text. Ursula said she was returning your call. Why'd you call that trick-ass bitch?"

"She's not a trick." He stood still and kept his sights on her hands, in case she started swinging.

"Oh, really?" She flung her hair from one shoulder to the other and aimed her right ear toward him. "So you're gonna defend her ass now? Then what the hell is she if she paid you to fuck her?"

"She didn't pay me. She's a friend."

"Make up your mind. Is she business or a friend?"

He looked frustrated. "You pick one."

Beryl tightened her jaw and squinted her eyes then said at the top of her lungs, "She's a fuck. You're fucking my sister, Kemba. And you're gonna stand there and get defensive about it? Like *I'm* the damn problem?"

"This whole thing is a problem. I have no privacy. You answered my phone and then you jumped the gun without giving me a chance to explain. I'm sorry if I made contact with your sister. I didn't even know you had a sister, black or white or anything else. I don't know much about you anyway," he yelled back.

The sound of the football game resuming sounded in the background. "Because you never took the time to ask! And I answered it because I saw the fucking caller ID read Dallas." She turned around and grabbed the remote to turn off the TV and threw the remote onto the carpet. "But don't you worry about that now. Things are gonna turn around. Your well has run dry. I can never be with you again, knowing you've fucked her nasty ass. That stupid bitch broke up my marriage, and I thought I'd cut her out of my life for good, but she shows up on a Sunday, calling on my man's phone." She paced back and forth from the TV to the sofa, shaking her head. "It's bad enough that I have to see her on TV, with the husband she snatched up just so she can be in the White House. That's all she talked about when we were teenagers was marrying a politician. I'll tell you one thing, I'm about to put a stop to that shit. You best believe that." She took fast, heavy steps back toward their bedroom.

He looked at her incredulously. "Beryl."

She turned on a dime as she hit the hallway, pointing back at him. "I give you thirty fucking minutes to get your shit out of here or else I'm calling the police. Don't play with me. I want your hooker ass gone."

"Wait. Please."

For every word she said she took a step toward him. "Get. The. Fuck. Out. Of. My. House. *NOW!*" Her eyes watered and her lips quivered.

"A'right. Damn." He walked past her and went into their room, where he packed some things into a large suitcase. He also made sure to pack the Bible his mother had left him years ago. He'd always had it; he just never opened it.

Ten minutes later he rolled out the large suitcase and a shoulder bag. He went to the sofa to get his phone, putting it in his pocket.

She simply stood by the front door, holding it open, looking anxious. Her cheeks were flushed.

He said, exhausted as he walked to the door, "I'd like to be able to get the rest of my things later."

She looked down at her phone with a scowl of disgust. "Don't make me call 911."

He stepped out and she slammed the door within an inch of the base of his suitcase.

He stood there for a minute, then headed to the elevator and took it to the lobby, and exited the building he'd called home for two years.

Having fucked up his sugar-momma good thing, all he could think was, *Damn, it's a small-ass world.*

And trip off of women. He'd been kicked out by his girl, and left by his own mom.

Fox News projects Senator Darrell Ellington has won the Nevada caucus, capturing twenty-eight delegates and knocking Kalin Graves down a peg in a close race that came down to the wire.

Twenty-Five

∽

Kemba

Super Bowl Sunday—February 5, 2012

That evening, after checking into the stylish Aloft Hotel on Frederick Douglass Boulevard, not far from the home he had once lived in, Kemba left the hotel and went back out into the thirty-three-degree weather. He wore gloves, with a knit cap over his head, easing himself in the direction of his place of literal physical therapy, the gym.

His mind was busy. He didn't dare call Beryl, and she hadn't dared to call him. Not even a text to cuss him out further. And as much as he wanted to, he definitely didn't dare call the tall, brown one whose oversized clit he fell in love with, sexy Ursula Ellington.

"Sisters. Of all the luck," he kept telling himself out loud into the still of the chilly night. "Who needs them?"

He entered the doors of Planet Fitness, and the club was

nearly empty. He scanned his membership card at the front desk and entered the men's locker room, placing his gym bag down on the bench. He removed his Jordans and took out his lock and towel, then pulled off his sweatpants, tossing them inside and locking them in. He used a safety pin to attach the key to his gym shorts. He sat down, lacing up his tennis shoes.

"You must come every day," he heard from behind him.

He looked back. "No."

Romeo stood near the water fountain by the door, not far away. "I know you. I figured it out. You're with Money, right?"

"Why?"

Romeo walked closer, wearing Under Armour gym shorts and a tight muscle shirt, exposing his buffed arms. "I know you know me."

"I do."

"Good. I mean, technically, you don't really know me. Only what you've heard. But, hey, I say we've gotta change that."

"Look. I'm about to go work out. Tonight is not the night, okay?" Kemba stood up, giving him a look of impatience.

"Wait. I just wanted to say, that, uh, I talked to Money the other day."

"Good."

"Told her I'm willing to bet you are her greatest asset right about now."

Kemba turned to him. "Romeo, listen. Please," looking like he was in no mood.

Romeo said, "Oh, it's cool. I understand. I just wanted to say, I have something to talk to you about."

"What?"

"Maybe we can talk when you're done. I know you're ready

to get your workout on. Me too. Maybe we could watch the rest of the Super Bowl game somewhere. It's dead in here. I can't believe anyone's in here at all with the game on. But hey, either way, I just wanted to let you know there's a whole other side to the game that Money plays. I think, with what you're working with you could be wearing a Rolex by now, living in Trump SoHo."

"I'm good." Kemba looked bored.

"I'm better." Romeo seemed to be kidding, but maybe not.

Kemba stood a few feet from him, managing a faint smirk. "Oh, so you're the shit, huh?"

"I can tell you about it. Let you decide."

Kemba took a step. "I've gotta go."

Romeo told him. "I'll meet you in the lobby of the Surrey, Upper East Side, in say, an hour and a half, two hours."

Kemba nodded. Then he said, "Two." He walked away, tossing a towel over his shoulder, ready to work out his frustrations.

Kemba had taken the short walk back to his temporary residence, showered, dressed, then caught a cab to the Surrey.

The formal-looking doorman held the door open as Kemba went inside, heading to the upscale but tiny lobby.

Romeo walked over to him after stepping out of the elevator.

Kemba asked, looking confused, "Funny. Where's the TV?"

"In in my room."

Kemba angled his stare. "You said watch the game in the lobby."

"I said meet me in the lobby."

"Look. You know. I'm sure that game is just about over.

On the way here I saw tons of people in the streets, hanging out, looking like they were celebrating. I hear the Giants are up."

"They are. It's not over just yet. So, you're not coming up?"

"Why? What's up with the hotel? You staying for the night or what?"

"I live here. Extended stay. Follow me."

Romeo turned back toward the elevator. Kemba looked at the doorman, who was watching them. He followed Romeo.

They headed up and walked inside the large, contemporary hotel room. Kemba looked around like he was in Emerald City. The last few minutes of the game were playing on the widescreen television in the living room.

Kemba said, "Sharp. You've gotta be paying at least eight thousand a month to stay here. Why?"

Romeo set his keycard and phone down along the bar that separated the kitchen from the living room. "Got my reasons. Sometimes I check into different places after a few months. I do have a spot in Harlem at the Langston, near the gym. It's cool, but you know, all depends on where I need to be."

"So life is pretty good to you then, hey?"

"Well, let's just say, with all the people I have working for me, I've got a good life."

Kemba still hadn't sat down. He just looked around. "I see. And all this is just for you? You don't live with anyone?"

"No."

"How many bedrooms are back there?"

Romeo walked into the kitchen. "Just two. I have company from time to time. Mainly when I want one of my girls to feel special. But they can't stay too long. The doorman keeps an eye on things. I like it uncomplicated."

"I see."

"Can I get you something to drink?" Romeo asked.

Kemba walked to the long granite bar. "What do you have?"

"What do you want? And please don't say beer."

"Beer and football go together, right?"

"Try something different. It's Super Bowl Sunday."

Kemba asked, "Like I asked, what ya got?"

"Everything."

"Really?"

"Really."

"Okay, how about, a Long Island iced tea."

Romeo nodded. "That's it. Good choice. I'm a New Yorker. If I know anything, it's Long Island. That's where I'm from."

Kemba said, leaning over the bar, "Really now? But you have everything to make it?"

Romeo looked over at the shelves and then opened a cabinet. "Oh, you mean vodka, tequila, rum, gin, triple sec, sweet and sour, Coca-Cola, lemons?"

"Okay. Excuse me."

"Yep. Got that. And more."

"I see." Kemba looked over at the TV and back at Romeo before taking a seat at the bar. Romeo grabbed a few bottles, and a glass from the overhead glass holder. He used a cocktail shaker, and once everything was added, he filled it with ice, shook, and poured, all while Kemba watched.

He set the tall glass in front of Kemba, upon a napkin. "There you go."

"Impressive."

"It's nothing. Just from my bartender days."

"So you had a life before all of this."

"I did."

Kemba asked, scooting the glass closer, "You gonna have a drink with me?"

"I don't drink."

"All that alcohol you've got up in here and you don't drink?"

"Nope." Romeo poured himself a glass of Dr. Pepper with ice and held up his glass. "Cheers."

"Cheers," Kemba said, holding up his glass, too.

Romeo added, "To you. To me. To us having what we really want."

"Looks to me like you've got enough." They raised their glasses and each took a sip. Kemba said, "This is cool, man. I like it."

"Good. But hey, as far as having what we really want, I'm not there yet. But I plan to." He asked, "So what do you want?"

Kemba managed to joke, looking over at the TV, "I wanted the Giants to win. Looks like I've got that." The crowd was going crazy. The celebrations had begun. The Giants were the 2012 Super Bowl champs.

"You can do better than that." Romeo looked uninterested in anything but Kemba. "You want more."

"Where my life is going right now is a mystery. Honestly, tonight, my woman found out that I was hitting her sister."

"Her sister?"

"Yeah."

"Oh, that's shaky ground, man. How mad is she?"

"Pretty mad. It's bad."

"And obviously she knows what you do, right?"

"Yeah."

Romeo set his glass down, saying, "You need to make that right. You need to let her cool down and then in a few days, get inside her head and convince her she needs to chill. Get back with her for a minute if you need to."

"Oh, I don't think she'll be letting me back into her head, her place, or anything else." Kemba took another sip.

"Her place? She kicked you out?"

"Yep."

"Man, you never move into a woman's place. Ever."

"I know. Needed to save my money. Did that."

Romeo explained, "Your focus should be on her squashing what she knows. If she doesn't, Lip Service is all up in there with you. You are part of the whole thing, so that's why I'm telling you that. Just keep it cool."

"I don't think she'd do that."

"Never underestimate a woman scorned. Period."

"True. Kinda like with you and Money. You two still trippin'?"

"Man, fuck Money." Romeo frowned.

"Damn. What's up? Money's cool people." Kemba sipped again.

"Money can't be trusted. Women can't be trusted."

"Okay."

"So, where are you gonna stay?" Romeo asked.

"I've got a hotel until I can figure things out."

"All right. Just wanted to say, you need a place for a minute, I've got room." He waved his arm toward his apartment.

Kemba looked around the suite. "I see that. I'm good."

"Okay. And I know you're making some good money for the old girl, but what you need to do is come and let me put you on trial over here."

"On trial?" Kemba asked.

"Just a couple of appointments."

"I thought you did more of the stroll kinda thing."

"Does this look like streetwalker money to you? I've come up. I might not charge as much as Money, but I get mine."

"What, you take 50 percent?"

"I do. But there's no 10 percent off the top. I do it all."

"I see."

"And, I have a lot of women who want a male like you." Romeo also threw in, "And men, too."

Kemba put his drink down and said right away, "Hey, I don't do that shit, man."

"You don't?"

Kemba sat up straight. "Hell, no."

"Never have?"

"Never have. Never will. I can tell you that right now."

Romeo raised an eyebrow and gave a chuckle. "Never say never." He took hold of his glass.

Kemba raised both eyebrows and his voice. "Dude. I'm not gay."

Romeo replied, "I didn't say you were. I'm just talking about filling a need. Won't mean you're gay."

"It would mean I'm bi. Same damn thing. And I'm not."

"You sure?"

"What are you asking me?" Kemba gave a look of disapproval. "Man, fuck you."

"Okay." Romeo's face said he was being playful.

Kemba was anything but. He noticed Romeo's pinky finger sticking out as Romeo took a sip of his soda. Kemba said as he stood up fast, "Look. It's about time I get on out of here. Thanks for the drink, dude."

Romeo put his glass back down and made his way around the bar near where Kemba had sat. "Okay. Okay. Relax." He looked at Kemba, who stood with his hands in his pockets. "Why are you mad? If you're straight, no need to get mad."

"I'm not having this conversation."

"Look, I apologize. But I'm telling you now. Honestly. I thought you were feeling me. It's just a sense I got. Nothing concrete, nothing definite, but you know, it's almost like when we men see a woman and we're attracted. I'm attracted. And I thought you were, too."

Kemba looked pissed off. "Then let me tell you this. I am *not* attracted to you. No homo here. Period. And if you got some gay-ass men wanting you to hook them up, then you bend your pimp ass over and do that shit yourself, or find someone who's into that. I know this business can sometimes mean some Academy Award–type performance shit, putting on an act and making their asshole dreams come true. But that ain't gonna happen here. Ain't no money in the world gonna make me rub up against some rusty-elbowed dude with a boner. Oh, hell no."

"Okay." Romeo just watched like he was even more suspicious.

Kemba turned toward the door and said, "You take care."

"You too. And hey. I'm sorry. Forgive me." Romeo put out his arms as though encouraging a hug.

Kemba looked back with an angrier face. "Later. Fag-ass pimp." He closed the door and said loudly, "Lord. I have seen it all."

A little after midnight, Kemba pulled back the white sheets of the signature bed in his king hotel room and stripped down from the day. Exhausted mentally and physically, he entered the oversized ebony shower.

Warm sprays of water spewed from the chrome ceiling-mounted rain-shower head. He allowed his dreads to drench, leaning his head back to feel the water upon his tired face. He rubbed his forehead and placed his hand against the onyx wall, feeling the sensation of the water saturating his muscular, dark skin.

He stood in thought, wondering if he really could move on from Beryl without even trying to win her back. There was a feeling coming over him that surprised him. He didn't think he'd ever really miss her that much if they'd decided to move on. Independence wasn't something he'd grown to enjoy.

He gave a long exhale and grabbed the blue body wash with the mandarin scent, squeezed a generous amount on his hand, and rubbed down his chest, shoulders, and neck, then turned around for the other shower head mounted on the wall to meet his back. He rubbed his hips and glutes, and then his penis, washing himself with his hands. The soapy bubbles cleaned his skin, but did nothing for what was on his dirty mind.

His penis began to grow.

He grabbed it and looked down, as though it needed to cut the hell out. He grabbed it tighter, massaging his shaft with his palm, rubbing his tip with his thumb. Taking a stance with his feet apart and a hand on his hip, his mind raced to Romeo.

He thought, *What if I had turned around before I left and he pulled down my shorts, taking hold of my dick and strumming it, then falling to his knees to apologize for thinking that I would even be amused by his stupid-ass "sex with a man" talk? What if he opened his mouth and began sucking my dick so I could feel the hairs of his mustache on my skin? What if I looked down and saw his male face pleasing me? What if his grip was strong, not like a woman's, and I liked it? What if he went deeper down his throat than anyone ever had, kind of like he would like it himself? What if he knew what he was doing so well, that even if I pushed away he'd pull me closer, grabbing my ass cheek with his hand, stroking me faster with his mouth until I couldn't take it anymore, and I looked down to see that he took his other hand, yanking his own long dick while having my dick in his mouth, and the anticipation of what that dick would feel like in my mouth made me come in his mouth like this?* He screamed out loud, "Like this. Like this. Ahhhhh, Dammit. Fuck. Oh fuck. Just like that."

Upon Kemba skeeting his last forbidden drop onto the shower floor, his phone rang. He listened to it and focused on his breathing, telling himself it could wait. It rang again. He continued to shower and shook his head over what madness had just occurred, and then his phone rang again.

He stepped out, snatched a towel, and darted to the bedroom to grab his cell from the nightstand. "Hello."

"Kemba Price?"

"Yes."

"This is Ty Ellis with TMZ. We'd like to talk to you about an unnamed source who has informed us that you are an escort who has been servicing Senator Ellington's wife. Would you mind if we ask you a few questions?"

His ears, head, and heart jumped, and he looked down at his phone as another call came in. The caller ID displayed a number he didn't recognize.

Who the hell is that? Aw damn!

Senator Darrell Ellington has won the Maine caucus with Robert Sally coming in second. Sally is from Maine and was expected to win, but Ellington campaigned hard.

Twenty-Six

∞

Money

Monday—February 6, 2012

Most of the lights in the hotel room were off. The lamps on each side of the bed were set to the most dim level. And Pretty in Pink, aka Mr. 31, didn't have his bag of tricks with him. He had his thick little wife instead. It was a three-some, with each one playing by the rules that applied only for this particular afternoon. Part of the new rule was that to-day, Pretty in Pink would go only by his real name, Tyler Copeland.

"So you're my husband's mistress, huh?" Tyler's wife asked.

Money, who was going by the name Queens, asked, "Did he say that?"

Tyler admitted, aiming his blue eyes at Money, "Queens, I told her everything." Unbeknownst to his wife, he'd already hipped Money to the deal. That his wife heard him on the phone booking an appointment. That she started digging into their finances and found thousands of dollars in even amounts debited from an account in his name only. But she wasn't able to access the payees, only the amounts and dates. She assumed there was a very expensive third party in their marriage. He came clean after arguing with her for two days. But one thing he didn't do was tell her about his other side. She did find a dildo under the sink of his separate bathroom years ago, but he claimed he bought it to use on her. Which he never did. She'd let it go. But this one, she just couldn't drop. This one she said she had to see for herself.

Today he'd asked Money to make it average, like everyday, normal sex. And she agreed.

Money asked Tyler's wife, "So, you just want to watch, huh?"

"I do." She seemed semisure.

"You sure you don't want to play?"

"I'm sure. He told me what he's been doing. I told him I want to see. If he's been living like this, seeing you, then I need to know it all. Just act like I'm not even here."

It was a different situation compared to their usual. There would be no submissive. No slave sex. No female domination. No bondage. There would only be vanilla sex with a man she'd known for a couple of years who'd never even penetrated her. But she'd need to play the role of the escort hired to sleep with the husband who just wanted some pussy on the side. No kink. Just good old-fashioned sex.

Tyler, wearing Jockey men's underwear, was barely hard when he stepped to the bed from where his wife sat on the guest chair. She was wearing the same outfit she arrived in. It was a blue-green wrap dress and heels, no stockings. She was in her mid-fifties, blonde, and pale. She had a bob cut, much like Katie Couric. She was conservative looking, wealthy looking, and almost square looking. Her face said she was a newbie, but she had her dress hiked up to her hips already, the finger of her dainty right hand rubbing her hairy vulva. Her slightly chubby legs were wide apart, cooperating by making room for voyeuristic playtime.

Tyler climbed on the bed with Money, holding a Magnum condom package in his hand, which he definitely didn't need. He was average, at best. It was like he didn't know what size to buy at the store. Money had always gotten them. But his wife made him get his own before they came to the hotel.

He lay next to Money, who crawled on top of him, and it was lights, camera, action. She began rubbing his forehead with her hand, massaging his hairline, and placing her hand along his flabby pectorals, coming to the level of his chest to kiss his nipples, tracing the roundness of his areola with her stiff tongue. She looked over at his wife, who was completely silent. Money wanted to see if she was buying it. She looked intrigued.

Money took a bottle of eucalyptus oil from the side table and rubbed it over Tyler's chest and even his beer-belly stomach. She moved on down to his thighs and then scooted herself to his calves, massaging his shins and ankles. She turned to aim her ass at his face, and again looked at his wife. Money shook her ass cheeks and rubbed on the front of his legs from his knees to his upper thighs.

Tyler showed little response.

"Doesn't that feel good?" Money asked him, making sure he remembered he was supposed to act like he liked it.

"Oh yeah, Queens. Ummm, that feels nice."

Money raised an eyebrow at his fakeness.

His wife was none the wiser. Her eyes had grown sexy with curiosity. She now had her finger inside.

"That looks good," Money told her.

She said nothing, she just continued to explore her pussy with her finger.

Money turned around and lay on her back along the width of the bed so the Mrs. could see them better. Tyler climbed on top of her, and Money brought her legs all the way back, exposing her pussy. It was wide open, and her wetness glistened. He removed his underwear. His penis was nowhere near as hard as it had been before. She pulled her legs all the way back, touching her knees to her ears, and said to Tyler's wife, "Bet you can't fit your whole hand in there."

She said, "No thank you. I'll let my husband have you to himself."

Money explained, "No, I meant you put your whole hand inside of *your* pussy."

His wife looked down at her vagina and right away, inserted two fingers, then three, then four. She adjusted her knuckles and turned her hand to make room, but she seemed to have reached her maximum.

Tyler said, "Good girl," and Money saw his dick jump to another level of hard.

Money said to him, "Now why don't you stick your dick all the way inside of me? Your pretty wife can fist herself while we fuck."

Tyler placed the condom on himself, got in position to give Money what she'd never had from him, then pressed his hips against her body. The two of them moaned at the same time.

When they looked over at the wife, her entire fist was impaled into her vagina. Her eyes were still sexy, her hand was devoured, and she started a soft, erotic groan that escaped from her throat while she licked her lips and scooted toward her hand as if excited to get it in further. All they could see was her wrist hanging from her pussy.

Tyler kept watching her and fucking Money and grinding himself deeper as his wife freaked herself.

Money kept an eye on them both, and her thoughts shifted to how this woman had no idea her husband, who was so in control and responsible for so much, was really such a sissy in his head, who had such a need to be the opposite of what he was, who was so conflicted in his manhood that he wore makeup and high heels and liked to get fucked with dildos.

Tyler pressed deeper and gave off a high-pitched grunt, kind of girlish, like he always did. And Money realized he had actually come. His wife kept her fist inside and rubbed her breast with her other hand. Tyler pulled out of Money and went over to his wife, taking her hand out of her wet pussy and sucking her fingers, licking all of her juices off of her palm and knuckles, before taking her entire hand into his mouth until it disappeared.

She gave off a giggle—"Look at you"—as if the sight did nothing to turn her on. She said to Money, "He always gives off that girlie groan when he's having an orgasm." She sounded so straight-laced, the complete opposite of her husband, who seemed to be enjoying her fist in his mouth. The Mrs. closed her legs and giggled again, tapping him on his shoulder. "Tyler, stop that."

Money lowered her legs and gave the wife a smile. "You're very sexy."

"Thank you." She blushed but wouldn't give Money eye contact.

Tyler stopped and looked toward Money, apparently realizing he'd gone just about as far as his wife could handle. He turned to get dressed.

When Money saw his now flaccid penis, she gasped. The condom was gone.

She quickly reached inside of herself and dug deep, bringing her legs back again, and she pulled it out. The way-too-large condom had slipped off, and it had Tyler Copeland's sperm dripping from it. "Oh, no," Money yelled.

His wife had begun putting on her clothes, but she froze when she saw the condom. "What?"

Money dropped it onto the sheets and jumped up, hurrying into the bathroom and slamming the door. She sat on the toilet to force out whatever was there.

She heard Tyler's wife ask him, "Has that ever happened before?"

Tyler gave off a panicked "No." Money could tell he was standing before the door. He asked, "You're on the pill, right, Queens?"

She said loudly, "I have a uterine device," wishing they would just leave.

The sound of her cell went off, and then it went off again. Money let it ring and ring and then heard Mrs. Copeland say, "Bye. It was nice meeting you."

Money said nothing.

The door closed.

When she came back out, her mind was filled with the fact that the condom had slipped off.

She picked up her cell and saw that she had a message. She pressed 1 for the voice mail and heard, "Ms. Watts. This is Detective Raymond Thompson. I need you to give me a call, please. We have some questions we'd like to ask you regarding a case that just opened up here. I'm with the New York Police Department, 67th Precinct." He left his number.

She stood frozen in a daze. "Shit."

Kemba's text came in next. Call me.

"Shit. Fuck."

The next morning, Money Watts sat in the police station in front of Detective Thompson. It was just the two of them in a small, barren room. And he did indeed have questions.

Her reply to what he'd said so far was, "Solicitation of sex and pimping? You are kidding me."

"Your employee is Kemba Price, right?"

"Yes."

He was older, with built-in frown lines. "He has a girlfriend named Beryl Thomas. Turns out they broke up. We've been given the name of a woman who Mr. Price was allegedly seeing on the side."

"Okay. What does that have to do with me?"

"It's not so much about the fact that he was supposedly cheating, but the reason we want to talk to you is because of *who* he was cheating with. We need to know if this person hired him for sex."

"I know nothing about that. If that happened, that's his business."

"Kemba Price is your employee, correct?"

She looked impatient. "I already said yes. He's an independent contractor."

"And you run an escort service, right?"

"Yes."

"Named Lip Service?" He wrote down notes when she spoke.

"Yes."

"Did any of your business dealings fall into the category of your clients paying your employees for sex?"

"Not that I'm aware of."

He asked, "You do know that's illegal, right?"

"Escorting is not. If anyone was involved in sexual acts it was against my knowledge."

"Very good. Interestingly enough, the woman involved who is said to have paid Mr. Price for sex is Ms. Beryl Thomas's estranged sister, Ursula Ellington. And as you know, Ursula Ellington's husband, Darrell Ellington, is running for president."

"Really?"

"Yes. Really."

"And?" She played it off.

"Well, you tell me."

"First of all, she's not one of my clients. And second of all, as per my Fifth Amendment rights, I have nothing else to say without having my lawyer present."

"You think you need one?" He looked like he knew more than he would say.

She told him like she was schooling him, "You didn't read me my rights, which means you might be able to use anything we discuss or act upon any knowledge gained, but you still wouldn't be able to use it in court. You don't want that, do you?"

He answered her question with a question. "Do you think there'd be a need to go to court?"

"I reserve the right to halt further interrogation, and you must exercise that explicitly. Do not ask me any more questions without my lawyer present."

"Fine."

"Now, am I free to go home?"

"Ms. Watts, we will continue to gather evidence. But you are not under arrest. I never said you were. You are free to leave. Therefore, the Miranda warning you refer to does not apply. Simply coming into the station for the purpose of answering questions is not an indication of custody and not entitled to Miranda warnings. We're not interrogating you. Did it feel that way? If it did, I apologize."

Money stood. "Good-bye, Detective Thompson."

"Good-bye, Ms. Watts. You smell good, by the way."

She walked out like he hadn't said a thing.

Damn, she thought, as she adjusted her purse strap along her shoulder. Why had she grabbed that bottle of fruity-smelling Gucci Guilty perfume instead of her usual, clean-and innocent-smelling Classic? *Kemba's sloppy ass is mine.*

The race will now head to Arizona and Michigan on February 28, giving the candidates a chance to get some much-needed R&R. Senator Darrell Ellington arrived at LaGuardia Airport this morning and stated that though he was in the lead, he still has a long, tough road ahead to win the nomination.

Twenty-Seven

Virgil

Tuesday—February 7, 2012

Virgil and his mother, Ursula, had talked for only a few minutes about a phone call she received, when Darrell rushed into their Scarsdale home with fifth-gear energy, slamming the door and entering the open-floor plan of the wide living room and dining room combination. He hurried over to the mahogany dining room table where his wife sat upon a black formal chair, sipping tea. Virgil was sitting on the living room sofa, pretending to be focusing on his laptop. They both looked up at Darrell, who aimed his quick words at his wife.

"The *New York Daily News* called my campaign manager. I've been getting call after call on my cell phone. And you know what I'm talking about."

"Yes, Darrell, I do. They've been calling the house, too."

Virgil sat back, keeping an ear on the conversation.

His stepfather pointed directly at his wife. "And?"

She admitted, "It's a mess. All of the media is going crazy."

"Then why is it that I got a call from everybody but you? You couldn't have possibly been that messy, Ursula."

Virgil was in total disbelief. He sat back and wondered how his stepfather had the nerve to react, since he himself had been sleeping with escorts for years. Yet there he was, throwing a guilt-ridden ball of blame at Virgil's mother, when he had no right to cast the first stone.

Ursula said with passion, "Let me tell you what happened. They've got it wrong."

"How wrong could it be that you've been seeing a male escort?"

She said, "I have not been seeing him. Well, not seeing him like that. I know how this sounds, Darrell. I know how important your campaign is. I would just ask you to keep an open mind."

He said to his stepson without even looking back at him. "Virgil, how about you leave us alone to speak privately?"

Virgil kept pretending to be working, but still replied, "I will if my mother asks me to."

Darrell said angrily, "I'm no longer asking you. I'm telling you."

Ursula said, without looking at anyone but her husband, "He can stay. It's going to all come out anyway."

This time Darrell's and Virgil's eyes met, and then both of them moved their eyes to Ursula. Her face was laced with regret. "I met this man in the lobby of the Marriott downtown. I was there with Nona, preparing for that Paine Webber speech. The guy and I talked. And we exchanged numbers. He's a personal trainer. It's not what you think. I had no idea he was an escort. He never told me that." She took a deep breath and closed her eyes for a moment. Just as Darrell was about to jump in, she opened her eyes and spoke as if she was only telling what she was willing to admit, "I only saw him that one time. He called me. I called him back, and, well...turns out..."

"Say it. He's Beryl's damn boyfriend."

"Yes."

"And you slept with a man you met in a hotel lobby just like that, knowing our life is an open book? And to top it off, it's your sister's man?"

"I didn't sleep with him. And I didn't even know Beryl was still in New York. I haven't talked to her in years. I called him back after he called me, and she answered and recognized my voice. I couldn't believe it myself."

"Oh, you couldn't believe it? What I can't believe is that you even had the nerve to exchange numbers with this guy. Personal trainer? You know how things are right now. We're so damn under the microscope. We're being watched. You don't exchange numbers like that. You needed a random personal trainer that bad? I'm the one in disbelief. Not you. Me." He pointed to himself.

Virgil fought back his words. He'd put down his laptop and got up and was now standing close to them. He was on edge.

Darrell asked, leaning his head closer to his wife, "What else happened?"

She said, "That's it."

"That's it? That's it! Like that's all there is, and now that we've got that out of the way, we can go ahead and finish this campaign. Finish our lives now? Well I don't believe you didn't fuck this guy. This will not go away, Ursula."

She explained, "I'm telling you, I did not."

He snarled his reply. "Well your own sister is saying he admitted to it."

"It's not true. I'm telling you this has been blown out of proportion. Beryl called the media, and they're running with it. She wanted it that way so she would hurt him and me."

"Well, it sure as hell worked."

"Darrell, I'm guilty of taking the time to talk to him, and call him back. I'm guilty of giving him my number. That's all that happened. And I know what this means."

"First of all, your sister has an escort, or—let's use the right words—a male prostitute, for a man. And you just so happened to meet him in a hotel lobby and the two of you started calling each other. Well, I guess you repeated the same thing you did to her years ago, huh? Brazen again?"

"No. I didn't."

"Is there any proof that you slept with him?"

"No. Because I didn't."

"Don't let this get worse. Get it out now, I mean it. My campaign has been at its height and now it's in trouble and I've gotta try to clean up this mess and answer some questions right away. Now's not the time for any more bullshit."

"I'm telling you the truth. Nothing happened."

He stared her down and Virgil stared him down. Darrell said, "I want to talk to Nona. I don't want you calling her before I do. Is that clear?"

"Yes," she said softly.

"Is that clear!" he asked again, louder.

Virgil jumped in. "Hold up. She said yes. Now back off. That's enough."

Darrell turned toward him, towering over Virgil by at least four inches. "Listen here. You don't tell me what to do in my own house, and how to talk to my wife. You hear me?"

Virgil stood firm. "You're talking to *my* mother, in *her* house."

"Your mother has fucked things up. This isn't the typical political story of the male politician who cheats on his wife. This is the politician's wife who cheated on her husband. And thanks to her, this is a first."

"She said she didn't sleep with him."

"I don't believe her." He shook his head stubbornly. "I just don't fucking believe her."

Virgil told him, "Well, this could be worse. It could be the male politician fucking escorts for years, cheating on his wife. It really could be. Ya know?"

Darrell didn't move. "Yeah. But it's not."

"Yeah. It could be." Virgil gave him a look as if he could tell it all if he really wanted to.

Darrell split his hateful, narcissistic stares between the two of them. "I'm going into my office. I'm not accepting calls. I'm not taking meetings. I'm not gonna play house like everything is fine. If I discover that you lied, Ursula, we're through. I'm not the type to stay. I'm telling you that right now."

She still explained. "I'm telling you, my sister is still mad for what happened years ago and she's making more out of this than there is. She's making a mountain out of a molehill."

"And if it wasn't for the molehill, there'd be no mountain to make. You need to take 100 percent responsibility for this. And when I address the media about this, you'll be the one standing right beside me disputing these accounts like your marriage depended on it. Because it does."

Virgil asked him, giving a daring glare, "You'd actually leave my mother for that? For exchanging numbers with a personal trainer?"

Darrell didn't answer.

He stormed off, looking certain that the bottoming out of his career awaited him.

Ursula's mouth was open, as if she still had something to say.

Virgil took the few steps to her and put his hand on her back as she sat, "I'm sorry."

Her voice shook. "I messed up, son. I plain old messed up."

"You're human." Virgil fought with telling his mother that his stepfather was the one who should be in the hot seat. Telling her things a whole lot hotter than what he was berating her for.

She hugged her son around his waist. She began bawling, crying so hard her body shook.

Virgil knelt down and hugged her. "It's gonna be okay, Mom. No matter what happens for now, it's gonna end up okay."

He said what he needed to say, but in his heart he knew the truth of it all would be their downfall. With the cat out of the bag, he wondered if he could continue to keep Darrell Ellington's indiscretions from the world and from his mom. But if there was still a window of opportunity for the White House, even with the news about his mother, then he would keep it to himself for now.

Breaking news: This morning in a special press conference in New York City, Senator Darrell Ellington and his wife, Ursula Jackson Ellington, denied recent allegations that Mrs. Ellington paid for the services of a male escort. They did not take questions, but said the false allegations would be cleared and that Senator Ellington will continue to move ahead with his campaign for president.

Twenty-Eight

∽

Midori

Friday—February 10, 2012

Three days after everything blew up, it was obvious that business at Lip Service was on hold. Plans to hire the new male IC, Bronx, for Kalin Graves were also canceled. There were no bookings, no calls, no nothing. It was as if Lip Service was holding its breath to see if it would ever live again.

The fallout from the accusations made by Beryl Thomas were all over the media, headlines reading, "Republican Candidate Senator Darrell Ellington's Wife Allegedly Paid a Male Escort for Sex." Darrell and his wife had given a press conference and denied the claims.

Virgil was at Midori's place. He'd spent a sexless night with her and was now dressed for work. Midori was still in bed, and Virgil lay next to her as they talked.

Midori asked him, "I know your mom denied it, but do you think it's true?"

"I have to believe her. I was thinking you'd know more. Thought you'd be able to find out if there was an appointment between her and this Kemba guy."

"No. I don't have access to that."

"Haven't you talked to him?"

"No. Not lately. I haven't talked to Money or anyone else. Haven't heard from the booker. Nothing. It's best to just lay low. No appointments. No phone calls. No e-mail, texts, nothing. There are still a few jobs I haven't even gotten paid for and I might not. It's just a mess, Virgil."

"Here I was worried about the mayor and about my stepfather, and what gets out is all about my mother, told by my aunt."

Midori asked, "Did you even know about her? Your aunt."

"I did. She was around when I was young. But they fell out when I was graduating from high school. The next year my dad died from a heart attack. That was about ten years ago. I never brought her up and neither did my mother."

"What happens now? I mean your stepfather's involvement could come up in all of this. The fact that your mother could be charged with patronizing a prostitute, if they really did have sex, is bad enough. And honestly, your association to me is just...I mean, what if we all get called to testify? Let's say there are charges filed against Lip Service. Your parents know you're dating me. I never did get close to them. I don't think they liked me the moment they met me. They'll know what I do. It'll all unravel."

He looked frustrated. "I don't care. I haven't done anything wrong. And I believe my mother. She said she didn't have sex with him, let alone pay for sex. The one who's got the most to lose is my stepfather. And he has the nerve to act like he's squeaky-clean. It burns me up inside to see him acting so righteous."

Midori rubbed the blonde hairs on the back of her head. "Are you gonna tell her? About what he's really done?"

"I can't do anything that would bring about more suspicions regarding what you do, what Lip Service does."

"Don't worry about me."

"How can I not? I just can't believe how this has blown up." Virgil reached into his pocket and took out his cell. He scrolled through his e-mails.

She asked, "You're done recording stuff, right?"

"Of course."

Midori leaned her head back against the headboard. "I wonder where my sister is. I called but she hasn't called me back. Damn." Then suddenly, her cell phone rang. She said to Virgil while grabbing it from the spot next to her on the mattress, "It's Money." She answered it fast. "Hi."

Money sounded serious. She spoke fast. "Midori, sorry I haven't returned your calls. Jamie's taking me to the police station. My attorney said I have to turn myself in before three o'clock. You need to stay in touch with Jamie because in a couple of days, I'll have an arraignment and bail will be set. He needs to post it. If he doesn't end up posting it, I'll need you to. My attorney will call you later today."

"Okay. Whatever you need. But what are the charges?"

"Pandering and prostitution for now. Looks like the FBI has been watching my bank accounts. And Senator Ellington's as well. He's been charged with money laundering. Just stay by your phone."

Midori looked at Virgil, who still scrolled through his phone. "I will. I love you. Sorry."

"Love you, too. Bye."

Midori hung up, giving an exhale.

"What?" Virgil asked, looking at her.

"Your stepfather's been charged with money laundering."

Virgil jumped up and put on his shoes. "I've gotta go." He darted toward the door and dialed his cell.

Midori heard his voice as he walked out of her front door. "Mom. Are you okay?"

And then he was gone.

Midori's first thought was to turn on the television. The local news station had breaking news:

> This just in. We have word that the FBI has been investigating Senator Darrell Ellington's financial dealings, as his bank reported suspicious activity on his account to their financial intelligence unit a while back. We have learned that the suspicious transactions have been traced to a company called LS Inc., which is Lip Service, an escort agency. The company is believed to be a cover for a prostitution ring. Oddly enough, one of the escorts working for Lip Service is the same escort who has recently been connected with Senator Ellington's wife, Ursula Ellington, charges that the Ellingtons denied earlier today. A warrant has been issued for the arrest of the owner of Lip Service, Money Watts, who is expected to turn herself in this afternoon.
>
> Senator Ellington is expected to withdraw from the presidential race and will make an official announcement this evening. He will be charged and arraigned in Federal Court on Wednesday.

Georgia, among other states, is gearing up for Super Tuesday, which is the first Tuesday in March. Ten states will be up for grabs, with Robert Sally and Kalin Graves expected to lead the pack in Georgia.

Twenty-Nine

∽

Leilani

Wednesday—February 22, 2012

Like Midori, Leilani had not heard from anyone at Lip Service. Her income had come to a screeching halt. The last time she had a hobbyist appointment was the day the story broke about Kemba and the senator's wife. That appointment had been with a popular, married rapper, Mr. 41, who wanted a massage in his hotel room, but with a happy oral ending. She was willing to bet that was one call he wished he'd never made.

Leilani hadn't heard from Shawn since that day he knocked on her hotel room door while she was with Senator Ellington. She called him a few times, actually surprised he wasn't begging her to come back as usual, but he never returned her calls.

Though one call was returned. Clean and easy Leilani,

as Money called her, had received a return call from one of many entertainment and national news services, including *Good Morning America*. She spoke to the producer at GMA, and the date was set. An interview for her to talk. She was about to add fuel to the fire, all in the name of setting things straight. So while Kemba and Midori weren't saying a word, Leilani was in it to win it, and her popularity was about to hit the roof. Her attorney was there standing in the wings, having already scripted her on what to say.

She had arrived at the studio in Times Square with her attorney at seven thirty in the morning. She'd worn a hot pink dress and pink ankle boots, sporting oversized white, glam sunglasses, looking Hollywood. She'd had her nails painted in a soft periwinkle color, her makeup was done with pink hues, and with less than one minute before showtime she was all wired up and ready.

Jasmine Hunter, the classy-looking, attractive host, sat facing Leilani under the bright lights as the crew around them did their jobs. After reading the segment's introduction from the teleprompter, the energetic host began asking her questions.

"Ms. Sutton, thanks for being here. You agreed to come on the show and talk about this company, Lip Service. Why?"

Leilani smiled brightly. Her heart fluttered though her voice was steady. "Thank you. I agreed to come on because, though I can't talk about the case itself, I can tell you about the world of being an escort."

Jasmine asked, "So, you're saying you are an escort."

"I have been, yes."

"Have you been escorting for Lip Service?"

"Yes."

"And have you had sex with clients in exchange for money?"

Leilani replied, her hands cupped along her lap, legs crossed, "I have gone out with clients and socialized and spent time with them. No money was exchanged."

"But do they pay someone for your time?"

She nodded. "Clients might pay for time, but the escorts don't handle the money."

Jasmine looked down at her index cards and asked, "I suppose the question is, is any of that money in consideration for having sex?"

"What two adults do is their business."

"Would you call that prostitution?"

"No more than I would if a woman was at a bar and a man bought her a drink, maybe even dinner, and they decided to like, go home together. It's silly to make it a crime. These people are consenting adults."

"Are you saying prostitution should be legalized?"

Leilani sighed and paused, then said, "I'm saying there will always be men, and women, who will seek the services of a prostitute. There will always be prostitutes. No one is getting hurt. I once heard that if a man talks dirty to a woman, it's sexual harassment. But if a woman talks dirty to a man it's like, $2.95 per minute. I'm just saying."

The host nodded. "I like that. Okay. So, what about the wives of the men, and the husbands of the women, who are getting hurt by them spending time with escorts?"

"That's between the husband and the wife. If the husband has a mistress who sees him on the side, does she feel guilty? Maybe so, maybe not. It depends on the individual." Leilani sounded certain.

"Do you think most men go to escort companies because there's trouble at home?"

"No. Sometimes they just want someone on their arm who's different. Sometimes they just want to talk. A lot of men really do have some things they want to get off their chest, you know, like share private things. It's well-dressed, educated men who don't want to get caught with the secretary. It's about companionship and just listening. Not all are married. When I escort, I make them feel important. Listen, smile, laugh."

Jasmine held her pen in hand, and followed up, asking, "Did Senator Darrell Ellington come to you for that type of companionship?"

"I cannot comment on the senator or details of his case or the charges against Lip Service. I'm here to reply to some of the speculation about the world of escorting itself. I've received phone call after phone call. I was photographed when I left my apartment this morning. It's been crazy."

"How did the authorities get your name?"

"I don't know."

"Will you testify in the pending cases?"

Leilani nodded. "I'm sure I will."

Jasmine straight-out asked, "Are you guilty of prostitution?"

"No," Leilani straight-out replied.

"Okay." The host looked at Leilani and gave a wide smile. "You know. Obviously, you're a very beautiful woman. You told our producer you're from Las Vegas, and you were a showgirl at the Flamingo. Is that true?"

"It is. I did that for a while, along with some burlesque. Then when I moved to Los Angeles I did some stripping and looked to get an agent to do some acting. Wasn't making much money. I moved to New York a few years ago."

"Did you move to New York to become an escort?"

"Yes."

Jasmine again glanced at her notes. "Was it Lip Service who hired you then?"

"Yes."

"Has it been lucrative for you? I mean, are you looking to stay in it or do something else? Acting again, maybe?" She put her hand to her chin, awaiting the reply.

"Well, I'm not sure how much acting I'd be offered after this, but I can't really say what the future will hold. There are obviously some things we need to get past first. So, I don't know. But yes, it has been lucrative."

She turned her head and looked playful. "Are you dating anyone?"

"I was, but no. Not at the moment."

A man near the main camera signaled Jasmine with a wrap-up sign. She said to Leilani, "Well, I wish you all the best, and thank you for coming on the show. I know this topic will be discussed quite a bit since it involves such a high-profile political figure and his wife. That's never happened before. But I thank you and wish you the best."

"Thank you, Jasmine."

Within ten minutes Leilani and her attorney left the studio. A crowd of photographers snapped pictures of her as she got in his black Audi, and then her phone rang. One call came in after another, and they were numbers she'd never seen before.

Her older, Italian lawyer said to her while driving, "You did good. But, you might need to get your number changed.

Honestly, it's your looks. The Flamingo hotel wants you to appear in their nightclub. Just show up for money. People are fascinated with you. Curious about why you'd even be in the business in the first place. They even want to know the name of the nail polish and lip gloss you're wearing."

"Oh my gosh." She glanced at her bluish nails and giggled. Then her phone rang. It was one particular caller she did recognize. She answered, "Hi, Shawn." Sounding unfazed.

He said, talking fast and loud, "Babycakes. I just saw you."

She smirked at his nerve to call her by a pet name. "Yep."

"I'm shocked."

She looked out of the passenger window. "I knew you would be. Things were about to be revealed so eventually you'd need to know. I'm sorry. But I hadn't heard from you anyway, so I figured the door was shut tight. We've been done for a while."

"And that's what you've been doing in New York this whole time?"

"Yes."

"Not catering?"

Feeling irritated, she said, "No, Shawn."

"Okay. Is that what was going on at the hotel?"

She changed his direction. "Where are you?"

"I'm still here."

"Uh-huh. I called you since that day, but you've ignored my calls."

"I know. Sorry about that. I've been busy. But I do have something to tell you."

Her attorney asked while they were stopped at a red light, "Leilani. You want to come by my office for a while?"

She looked at him. "Ah, yes. Sure." She then said to Shawn, "Okay. What?"

"I was about to work for Lip Service."

She darted her head back. "Stop lying."

He continued. "I'm not. I met Money and another woman at a restaurant and they asked me to work. I talked to the booker one time, and then all of this shit hit the fan."

She rested her elbow along the door. "Is that why you came here?"

"No. I came here to model. A friend of mine hooked me up with an agent, but nothing panned out. I had just thought about trying to see if any other options might work, and bam, there was Money. See, I got fired from the casino. I just didn't get a chance to tell you."

She gave a look of disbelief. "And here I was worried about you knowing my business."

"Leilani. It's okay."

She gave a long sigh. "I'm going to talk to you later. I've got to go. I wish you luck."

"Babycakes, wait."

"Bye, Shawn. Don't call me again." She disconnected the call. Her attorney continued on, headed to Park Avenue.

Another call came in. It was from *The View*.

The secret was out and the whole world knew, just as she now knew what Shawn was up to.

But what Leilani was now up to was about to make her very rich and very famous.

While in Michigan for the primaries, Republican candidate Robert Sally spoke about the importance of family values, saying candidates must have a good moral compass. It is believed that Sally was referring to former candidate Darrell Ellington and his alleged connection to a prostitution ring.

Thirty

∞

Kemba

Saturday—March 10, 2012

More than a month had gone by since Beryl had spilled the beans on Kemba's profession. He made sure to watch the latest newscasts to stay informed on the case. He knew that Money was still in jail, so his stream of income was cut off. He received e-mails from media outlets that he ignored, and he had not yet heard back from investigators.

He was still renting a room at the Aloft hotel in Harlem. He kept a close eye on his bank account to make sure it wasn't frozen. He didn't want to withdraw his funds and possibly raise a red flag by removing any amount in cash over ten thousand dollars. He just hoped the charges against Lip Service would be dropped, or some deal would be struck, and it would all go away, and that all of the unfolding caused by Beryl would be zipped up.

When he'd come to New York from Kenya with Beryl, he came to a new world and hadn't taken the time to build up a social circle. He hadn't heard from his mother since she left him, and he hadn't seen his father since he was twelve.

All he did now was work out at the gym. He kept an eye out for anyone who might try and get a picture of him, who might find out he was registered at the hotel or had the gym membership. For the most part he sat in his hotel room, worked out, ignored unknown calls, and just waited.

The one person he did talk to a lot was Romeo, who seemed to be living on cloud nine since the scandal broke. Romeo's workload had increased significantly, even though it appeared the world of escorting was under a microscope. He told Kemba that people were more curious than ever about it. More people, more business, more money, and more of a desire to fill the need.

On a rainy afternoon, Kemba lay across the leather sofa in Romeo's living room. Romeo said, "You're sitting up there worried about Money Watts, who doesn't give a damn about you."

"I'm not worried about her at all. I'm worried about this coming down on me." Kemba massaged his forehead with his left hand.

"She runs the risk of being convicted of pandering. She committed the act of arranging the appointments, she was the go-between—or procurer, as they say—of the sex. Not you. No money exchanged hands between you and the clients, right?"

"Right."

Romeo sounded sure. "So lighten up. If anything, you'd be a material witness. Nothing more."

"You can't guarantee that."

"Dude. Prostitution's the act of providing sexual favors to another in return for payment. You didn't get paid by the client for the act."

"Yeah, but I got paid."

"You got paid as an employee. Trust me, man, I've seen this before."

Kemba turned to Romeo, who sat in the recliner. "You should be a damn attorney then. It's not that easy."

Romeo broke it down. "Most of the hookers you see are streetwalkers, getting handed cash. Like in some of my cases. You rarely see them spend more than a night in jail. The police aren't looking for them unless they're looking to see the trail that leads from them to the top person. The prostitution ring. Money and I, we're the ones they want. The big fish. We take the risk and we get the money. In New York with budget cuts, they're not doing all the stings they did or patrolling the streets like they used to. I know some folks who tell me things." He stood and walked to the sliding glass door of the balcony, looking out. "Now enough with Ho-ing Law 101. What you need to do is get your big ass up and come to work." He turned back to Kemba.

Kemba picked up the remote but didn't turn on the TV. He tossed it up and caught it as he spoke. "Man, I don't know. I think I should just stay low-key a while longer until they subpoena me."

"They're working on the senator, dude. He's a really big fish. And I guarantee you, if he was a client of Lip Service he was a client of other escort companies, too. And besides, I heard about some pink book Money has. If there's mention of sex acts and names in there, she's done."

Kemba set the remote back down. "Pink book?"

"Yeah. Never heard of it?" Romeo asked, sitting back down.

"No." Kemba turned onto his back again. "Damn, man. Obviously, you're cool with her being in jail. You're happy Money's going through this."

Romeo gave a half laugh. "True. I don't give a fuck about her. She took Midori from me. Or should I say, I handed her over for a whole lot less than she was worth. Then she talked shit and got her business going using one-quarter of the people I had working for me. But you know, I was trying to get Midori back, but I realize now, with all Money's going through, Midori's blood and that's thicker than water, so she'll be the devoted little sister for the time being. I'm not thinking about her. I want you. I want you to work for me. So get your ass up and make us some money. Tonight."

Kemba eyed him down. "With who?"

"I have a woman staying at the Marriott downtown."

Kemba adjusted the soft pillow under his head, giving a heavy sigh. "Marriott? I don't know if I should go there. That's where I met Ursula."

"I heard. But hey, you don't need to check in. She's checked in so just go right up. Be there at nine. I've got the payment handled. You get half. And by the way, she's in drag," he said as if it was nothing.

Kemba raised his head and gave a crazy stare. "By the way what? In drag? She's dressed as a man?" His three questions sounded like one.

"No. It's a he. A TV. He's a transvestite. He dresses as a woman."

Kemba moved his legs from the sofa and sat up. "Again with this shit? Here you are trying to get me to work for you, and you have the nerve to assign me to a man!"

"You don't have to do any penetration. You don't have to do him. He's dressed the way he's dressed, just like a chick,

but with a dick. He does you with his mouth. I've got a couple of guys who do him, but he wants someone new. He pays a
lot. He's an ex–soccer player. Freaky, I know, but you've seen
freaky before in this business, I'm sure. You're in the biz, you
know the kink. So, you down with it or not?"

Kemba's bare feet were against the expensive carpeting.
His toes dug into the pile threads. He put his hand to his forehead again and asked, "How much?"

"You get fifteen hundred."

"Damn." His brain wheels were spinning. He was search-
ing his thoughts to see if he had enough nerve.

Romeo said matter-of-factly, "Kemba, get with it. Women
seek men more than ever now, but most men in this business
go both ways. They just make sure to protect themselves.
Whether it turns them on or not, it's up to them. But, its
money. It's work. It's reality."

Kemba released the deep sound of exasperation mixed
with acquiescence. "How will you let me know the room
number after check-in?"

"I'll text you. I do this all myself. No middle person. A
middle man just makes for one more person to cave in when
the heat gets hot. You just text me when you get there. Your
name is still Harlem. Just text Harlem."

"Got it," he said, though his face looked unsure.

"Good."

Dammit.

Three hours later, big-ass butterflies banged around in
Kemba's stomach. His penis was saying, *I don't know about
this.*

He rode the elevator to the fifth floor and exited, noticing
wall signs pointing the way to his destination. It was 8:59,

and he wished the one minute he had left until he had to knock on the door would never pass. The thought of having sex with men, money or not, had him messed up.

He stood next to the hotel room door, not quite facing it yet, just in case someone looked out of the peephole if he decided to run.

He took a deep breath, twice, with long exhales, gathered his nerve, his guts, his gumption, and took the step to face the door, knocking once. And he waited. Blue jeans, green shirt, white Nikes, blue bandana.

He heard, "Just a minute." The deep voice of a man who had awaited another man's arrival for sex.

The door opened, and a figure stood before him with dark olive skin, very tall, in women's black pants and a purple blouse with ruffles. Kemba looked down at the pumps he wore and then up to the face. They looked each other eye to eye.

"Hello," the transvestite said to Kemba. "Harlem?" Then he tilted his head. Their aquiline noses as well as their eyes matched.

Kemba's world stopped. He tried to swallow but his saliva got caught. He gulped to get it down, gave a deep, cutting stare. Neither said anything else. Kemba's right hand tightened into a fist with the same pressure that his heart squeezed into a knot in his chest.

He forced his stunned feet to snap out of it, then abruptly did an about-face. At first he walked fast and then he ran to the elevator, pressing the button over and over, and darting inside as soon as the doors parted, pressing the lobby button repeatedly and stepping back, collapsing against the wall of the elevator as it made its way down.

He hurried out and ran through the hotel lobby to the

front door, escaping from what his eyes had seen, into the light rain of New York's evening hustle and bustle, one block, two, three, not a second of taking a moment to hail a cab, he just hurried. And then he stood on the corner, waiting for the traffic light to turn green, but wanting to cross anyway, as if maybe he'd get hit by a truck and the burning in his heart would cease with his death.

His cell rang in his pocket, and without even looking to see who it was, he answered it with extreme panic in his voice: "That was my father."

Mayor Kalin Graves and his family paid their respects on the anniversary of a fallen soldier from Philadelphia. Graves has been a supporter of ending the war and has publicly made that known.

Thirty-One

~

Kemba

Saturday—March 10, 2012

The rain had stopped.

It was midnight, and the floor-to-ceiling windows in Romeo's dark hotel room exposed the glistening view of the New York skyline.

From the balcony, where they sat sipping cognac, the clouds had cleared and the neighborhood view of the adjacent tall, diamond-lit buildings that reached into the almost black skies was breathtaking. Kemba's eyes were red.

He sipped faster than Romeo. Noting Romeo had a glass of Hennessey as well, he said, "I thought you didn't drink."

"Tonight, I changed my mind. Sorry about what happened."

"No need."

"If I hadn't talked you into it, it wouldn't have happened."

"If I hadn't agreed to go, it wouldn't have happened." Kemba took a gulp and popped his tongue as he swallowed.

"But you did. It was meant to be, I guess."

Kemba looked at Romeo and asked, "Meant to be? Meant to be that I now know my father is some freak who dresses like a woman but fucks guys?"

Romeo shrugged. "Hey. That's not only the world of this business, that's the world we live in. Half of us have freaky uncles who might be into pedophilia, and aunts who are swingers, or parents, siblings, children who have fetishes. It is what it is." He sipped his cognac, too.

"Maybe. But I sure as hell don't wanna know about it." He had his bare feet on the glass patio table. "Damn. And he looked at me like he didn't even know who I was."

"Would he have known?"

"Please. A man knows his son like a son knows his father. It's been seventeen years, but I know that face. With his freaky Egyptian ass."

"And you're 100 percent sure?"

"Man, not even a question. His eyes and his nose were like mine. He was my height. He had dark straight hair like I remember. Plus, I knew he played some sport. Didn't know it was soccer. But shit, looking at him was like looking at myself in twenty years. That was him."

"Well, if he knew you, he said nothing to me. I offered to rebook and send him someone else. He said he'd be out of the country and just said forget it. I refunded his money. No questions asked."

"What country?"

"I don't even know. Been coming back every now and then for about a year now."

Kemba said nothing. Instead he took another gulp of his drink and stared out at the city.

Romeo looked at Kemba. "In deep thought?"

"I am."

"About what? About your dad still?"

"About men who sleep with men. Why?"

Romeo held his glass with both hands. "It's a preference. An attraction. Just like a man sees something about a woman that he's attracted to, a man sees another man and he's attracted. Ain't got nothing to do with a tug of the ear, or a wink, or an earring in the left earlobe, or a handkerchief in his right pocket. There's no signal about whether or not they'd be down, no meeting up in the restroom, no tests to see if they're gay or straight. It just happens. It's a stare that lingers for a few seconds. It's a feeling below the waist. A man may think he doesn't want a man based on what his brain is telling him, but his dick won't lie."

Kemba pressed a disagreeing breath from his lips. "Please, a man can watch a porno movie where there's a man masturbating and still get hard. That don't mean nothing. It's just the sex. We're just wired that way."

"Yeah. Maybe. But when a man thinks about it and wonders, and the curiosity is there, and he acts on it, and he's with women too, he's bi and he just needs to face it. He may never go back."

Kemba turned his head to look at Romeo. "How do you know all this philosophy of the gay male?"

"I'm bi. Been bi since high school. No big deal. I'm not afraid of the label. Hell, my friend from college is the biggest stud in Los Angeles, big pimpin', got all the ladies, but hell, I sucked his dick a few times back then. What does that mean, really? That he's a fake? That he's a fag?"

"That he's in the damn closet. I'll bet he won't admit it to those women who think he's a playboy. Shit, not me. I'm not down."

"How do you know? Kemba, you were just headed to a man's room for oral sex for money."

"Yeah. Well. Hey. Like you said, that's business."

Romeo pointed at him and smiled, "Okay, now you, you need to stop fighting it so tough. Makes you look way too suspect."

"Whatever." He gulped again.

Romeo sipped and said, "Maybe one day you'll let me do it to you so you can get past all that macho 'society will think I'm a punk' crap."

"Hell no. We are two dudes. And while it's true that I like getting my dick sucked, I'm sorry. I can't see it." Kemba looked back out beyond the balcony.

"Okay. You stay out here." Romeo put his glass down and stood. "I'll be in my bedroom. I live like a king but bottom line is, I'm a pimp and I'm always working. I'm going to sleep before my phone rings with some bullshit." He took a step and then looked back. "Now you? You might want to check out of that expensive hotel you're in and come stay in the spare bedroom here. I'm not gonna let you stay for free like your sugar momma did. But it'll be something reasonable. In the meantime, good night." He stepped away in his gym shorts and muscle shirt, past the sliding glass doors, but kept talking. "You need to get your mind off of all this bullshit you got going on before you have a heart attack. You need to relax and let off some fucking steam. And if for tonight, you want to sleep in my room, I'll have the covers pulled back for you."

Kemba shook his head and took the last gulp, thinking, *Now that is some smooth-ass, brother-to-brother seduction shit there.*

Hours later, the ivory pocket doors to Romeo's spacious bedroom were open. He slept quietly upon his belly, along the snow-white duvet, wearing only black briefs. His rear end was muscular and round. He had a wide tattoo of an eagle that spread across his defined back. On his right bicep he had the image of the New York City skyline with a crown over it. And on his right forearm, his name was written in bold script.

The beige linen lamp beside the bed gave off sheer ribbons of light. Gray and white pillows surrounded Romeo's face, though he didn't rest his head upon them. One hand was along his side, the other reached up and onto the taupe leather headboard, his fingers spread apart as though he'd dozed off while stretching out.

Though he claimed he didn't want it to happen, there were two dicks in the room. Kemba, totally nude, stood tall with his large bare feet pressed on the charcoal paisley carpet, at Romeo's side of the bed. The other side indeed had the covers pulled back, but Kemba didn't go there. He flung his dreads toward his back and put his right hand on his hip, his left hand holding his fully hard penis, and he eyed down Romeo's fit body, wondering why it did so much for him. He could have released himself right there.

He began to stroke, when Romeo opened his eyes, and gave a welcoming smile as if he'd been awake the whole time. He inched himself along his stomach like a snake so that he was facing the side of the bed, right at the height of Kemba's dick. He looked up, rubbed his mouth and his perfectly trimmed goatee, and said, "Damn, man. I should've asked to see this trophy before I sent you anywhere. Folks had better have some miles on them before they dare to venture with this."

"You think so?" Kemba looked dead serious. Or dead nervous.

"Luckily, miles is exactly what I have." Romeo still had a big smile, but quickly lost it as the skin of his face switched in design to make room for opening wide, accommodating Kemba's gift. Kemba moved his hand and simply watched, as Romeo, the pimp, the stud, the man, the one running the streets of New York, the king, the panderer, clamped down on Kemba's dick with his entire mouth, and bobbed his bald head.

Kemba bit his lip and gave a deep sigh like he was holding his breath as though he should yank himself from Romeo's mouth and beat the hell out of him, but the deep sigh overrode his notion. His turn-on feeling surprised him. Dare he go there, where his own father had gone before? Did he inherit this wonder? Would he have to get it over with in order to get used to what was requested in the world of escorts? A world of male-male he never heard of while in Kenya. If he could only deal with the wrongness, the guilt, the shame, the label, what it meant. The punkness of it all. For the moment, though, what it meant seemed to come second to what it felt like. And so, he let it be, and played along. His hips pumped all by themselves, betraying him.

Romeo served him up like he was dying of thirst, at times reaching down to soothe his own excitement, and Kemba saw it, only a couple of inches shorter than his, but wide and ready. Romeo's dick.

He thought as to whether or not he should or could return the favor, but was interrupted by his own powerful blood-flow that traveled at breakneck speed from his scrotum to the entire length of his penis, up to his tip where it thought for a minute. His pumping ceased and he looked up to the ceiling, as if saying, *No.* But yes, it was true, his semen escaped, right into Romeo's mouth.

Romeo moaned, squeezing Kemba's penis from the base to drain it all, licking the tip, saying, "Now, you're ready."

And that was Kemba's green light into gay-for-pay.

He stayed right there in the bed with Romeo, now under the covers with him for the rest of the night. He barely slept from the combination of his confused mind racing, and the fact that Romeo kept getting calls all night long. Kemba's phone was in the other room shut down. He'd turned it off in anger right after CBS News called, when he realized Beryl finally had had the nerve to call and leave a message, asking why he'd changed cell phone providers.

By six in the morning, it was a new day. Romeo had on a condom, lying on Kemba, who was on his stomach, and showing him the transformation of exit to entrance. Kemba realized then that he wasn't a bottom. But by the next day, he'd learned to live with being the top. Romeo accommodated it all.

Kemba was now officially bisexual.

Praying the gay away or not, the bottom line was that Kemba had slept with the enemy.

And he found that he liked it. A lot.

Thirty-Two

∞

Money

Tuesday—March 13, 2012

A few days later, Midori put up the one hundred fifty thousand dollars to get her sister out.

The entire time Money was in jail, Jamie was available only to answer three of her calls. Midori hadn't heard from him once about the bail. And Money was not happy about that one bit.

Jamie did, however, pick up once she was released from jail that morning.

They rode to her place in his black Lexus ES 350. Money was on edge. It showed on her makeupless face and in her disappointed voice. She looked thinner, tired, and troubled, and said, "Jamie. I want to know. I can see that I'm not going to be able to depend on you. Needless to

say, this is important, and I need someone who's got my
back. If the whole world turns on me, you and my sister
cannot."

He said with certainty, "I've got you. It's just that this
has been hard on me, too. I know you're on the front line,
and you've got a lot to lose. And I know if people get
called in to testify, I'll be on that list. It's getting heated.
You've gotta expect me to be a little nervous. I work for
Lip Service, too, and I know some things. They know me.
People know my face. They could be watching me for all
we know. I did bring you to turn yourself in. Now don't
make it sound like I'm a total no-show. I mean, I didn't
get around to calling Midori more than once, but hey, I'm
here now."

She sounded exhausted. "Excuse me, but right now this
isn't about you. And that's no reason for you to not take my
calls."

He continued explaining, "Every time I got a call from
the jail, I kept getting the message that I'd need to wait
until the prison released the caller's authorization, or some
shit."

"Jamie, I set up a prepaid account through the jail, so
that call was paid for by me, handled before I placed it.
Don't give me that crock. All you had to do was pick
up the damn phone. Shit, mighty funny how my calls to
Midori went through just fine. You need to cut this mess
out. I have no idea what you're up to. But I'm telling you
now, if you don't show your true colors, you will be cut
off. Your payroll is the only one still going through, but I
will have it canceled in a heartbeat. Did you handle that
situation with the fifty thousand? I'm sure you got that
money."

"I did. It's done. It was money well spent. I was able to help my sister out."

"Money well spent? It's all gone?"

"I told you that's the exact amount I needed to get things straight for now. But hell, since then there's some more mess happening. Everybody looks to me. Years ago, I could always help whenever someone needed something. But that's not the case now."

She looked impatient. "Well, guess what? Tell their asses no. Shit. You kill me with your stories about helping people, yet you can't help yourself. I'm fighting for my life right now. I've got to pay Midori back when I get home, and take care of my business. You need to take care of yours."

"I'm trying." He drove faster, trying to merge into traffic.

"No you're not." She cut her eyes sharp. "And what the hell is up with Leilani's ass? She's running her damn mouth about the business, acting like if she doesn't say anything specifically, she'll be a do-gooder by educating people on what the word *escort* means." She folded her arms. "Money-hungry bitch. I can't believe her. She really surprised me." She looked out the window. "Clean and easy. Try dirty and hard. She'll get hers, though. Yes she will. And you haven't heard from Kemba?"

"No. I'd be surprised if he still has my number. He's never called me once for a ride or anything else."

"No telling what his ass is doing. And I'm 100 percent sure Romeo is doing backflips right about now."

"I'm sure."

She rubbed her eyes. "Just so you know, I'm going to my mom and dad's house in Atlanta for a while."

"Okay. Are you allowed to fly right now?"

She explained, "No, I'm not supposed to leave but I have

to go. I'm driving. I won't be home. I'm just letting you know."

"Got it."

"Gotta clear my head. Gotta get away."

"I got you."

"No you don't. *I've* got me."

The Pentagon is declaring war on prostitution with a campaign of awareness and punishment aimed at service members and their families, federal civilians and even government contractors. Mayor Kalin Graves encouraged the same declaration for the homeland.

Thirty-Three

∽

Money

Friday—March 16, 2012

Money's parents, Beverly and Arthur Watts, lived in a modest area just south of Atlanta in a suburb called Fairburn.

They had a large ranch home that would've been twice the price or more in most other states, but because the prices of homes in Georgia were so cheap, they got it at a steal. It was a brick house, three bedrooms and three baths, which worked out because her mom and dad slept in separate bedrooms.

Neither of them was old enough to receive Social Security just yet; neither worked outside of the home. Money's mother, Beverly, was the only one with income.

Money had been home for a few hours. Her platinum 7 series BMW was in the driveway. Her father stayed in the back bedroom with the door closed and hadn't come out even once to say hello.

She sat at the kitchen table, looking out of the bay window, taking in the sight of the tree-lined scene along the cul-de-sac street in the tidy subdivision. Her mother, Beverly, whose figure had expanded from model-like to a size sixteen, sat across from her sipping hazelnut coffee from a bright yellow mug. She leaned along the long glass table with her elbows, looking at the same view as Money.

She said, "I believe you'll be fine. We'll be fine."

"I hope so, but, I'm not so sure."

"You have to know. Believe."

"It's big, Mom. Big falls hard."

"It won't fall. No proof of anything, just keep that in mind."

"That's what I keep saying. That's what my attorney keeps saying."

"He's right. You pay your taxes. You report your income. You run your business. Your business is legal. What can they do? The rest is hearsay."

"Mom, if Midori, or Leilani, with her starstruck behind, or Kemba come forward and say that they received money from Lip Service specifically for having had sex, all bets are off. If Leilani admits to sleeping with the senator for money, that they came on board knowing that or that I asked them to do that, it's really all over."

"Like I said, it's hearsay. No proof."

Money looked directly at her mother. She took a deep breath before asking, "Mom, where's the book?"

Her mom replied, "I've got it."

"We've got to get rid of it. What do you write in it?"

She avoided the question. "First of all, no one is going to be able to trace any incoming calls to the number I answer. That's all I know."

"Mom, you being the booker may not be a secret any longer. They might already know."

"We've kept it a secret all this time. Even from your employees."

"True. If Midori found that out, oh my God. Who knows what they know? We don't know how long this investigation's been going on. My attorney still doesn't have all the evidence against me. We're just waiting and wondering. I don't know who to trust." Money looked over toward the kitchen door and saw her father walk in. She offered a casual "Hi."

He offered no reply, no greeting, no *good to see you.* All he said was, "You got your mother into some real shit. I can't *believe* you came here." He was tall with salt-and-pepper hair, and heavy-set with a beer belly. A frown was pasted on his face.

Beverly frowned. "Arthur, I'm not a child. And the least you can do is greet your daughter the right way."

"Why? She never comes here anyway. Never see her until now, with all this mess on every damn channel on the TV—so damn much I can't even turn it on. My phone's been ringing every day. People want to know about your childhood and ask questions about what you really do. And all the while, to know my wife could be doing time, and here you are sitting in my kitchen, leading all of the legal mess right to her. Why'd you come here? Do you really think you're not being watched?"

"Damn, Dad. Okay. I deserve that. But, I guarantee you, Mom is fine."

"You can't guarantee shit. I looked up the meaning of *pandering*. She's been the arranger, so she's pandering just like you. You two sitting in here talking like you're trading recipes. Probably trying to figure out ways to beat this shit. This is big-time. You could get a decade in jail and your own mother could get time, too. Wake the hell up."

"Dad, I'll make sure that doesn't happen."

He looked hateful. "You can't make sure of anything. You might think you have power. Maybe you had power when you were talking half of the money and breaking your mom off 10 percent, but now you have no power. *They* do. Stop fooling yourself."

Money felt herself heating up. "Dad, that 10 percent has been providing a pretty good lifestyle for both of you."

"Yeah, well, shit. Maybe that means I could get time too. All three of us. Oh, hell, let's not forget Midori. You went and found her and pulled her in." He stabbed her with his eyes. "I give you one week here, and then I want you gone. In the meantime, stop sitting up here trying to figure a way out of it all with my wife. She and I will find a way between the two of us. No more of this talk in my house."

Money turned away from her father as her head began to ache. "You always were evil. You got arrested for the crap you pulled years ago with those hookers. On tape. Don't act like you're the saint in the family now. All of us are the sinners." She looked back at him.

"You're right, we're all sinners. We've done our mess. But right now, you're the ringleader." He slid his eyes from her. "One week. Period. Beverly, no more escort talk." He closed the fridge, never taking anything out of it, and headed out slowly, going to the back of the house, shutting his bedroom door with force.

Her mother said, "I'm sorry. You know how he is."

"Yeah, well, sounds like he's gotten worse. I don't know how you've dealt with him all these years. His anger has always been sitting on his shoulder."

Beverly stood up and walked over to the pantry, opening it up. "What do you want for dinner?"

"Whatever is fine." Money looked back out of the bay window.

Beverly glanced back at her daughter after taking out a box of spaghetti and a jar of Ragú. "I wanted to tell you that just as everything started to come unglued, I got a call from Kalin Graves to do a phone call with the new guy. But I never followed up, and obviously, neither did he."

"Wow. We could have our first closeted president."

"That's what I was thinking, too."

"Interesting." Money still stared.

"I love you, Money," Beverly said as she placed a skillet on the stove, "and I love your sister, too. Always remember that. I reached out to her to tell her that, but she won't call me back. And I wanted to tell you that just before all of this happened, the guy, the surgeon who asked her back the second time to spend the weekend in Puerto Rico? He called again, but this time asking for her number. He said he wanted to take Brooklyn out."

"What'd you tell him?"

"I told him I'd check and see if we could ask her to call him."

"Wow. She'd be glad to know that. But yes, let's wait."

Her mother took out some seasonings. "I really pray she

forgives me for everything. For keeping something so important from her for so long."

"Then ask her to. Keep calling. If none of this other mess goes away, at least work on that."

"I'll call her again tomorrow."

"Good, Mom. Good. She really needs that."

A new statewide poll shows a toss-up in the Alabama primary, with Robert Sally receiving 30 percent of the support, running slightly ahead of Kalin Graves, who has 28 percent. Alabama is a must-win state, and candidates are looking to continue building momentum in the South.

Thirty-Four

❧

Midori

Saturday—March 17, 2012

Midori was surprised and upset that he called. But with all that was going on in her life with her sister, Lip Service, and Virgil's family, she still took the call from Romeo—and surprisingly, she didn't curse him out.

He made her an offer, saying he would match whatever Money was paying her.

Her first question was how he got her number, which he never answered. Her second question was why he hated her sister enough to stab her in the back. He denied that he hated her. Denied he was stabbing her in the back. Said he was only trying to help.

The third question was to herself. Why still agree to work for him or anyone else just to meet men in hotel rooms?

POLITICS. ESCORTS. BLACKMAIL.

And her answer was that she couldn't think of anything else she'd be qualified to do where she'd make that kind of money.

Despite her gut feeling, she said yes to Romeo setting her up on appointments.

The agreement was that Money would never know.

And so it was set.

The St. Regis at eleven that evening. The payment was already sent to Midori's new PayPal account. Her income was back on.

Done deal.

Midori called Virgil to check in with him, but he didn't answer. She knew he was going through a lot with his mother and stepfather. But she didn't know what to tell him as far as where she'd be. She couldn't use the real estate excuse anymore. So she just left a message on his cell. "I'll be out. Talk to you later. Love you."

She arrived at the boutique hotel Kitano in Murray Hill, paid the taxi driver, and went up to the six-hundred-dollar-a-night junior suite on the fourteenth floor.

She knocked once, and pressed her lips together to smooth out her sheer sienna gloss. She wore a light musk oil and a peach sweater dress.

She knocked again.

In one fell swoop, the door to the swanky hotel room flung open and a strong hand was on her forearm.

She was yanked into hell. And the door shut behind her.

"What the—?" she asked loudly. Her panic-mode indicator hit full tilt, and she realized she'd knocked on evil's door. She opened her mouth again and a hand was pressed against it.

"Hi. I missed you."

Her eyes went wide with shock.

Oh the fuck no.

Tall, dark, and odd, Bailey Brenner said with a nervous anger, "Yes. You wouldn't return my calls. I've been cheating on you. Just minding my own business, seeing other whores by using your new employer's services. None of them compare to you, so when he told me Brooklyn would be coming, my dick got so hard I couldn't help but to jack off while I was still on the phone. You could have at least changed your name, Brooklyn." He slowly removed his hand. "You scream and it'll be the last time you ever scream again in your life."

She looked like she believed him and swallowed deep, taking a step back, but he still held on to her arm. "Please let me go," she begged.

His eyes were livid. "No. Not until you step toward the bedroom, away from the door. You won't be as slick as you were last time. Now send a text and let him know you're here. Actually. No. Don't do that."

"I have to."

His voice was piercing. "No. You won't be here long. You'll be able to leave in half the time you thought you'd be here. Just do as I say."

"Okay." Her one word was laced with fear.

He dropped the sharpness of his tone a bit. "Sorry to hear about Lip Service. I guess they'll be coming around to ask questions soon, huh? Or maybe not."

"I don't know."

As he spoke, he backed up, eased her into the mahogany-and-cherry bedroom area. "Lighten up. You look way too scared. You know me. I just like to have a little fun. And I've planned a very special time for you."

"What?"

"I know what you're thinking. Don't worry. I'm not going to play rape games." He now backed their way into the oversized bathroom. "Come in."

"What?" she asked, looking around, feeling the sting of his firm grip on her arm.

He backed up more. "Come here." He looked down and her eyes met where his aimed.

She looked into the square ceramic tub. "What is that?"

"It's a bathtub, silly." He sounded sarcastic.

"What's with the ice?" The tub was filled halfway with ice cubes.

"Take your clothes off."

"Bailey, no. I can't get in there."

"You can and you are."

"I'm telling you now. This is not cool."

"Let's get this over with. Take your shoes off."

She looked back at the tub and shook her head while stepping out of her high heels.

"Remove your panties."

Reluctantly, she did, bending over and stepping out of them, leaving them on the white porcelain floor.

"Test it. Step in."

"Bailey, please."

"Brooklyn, you know it's okay. You know I still love you. Just relax. Why are you so uptight?"

He pulled her closer to the tub. "It's not that cold."

She took a deep breath and looked up at him. Still wearing her dress, she lifted her right leg and lowered her toes close to the water. She pointed her big toe, the one with the wildflower tattoo, and jerked it back out. "No way." She shook her head and brought her foot down on the floor again.

He demanded, "Put it back in. I'm not going to let anything happen to you. Just get in, as slow as you want to, and sit, just for a few minutes."

"And then what? Until hypothermia sets in, is that what you want? Then what?"

"You won't be in long enough for that. I just need you cold. I need your body ice cold."

"And then you're going to do what?"

"Get in."

"No." Her neck told on her tension.

"I went through a lot of trouble for this. Get in."

"No." Her shoulders were tight.

He took her by her upper arm and yanked her toward him. "You know what happened the last time you said no. What is wrong with you? All this time we've been together, you were a lot more cooperative than you are now. You know you're a freak. You know you like it as much as I do."

"Bailey, stop." Her nerves were on edge.

"Take your dress off."

"No. I want to leave." She gave off a begging stare.

He pointed his finger within a millimeter of her nose and his eyes frowned with impatience. "You will get in. Now!"

She again shook her head and squinted her eyes, bracing for what he might do.

"Don't play with me. Get in."

She began to shake, her eyes watering but her voice was firm when she said again, "No."

He placed his hands along her throat as he spoke. "Now you will get in this tub like I said. I put a lot of planning into this. I had to get eighteen buckets in here. And you're not going to ruin all the time and work I put into this. You told me you liked being scared. You told me your first lover would play games with you and get you to the point of fear. That's why you had me fight with you in that hotel room when I told Money you tore the room up. You got off on this for years and now you don't want to play along?"

"I told you, that was my father. I had sex for the first time in my life with a man I didn't know was my father. I was too young. I did it to get back at the man I thought was my dad. I had sadistic sex and I thought that's how sex was supposed to be." She continued to explain, filled with fear. "I thought you had to be scared to get off. He abused me, and here I am fighting you off because I don't want to live like this anymore. I can't do this anymore. I don't want it. Can't you see that? I beg you to let me go home. I won't tell anyone. Just let me go. Please."

The lines in his face were etched to their depths. The anger in his voice raised to its max. "I really don't give a fuck! You will do this because I have paid for you to be here. I don't give a shit about who fucked you up. I tried to love you but you didn't want it. Now you will do what I say, and you will like it. Just like every other time. You will like it."

She struggled to free herself, twisting her arms and yanking at him, and then she kicked him, yelling "Fuck you" as if she'd had enough.

His eyes leapt with hate. "What?" He began shaking her like she was a rag doll. "Do it again. Kick me again. I've got a gun beside that bed and I will shoot you in your fucking pussy, bitch."

"You heard me. Fuck you. You are one sick asshole." She gave it all she had, hoping he'd slip back into his turn-on from the drama of it all, as if maybe it was just a masochistic act.

"Did you say 'sick'?"

"Yes," she replied with as deep a stare as his.

"Are you calling me sick? Please say you did because you're making me rock hard."

"Yes. I did."

The more she replied the more he squeezed her throat.

She grabbed his hands, wanting to fight again, but felt her airway tighten. "Stop." And then she tried the word "When," just in case. But he kept on.

He used his other hand, too, squeezing her neck as her knees weakened. Her body gave way to the floor. He lowered himself to her level until she lay on her back along the floor tiles, him on top of her, still squeezing.

She took in his psycho stare, her eyes bugged in fear as she said in a muffled voice, "I love you."

He still didn't stop. He only said back, "I love you, too," breathing harder than she'd ever heard him breathe before.

Panic owned her face. She realized he had it in him. Not just for the sadomasochistic part of it, but for the illness in him. He'd gone too far.

All that could be heard coming from her mouth was a gurgling sound. Her mouth was open but no more words would fit. A fading look of shock shown on her face. With each continued grip, her eyes closed more and more. Her fists were tight, digging into his skin.

She took a tiny swallow. Her eyes burst open again and then she gave a faint whimper. He released his hands. Her head fell limp to the left. She lay in the bathroom, on the floor, having taken her last breath.

A moment later there were two sounds.

A knock at the door.
And a gunshot.
No Cinderella story.
No dreams coming true.
She danced with the devil and the devil had won.

Robert Sally and his wife, Helen Sally, a former elementary school teacher, joined Piers Morgan on CNN for an up-close and personal interview about his past, his present, and his future, and the making of a lasting marriage, including the topic of infidelity and why so many politicians seem to get involved in cheating scandals.

Thirty-Five

∞

Money

Sunday—March 18, 2012

The next day, tragically, Money's trip home was cut short. Her sister Midori had passed away on March 17, 2012, at the Kitano Hotel, the victim of a murder-suicide.

Money drove back to New York, while her parents flew together.

It was a long drive home for Money, almost nine hundred miles, and more than fifteen hours. Most of it was spent grieving in disbelief, her tears flowing so hard she could sometimes barely see the road and had to pull over. She prayed for someone to take the knife out of her heart. Her head pounded in pain. Her gut was tight. She felt the intense weight of guilt. She should've run a background check on that stalker freak Bailey Brenner. Then she would have found out that after he requested early discharge from the Navy to run for a New

York congressional seat that he lost, he served time in prison for involuntary manslaughter. He had killed a man when his car went barreling through an intersection while he was chasing his ex-girlfriend, who had a protective order against him. He'd tortured his ex for two days in a motel in Florida until she managed to dial 911 on his cell phone. He was sentenced to ten years and had served only five before being released and moving to New York. He'd been spending the quarter-million dollars he'd inherited after his grandmother passed away.

Money couldn't figure out why Midori would've lied about still seeing Bailey. The police weren't sharing much with the family. In Money's heart, she knew there had to be a reason why Midori would meet Bailey on the side. She vowed to find out on her own.

Money's world was dark and lacked hope. She was filled with regret. The person who had called her the most since he found out was Virgil Daye. He was devastated. Nearly inconsolable. He had told Money that he and Midori were seeing each other again. That he'd bought a place near the water that he'd chosen with her in mind for them to have a future together. That she'd called that evening and left a voice mail telling him that she loved him. That he had sent her a text message that evening in reply, asking to see her later. Money cried with him over the phone, and felt for him, sensing his sincerity. She also felt kind of bad for judging him because of his plans to tap into Mayor Graves's accounts. He asked her how she could've gotten her own sister into the business, and she admitted that she shouldn't have. That she would have to live with that decision for the rest of her life.

Money felt that she had no one. Her father was even more distant now, blaming Midori's death on her for setting Midori up with Bailey Brenner in the first place, even though Money had forbidden Midori from seeing him.

Mr. 31—Tyler Copeland—had dared not call since the heat was on. She just had to believe that maybe he'd do all that he could. And once again, Jamie would call when he wanted to and not answer when he didn't want to.

After placing calls to him at least five times since she began her road trip home to New York, he finally called when she was almost home. She answered using the speakerphone as she drove. "What do you know about Midori seeing this psycho asshole, Bailey Brenner?"

"Absolutely nothing."

"You have to be able to call someone. You were a sheriff, Jamie."

"No one there talks to me. After the internal investigation when I was there, everyone cut me off. I was gonna ask you if the police told you and your parents anything else. You said a guest in the hotel heard them arguing and called hotel security, who found them. But I was thinking maybe your lawyer told you something."

She explained, "I'm not even supposed to be out of the state. I just need to know how she connected with him. Jamie, I can't take this. I just can't. You hear about stupid-ass Johns killing women out there somewhere, but you think it will never hit home, killing you or your family. What in the hell am I going to do? How can I live with myself after this? I can't." She screamed out loud.

He yelled, "Money. Money, listen. You have to stop. Don't do this to yourself. You've got to keep it together. There's too much going on right now. You have to push all of that aside, no matter what else, and focus on Midori and her funeral. That's it. She'd want you to be okay. You have to know that."

"Dammit, Jamie." Money began crying again and coughing like she could gag herself to death. Sharp pains in her stomach stabbed at her. She kept driving, kept crying, and Jamie kept on the phone with her until she arrived at her house, consoling her.

After they hung up, she took herself straight to bed and prayed that when she woke up, it all would be a dream.

Saturday, March 24, 2012

The funeral was at First Baptist Church in Manhattan, though Midori had never attended services there. She wasn't one to go to church. Her mother had arranged everything according to her daughter's wishes.

With Midori born in London, her mother had originally wanted her buried there. But it turned out Midori had drawn up a will only weeks prior to her death. She wanted to be buried in New York. In Manhattan. She made Money the beneficiary of her life insurance and also the executrix of her estate.

Money's real father, sadomasochistic Jimmy, attended the funeral, but he still didn't know he was Midori's birth father. He attended as a friend of the family. He and Midori's father, Arthur, had fallen out years ago about Jimmy having had sex with Midori, but they got past it, though their friendship was never the same.

Virgil and Money and Jamie and Kemba all sat in the same row as Money's mother, heartbroken over not being able to talk to her daughter before she died, and Money's stepfather, silent and even more distant with everyone but his wife. Leilani was a no-show. Jimmy sat in the very back.

Standing strong, Money spoke about her sister to the small

crowd of a couple dozen people, mainly family and neighbors, including the man in drag Money had met the day she took Midori from the streets.

Money kept her sights on her mother and said, "My younger sister and I were born in London. We traveled a lot and went to many different schools, but we were always together. When we were young I made sure to try and keep her out of trouble, as she was very adventurous.

"I remember one time when she ditched school, and I couldn't find her when it was time to walk home. Turned out she was at this ice cream shop, sitting with the old lady who had dementia. Midori waited with her after having the ice cream shop owner call the police because the lady couldn't find her way home. My sister had a heart, she was always willing to forgive, she was beautiful, and she was too young to die." She looked over at her sister's shiny white casket with a spray of colorful wildflower variations, and she said with a shakiness to her voice, "I love you, Midori. God rest your soul, now you're free. I'll see you again. One day."

As Money stepped down from the altar, she passed the closed casket with a tear in her eye as the song "Wildflower" by New Birth began. As the song continued, her tears geared up into full-on streams of sorrow and regret, for not saving her sister one last time.

The caucuses started on January 3, 2012, and will end June 5, 2012, with the presidential election on November 6, 2012. The list of Republican candidates is down to Kalin Graves, Seth Taylor, and Robert Sally. Darrell Ellington dropped out of the race following a scandal involving prostitution and money laundering.

Thirty-Six

∞

Leilani

Wednesday—March 28, 2012

In spite of all that had gone down with Midori's death and Money's pending trial, which kept getting put off due to the defense lawyer's requests for continuations, Leilani kept her aim focused on making the most out of the attention. The media and the public were still curious about her and her past. It was her fifteen minutes of fame, and she was ready to milk it.

Today, it was *Access Hollywood*. They actually came to her home to set up for the interview. She sat tall, as if proud of her life's accomplishments, basking in the attention. This time a male interviewer asked the questions for a special show they were doing on men of power.

With porcelain skin and perfect hair, Leilani was dressed

in a short, low-cut plum dress, showing off her firm legs and looking proud.

They sat on her sofa as a room full of people looked on. The interviewer asked, "Are you amazed by all of the attention coming your way since the allegations against the escort service you worked for came to light?"

"I am."

"I'm assuming you no longer work for Lip Service."

"You're right. I don't."

"Did you quit?"

"Well, it was a contract gig, so the work stopped, and I suppose the contract basically, like, ended because of all that's been going on. I had signed for another six months, and I guess you could say it technically expired."

"So, you weren't technically an employee, I suppose. Did you get a 1099?"

"Let's just say I pay my taxes."

"Got it. We understand you've been offered a job to write a sex column for *Climax* magazine."

"Yes."

"And you're going to do a layout for them?"

"I am."

"I see. Tell us. Is it true that nude photos surfaced that will hit the Internet soon? At least that's what TMZ reported."

She replied like it was no big deal. "Yes."

"How do you feel about that?"

"I'm doing a nude layout with *Climax*, so it's not like I'm shy about showing my body. I don't think *Climax* will be in competition with pictures I took years ago. They were taken with a digital camera. The *Climax* photos will be professional and beautiful. I'm not worried and I don't think they are, either."

"Who took the photos?"

"The same person who is releasing them. An ex-boyfriend I had while in Vegas. We broke up and, well, I guess this makes him feel like he's getting me back for whatever. I don't have time for him. I guess he got paid. At least I hope so."

"There's also rumors that you dated a top basketball player in the past who still plays for the Lakers. Is that true?"

She gave a nervous giggle that had a triumphant edge. "Yes. I dated a lot of athletes. I have a past like anyone else."

"Would you tell us who it is?"

"No. I can't. Sorry."

"Okay. Why do you think everyone is so interested in you?"

"I think originally it was because I kind of shed so much light on a dark world that few get to see; the world of escorting with high-profile names associated with it. Plus, I don't know, some say my looks are marketable. I guess some wonder how I ended up on the road I was on. I don't consider it a bad road."

"I also understand that there's a sex tape out there as well."

Leilani explained, "You have to understand, if I were a news anchor or politician, it would matter. But I've been a showgirl and a stripper. I worked in burlesque. My mother gave birth to me in jail, God rest her soul—she was drug addicted and arrested for prostitution. I watched my mom die from a drug overdose. Now people can add that up any way they want, but the bottom line is that a video or photos do nothing to damage me in any way. I'm not ashamed. I was dealt these cards in life. I've had to survive."

"I understand. But is there really a video?"

"I don't know. Like, he may have recorded me on his laptop or some other way. Nowadays, women need to be totally careful before they take their clothes off. I'm just telling you.

I mean, you never know what device is in the room of anyone you're with, your sweetheart or not. Honestly, nothing
surprises me."

"What direction are you going in now?"

"First is the *Climax* spread and the column for them."

"Is it true that they offered you one million dollars?"

"I can't say. What I can say is that I'm very happy about it."

"You know, I'm wondering." He gave a chuckle. "Maybe
you should go into politics. Your answers say just enough to
not say too much."

She laughed out loud. "Oh no. That's one direction I'll
never go in. Politics. Guaranteed."

"Okay. So what else is going on with Leilani Sutton? Anything we missed?"

She sounded vague. "Well, like, I'm hearing from some
people about doing some things. We'll see."

"Are you dating the owner of Strip Video in Las Vegas?"

"Yes."

"Okay. Will you move back to Vegas?"

"Probably."

"And, are you thinking about doing work for Strip Video,
his adult video company? Maybe porn movies? You said in
one interview that your bedroom skills have been compared
to Linda Lovelace." He smiled like he was impressed.

She uncrossed her legs and crossed them the other way.
"No. But I do have an offer to work for a female-owned video
company. We'll see. I will say I have some tips for people who
are curious along those lines."

He gave a look of curiosity. "Like what? I mean, if we can
keep it clean, perhaps you could share maybe?"

"Well, for guys, I will say, stop pushing the woman's head
down, please. Most women really don't like that."

"Oh wow. Okay." He looked around at the crew who looked at each other. "Dare I ask for another?"

"And to the women, totally concentrate on your breathing. Your viewers can keep up with me on ClimaxMagazine dot com for more info. The column is called 'Sex-corting by Leilani.'"

"Clever. As in 'escorting'?"

"Yes. It's meant to be along the lines of someone, like, sort of talking you through or escorting you through sex topics. You know."

"Clever. I think." He gave a nervous laugh. "Okay. Last questions. What do you have to say to the critics who are upset that, as they put it, you're getting so much attention stemming from a possibly illegal activity? Especially in the wake of one of your fellow escorts, Midori Moody, being killed during an apparent visit with a former Lip Service client. And considering that the owner of Lip Service is still under investigation with charges pending. And considering what Darrell Ellington and his family are having to face in terms of the allegations against him. Are you making money off of everyone's misfortune?"

"What people don't understand is that I totally didn't ask for this. People came to me from the moment this story broke. I'm sorry for what everyone's going through. I'd only met Ms. Moody a few times, but I pray that her family will stay strong. That's one of the risks for women who play for pay. Women need to think twice, whether it's streetwalking or the supposed high-class call girl. Women can find themselves in compromising situations with men. Our safety should be the priority, not the money. Actually, I hope to be able to help. I do think prostitution should be legalized. Certain states have legalized it and studies show they have fewer crimes against women."

The host asked, "Don't you think some will say you only stopped escorting once everything came unraveled? I mean, you haven't admitted to sex for money, but your warnings might seem opportunistic to some. You must admit that."

"No. I have stopped because I was meant to stop. It was time for me to move on. I don't wish to go back. If my knowledge and experiences can help others who might think it's glamorous, I want them to think again."

"Sounds to me like you're admitting to exchanging sex for money."

"No. I'm not. I've been an escort. I'm just telling you about what's going on out there."

"Well, you do have a lot of knowledge about the business, I will say that, and interest in this case and your life has been tremendous. Your name is the number one search on Google right now. We're all curious, I suppose. Hopefully some of this will shed light on the situation as to what escorting is and isn't. Thanks for talking with us, Leilani."

"Thank *you*."

She had finally gotten what she wanted. Fame.

Republican Kalin Graves says the death penalty should be dealt with on a state-by-state basis, but he supports the decision to uphold the death penalty, calling it the "ultimate justice."

Thirty-Seven

∞

Money

Saturday—March 31, 2012

Money's life was more entangled than ever before. Midori's death did something to her. She just couldn't put her finger on it. It made her nervous. Shaky.

She sat under the gazebo in her backyard again, in deep thought, when her mother called.

"Money."

"Yes, Mom."

"You okay?"

Money was honest. "No. How are you?"

"Sorry. Listen, Money. Your dad and I are going away. We're leaving Atlanta."

"Why? Where are you going?"

"We're not sure."

Money thought her ears were deceiving her. "How are you not sure? What is going on with you two?"

"That's all I can tell you."

"Mom, that makes no sense. What do you mean you can't tell me?"

"I just can't."

"Dad has you doing this," Money said. "Are you afraid of what could happen? Is that it?"

"I'm going to have to go now."

She begged, "Mom, you can't just leave like this. You can't. You're not even going to be here in case there's a trial? How will I reach you? We're family. I need you, Mom. Please. I'm in hell."

"So are we. I'll always love you. Good-bye."

"No!" Money screamed, but her mother had already hung up the phone. Money pressed Redial as fast as she could, but the call went straight to voice mail. She then dialed her father's number. It was disconnected.

Money spoke aloud as she again tried to call her mother back. "What in the hell are they doing? Shit. That man has my mother acting just as crazy as he is. How could she not know where they were going?"

In Money's head, it was all too confusing. She knew something bad was happening. The tides felt as if they were turning against her for good.

And in that moment, her cell rang again. She answered in a split second.

Her attorney spoke slowly. "Money, are you sitting down? Are you alone?"

"Yes. What?" She held her breath.

"Well, three things. One, the prosecutors have a recording of you speaking to your sister about Senator Darrell Ellington paying Lip Service for sex. A portion of the recording has been erased, but they claim to have enough of you talking to your sister. They said they got it from Darrell Ellington's step-son. Do you know anything about this?"

Her exhale was loud. She cursed Virgil in her head, knowing she was correct to not trust him. Knowing if he'd turn in his own stepfather, he'd turn her in, too. "No. But if they do, is that even admissible? How do they know for sure it's me and Midori?"

"They'll submit the recording to voice analysis experts who will determine if it's accurate. If it is authenticated, it can be allowed as evidence."

"Okay. What else?"

"Second, they have been able to track down a payment made to your sister the night she met her killer in that hotel room. The credit to her PayPal account was from Oemor Productions. *Oemor* is *Romeo* spelled backwards. That is the business account name of the pimp we talked about, Romeo Butler Martinez."

Money closed her eyes to steady the vision in her head. She fought hard to focus in order to keep from exploding.

"Are you okay?"

Her voice was now weak. "Go on."

"And lastly, they have a pink book. It is listed here as having client ID numbers and information about their sexual preferences. It has dates up to a certain point as well as amounts. And it says they received it from your mother. That she mailed it to the detective who's handling the case. Also, six figures was paid from Oemor Productions to an offshore account in your father's name, Arthur Watts."

Money still said nothing. Her blood boiled.

"Are you there?"

With a monotone voice, she stared into nowhere. "So what next?"

"I'm sorry, Money. You need to know that you are going to be arrested. Chances are they will come there and attempt to make the arrest. When this happens, don't say anything. I'm on my way. If they get there before I do, just make sure that I'm your one phone call. Do you understand?"

"Uh-huh. I have to go."

She hung up before he did. Her soul felt sold. The road taken in her life was down-spiraling fast, as if she'd jumped out of a plane without a parachute. The anger in her churning gut was deep enough to cause injury. Not to herself, yet, but to someone. There was nothing left to do but take care of the one who found a way to reach out to her family and tear them apart at the seams.

Prison time felt certain. There was nothing left to do but face doom and visit revenge.

She dialed.

He answered. "Hello, Money."

"Jamie, I'm about to be arrested. Everything has come to a head. I want Romeo killed within twenty-four hours. I have a quarter-million dollars here in cash. It's inside of the grandfather clock in my living room. I will leave the door unlocked. Come by later and get it. If you don't hear from me by midnight that means they've arrested me, so make it after then. And, there's twice that much in a safe waiting for you once I hear it was done. Then and only then will I find a way to get you the location and combination. You're going to have to trust me about the money in the safe, just like I have to trust that you won't come in here, take the money, and run. Remember—I want Romeo killed within twenty-four hours."

Click.

Thirty minutes later, after she quickly prepared herself for the inevitable, the doorbell sounded.

She opened the door holding only her driver's license and cell phone, wearing a burgundy sweatsuit and flats, hair in a ponytail. No makeup.

Two male officers stood before her. One spoke. "Money Watts?"

"Yes." She stepped outside and closed the door.

"Ms. Watts, we have a warrant for your arrest."

"Yes."

"You are under arrest on charges of pandering and prostitution. You have the right to remain silent. If you give up the right to remain silent, anything you say can and will be used against you. You have the right to an attorney. If you cannot afford an attorney, one will be appointed to you by a court of law. Do you understand these rights?"

"Yes."

The other officer handcuffed her and she went quietly with them down her winding walkway.

Her neighbor across the street stood on her porch and watched. Money walked on, expressionless.

Just as one of the officers opened the door to the backseat of the police car, Money leaned over and vomited along the curb.

"Ma'am, are you okay?"

She stood and looked as though it was nothing.

"Yes," she told him simply. "I'm pregnant."

She got in the car and was taken to jail.

Yesterday, November 6, 2012, Republican candidate Kalin Graves won the 2012 presidential election. Graves's running mate, Lois Carter, will be the first female vice president in U.S. history.

Thirty-Eight

∽

Money

Wednesday—November 7, 2012

W e the jury of the above-entitled action, find the defendant, Money Watts, guilty of murder in the first degree as charged in count one of the indictment." Those were the words of the female bailiff who had confirmed the guilty verdict with each of the jurors one week earlier in Manhattan Federal Court, and today was the day of the sentencing. The jury of nine men and three women had unanimously spoken, and after the presentencing reports were reviewed by the judge, it was time for Money to learn the terms of her fate.

She had been held without bail for almost eight months since the officers picked her up from her home that day, taking her in based on new evidence of pandering and prostitution. But within days after the murder was committed, those charges were dropped. In addition, the misdemeanors that would have been filed against Leilani and Kemba as sex workers, and even Money's mother, Beverly Watts, for answering phones and making appointments, were never filed. And since then, Money still claimed to not have arranged for sex. She consistently denied any involvement in the murder, especially after Jamie Bitters was caught and testified against her at the trial. Her claims remained that Jamie Bitters acted alone after Romeo Butler Martinez refused to pay him for information Jamie provided on Money's company. And that Jamie broke into her house and stole her cash.

Kemba Price, a witness for the prosecution, was a regular fixture in the courtroom each day. When called to the stand as an eyewitness to the murder, he testified he had been sitting in the car with Romeo, who was distraught over investigations into his own activities, when a hooded man wearing sunglasses walked up to the car, pulled out a gun, and fired two shots, killing Romeo instantly. The man ran, but surveillance cameras captured images of him getting into a black Lexus in a nearby alley and speeding off. Kemba immediately identified the car of Jamie Bitters, Money's lover, from the surveillance video. The jury bought the prosecution's claims that Romeo set up Midori to be killed to get back at Money, and that Money was also upset about Romeo buying the pink book from her parents. The jury agreed that Money had enough motivation to have Romeo murdered.

Kemba sat in the front row of the courtroom with both Romeo's elderly father and teenage daughter, who cried heavily. During her victim impact statement she told the court that she loved her father from a distance. Through heavy sobs, she said he was a good man who didn't deserve to die. She asked the court for a sentence of life without the possibility of parole. Kemba hugged her and cried often, hiding his face as though it would hide his feelings.

Jamie had pleaded guilty to first-degree murder, weapons charges, and various drug charges. Because of his priors, he was sentenced to life but without possibility of parole because he testified against Money. He had made the hit like she told him to, but never got the call about where to find the half million in cash. He had been on the run after Kemba identified him, but was extradited after his arrest in an undercover drug buy, when he paid two hundred thousand in cash for four hundred pounds of marijuana in California.

The older black judge told Money in the packed courtroom as he announced her sentencing, "This was a contract killing. It was a murder-for-hire for a quarter million dollars with the promise of more money. This was premeditated. Carefully thought out. Though you don't have a prior record, this was a cold-blooded hit for revenge. You will dodge the death penalty, but you are hereby sentenced to life in prison, eligible for parole in twenty-five years. You may file an appeal within thirty days. Ms. Watts, if you had not ordered the hit, you might have only gotten six months in jail and three years' probation if the other charges on pandering had been tried in court, *if* you had even been found guilty. Evidence is key, but because you took the life of another, you will be in prison for at least twenty-five years. You made the decision. Now you must live with it."

Money sobbed and shook her head in disbelief, looking back to not see one person in the courtroom to support her. Devastated about losing their case, her attorney hugged her, and Money was taken away to start serving her sentence for her crime.

Coincidentally, this was the day after the new president-elect of the United States was decided by the people. There would indeed be a Republican president, at least through 2016. Kalin Graves had been elected by a wide margin.

It was historical in that it was the first time in history that a white president and a black First Lady would occupy the White House.

Virgil sat in the back of the courtroom that day, even though he'd turned in the audio file to the prosecutors. Money never looked at him. His home and his heart were broken. He did buy the waterfront condo overlooking the East River. He visited Midori's gravesite every weekend, and even joined the cause to tighten laws against prostitution. He'd sold his hacker program idea for millions and was promoted to vice president of engineering at Google. He was a wealthy man who vowed to share his life and his body with someone someday, even though in his heart Midori earned the title of his first love.

Sugar momma Beryl moved her lover Ryan in. She and Ursula hadn't spoken since the night Beryl answered Kemba's cell phone.

Turned out Ursula really did see Beryl in the taxi with Kemba that day. She went after him on purpose, having always felt inferior to her sister. She moved in with Virgil until her divorce was final. She'd then filed a petition to get half of Darrell's fortune.

Darrell Ellington, the former senator and now reformed sex addict, ended up staying in the home he'd shared with his wife and stepson, and was dating a new, young stripper girlfriend whom he'd met while in Indianapolis for the Super Bowl. It was discovered that he did pay four different escorts over a three-year period. But there was not enough evidence to prove that he actually paid for sex, or that he laundered money, even though a recording had been provided by his very own stepson.

Just another instance of failure to prosecute the rich and powerful. A double standard in the criminal justice system when it came to men and prostitution. Hypocrisy at its height. The arrogance of power. It had gone on for ages, and would continue.

Money was set to do her time, and Lip Service was no more.

Epilogue

Money

So, Mr. Big, that's my story, and I'm sticking to it. You'd better be careful. They're cracking down on prostitution out there. I hear that you're running things in your boyfriend Romeo's place now. You really did earn that name, as well endowed as you are, but to find out you went out like that, Kemba, in love with a man; wow! Well, what can I say? I didn't think you had it in you. Oh, excuse me, I guess you did. It's just that I'm blown away. Oh, I'm sorry. Please forgive me.

You should know, we filed an appeal based on lack of evidence, so it looks like I've still got another shot. I could get out and give you a run for your money, you think?

A bit of bad news: Mr. Pretty in Pink, Tyler Copeland, was relieved of his duties as New York City's police commissioner. He's currently under investigation for professional misconduct.

But a bit of good news is, Tyler and his lovely wife are raising my daughter, little Yardley Elise Copeland. She was born in prison. I suppose that's just like Leilani, who is now one of the highest-paid porn stars in the world, using her talented jaw as a cash register. God, I hope my daughter doesn't turn out like her. Bless little Yardley's heart, she looks just like me, only she has her daddy Tyler's blue eyes. I guess even condoms aren't safe anymore. Let alone IUDs.

Mr. Big, did you ever get square with your parents who left you? Probably not. I will say it's a shame that my fugitive parents won't even get a chance to see their granddaughter. That's kinda messed up. They've probably gotten new identities by now, what with Dad being a spy and being good at all that undercover crap. They also have all the money your dead lover Romeo paid them for the pink book. You'd think they'd give a damn about their daughter, who's been wrongly sentenced to life for murder. I mean, I'm not doing well. I'm on meds because of this eleven-by-thirteen, 143-square-foot cell on Rikers Island. My claustrophobia is sending me over the edge. At times I can't even breathe. The only good thing is that I get to work out. The food sucks. I knew I'd never survive in prison. No dicks. But I bet you could. LOL. I give myself one year before I crack. But surely you could not give a damn about that, right? I mean, you're big pimpin' now.

Another person who doesn't give a damn is Virgil. He provided evidence against his stepfather that didn't do a damn thing. But it helped to build a bogus case against me. I knew he blamed me for Midori's death. I could tell, even at the funeral. Fuck him! If he wanted my sister that bad he should've saved her from herself and answered the phone when she called him that fateful night.

One last thing, I think I'm about ready to say who's who from the client numbers in that little pink book. I hope the world doesn't come undone, but here goes:

Ms. 111—Emma Grier—Retired Supreme Court Justice

Ms. 101—Temeka Palmer—WNBA

Mr. 91—Chris Lavelle—Comedian

Mr. 81—Dr. Feelgood—Can't remember his name

Mr. 71—Deceased

Mr. 61—Congressman Eric Walters

Mr. 51—Former Senator Darrell Ellington

Mr. 41—Freestylez—Top Rapper

Mr. 31—Can't remember his name either

Mr. 21—Walter Williams—Head of Homeland Security

Mr. 11—Former Mayor Kalin Graves—Newly elected President of the United States

Ha! Looks like we have a bi President who's in the closet. Don't shoot the messenger. You'd like him.

There, I did it. Whew! And the very thing I never wanted to do above all else was expose my hobbyists. But, oh well, what the hell? Never say never, I guess. Wow, these feel like my acknowledgments, but turns out it's a letter to you, my former employee who turned witness for the prosecution. You big-dick asshole. Oops, sorry! Well, I guess to you the word asshole is a good thing.

I guess I've pretty much admitted to the whole escort thing already, huh? But I mean, how much more time can I get? Besides, you can't believe everything you read, now can you? I guess I should've changed the names to protect the innocent. Or maybe I really did, because you know this is a novel. Yeah, I'm smart enough not to write a memoir. I mean

*after all, I do have that one last chance at an appeal com-
ing up.*

*Well, I hope you enjoyed this little bit of madam soul cleans-
ing by a not-so-happy hooker.*

Ciao.
Or should I say,
until next time?

This is a woman's world, but it wouldn't
be nothing, nothing, without
a man or a boy!

Sex-Corting

by Leilani

The Girlie Happy Ending:
The Movie's Not Over until the Woman Climaxes

Aloha! This is my premiere article for Climax and I'm happy to be part of the Climax family. I believe that talking about sex as opposed to making it some dirty little secret is very important. It's true that the majority of Climax readers are men, and therefore my articles will be geared toward men, but I ask you to share my information with the women in your lives because women tend to be a bit more uptight about sex than men. We women are supposed to be the virtuous ones who save ourselves for marriage. If we're not fitting that mold, we fear being judged.

That's the reason why this article is about the porn industry and women. Porn can be liberating, and it can improve your sex life by increasing your sexual desire through stimulating visual images of positions and techniques that lead to more intense climaxes. One benefit to watching good porn can be that seeing and hearing sex can stimulate your libido, and for women it can stimulate natural lubrication. Plus, it can be plain old erotic for those who focus on their partners while watching the movie, not just focusing on the screen. All of this is true and healthy—but beware when it is used excessively, as in an addictive manner. Moderation is key.

After having been a high-paid escort in Manhattan for a few years, I am now an adult video actress, working in the porn industry in Las Vegas. I was just nominated for three Adult Video News Awards. I was nominated in the categories of Best New Starlet, Best Oral Sex Scene, and Best Girl on Girl.

I have found that women are just as stimulated by porn as men are. Researchers have methodically monitored our genital temperature changes and brain-wave responses and found that women do get turned on by watching people fuck. Imagine that. Women account for 56 percent of purchases at the Climax video stores, and the female audience is increasing. Women are buying more and more porn. And one in three visitors to adult websites are women. Sex on the web makes for easier and more private, instant access for everyone. We women love to watch sex, too, in the privacy of our own homes, though sometimes we won't admit it. Some women tend to watch porn by themselves and aren't as comfortable watching it with men, so men may think their women don't watch it. Well, we do!

But just because we're watching it doesn't mean we're necessarily enjoying the scenes. Women are first to press the Eject button, especially if we feel women are being adversely degraded or if the scene does not visually contain what we'd need in order to feel ready for pleasure.

We always see gangbangs, or the hot pizza delivery guy or the maintenance man coming to the door, and he ends up being seduced by the sexy, scantily clad woman with the perfect body and fake tits who pleases him, first by getting on her knees to suck his dick and then by straddling him, doing all the aerobic work. And of course he fucks her in every position he wants to fuck her in, and just when he's about to come, she gets back down on her knees and he jacks off on her face while she smiles sweetly and tries not to get it in her mouth or her eyes, and she spits it out while trying to look submissive, ready to please, and turned on. NOT!

Hey guys, women want to be pleased, too. Sometimes, the video shouldn't end until the woman gets the last orgasm. Most traditional hard-core videos are made for purposes of masturbation, but with women watching more porn than ever before, you'll start to see more and more videos where the woman gets hers first and last.

The adult video company I work for, Ladies First, sells more than twenty thousand copies per month. The company is owned by a woman. Allow me to escort you through how one of our scripts is written—specifically by women for women:

We focus on a plot and good storylines—something that's not hokey, like the pool guy with the big dick. We want great acting. And we don't want women to feel like the bodies of the freak-of-nature women in the movie are ones they cannot stack up against. Men, please don't compare the bodies of the porn stars to your women's bodies. You might want to try to compliment your woman while watching an adult movie. Make a comment about her supple breasts, or how you like her legs, or how her backside is. I promise you, she'll appreciate the flattery.

It is true that porn actors need to look appealing and desirable, so they do shave, wax, and wear makeup, even on their private parts. It is all about the fantasy, but we at Ladies First add a bit more reality to it.

We like to focus on outfits and music, sensual settings, and great cinematography that doesn't look like Joe Schmo walked in and shot it with his BlackBerry. It's high-quality, as close to real sex as possible, and it's instructional. One reason I enjoy performing oral sex scenes is because we get a lot of viewers who send e-mails asking how I go so deep with the dick and how I treat a pussy like I'm savoring my last meal. We also add humor, showing people who are not being so serious but are enjoying each other, taking time to bond and laugh. We use sex toys at times between couples, as well as in solo scenes. We have group sex scenes with couples who you will get to know first, so there's a connection with them; there's even jealousy and arguing and makeup-sex scenes. Some of our actors' genitals are clean shaven, some are natural. Some men have big dicks and some have wide dicks and some have average to small dicks.

What's really important is that we like to show foreplay, and the woman getting eaten out first. The woman has her orgasm early on so that she is wet and ready for the dick. Isn't that how it's supposed to be? The pussy is lubricated for insertion. The man always wears a condom in our movies, and the movie doesn't end when the man is about to bust his nut. The sexual encounter is not over when the man is finished. If he comes and the woman still wants to sit on his face, or give him head until he gets hard again so she can come vaginally, or if she wants him to use a bullet on her clit while she comes in his face, instead of him coming on hers, then it's over. That's just how our movies are written and produced. We hope you, as men, will check them out. Your lady just might thank you for it. And if the lady is turned on, you know you'll benefit greatly. The point is, you give, and we give back.

I'll be back next month to go over the proper way to go down on your lady so that she comes within five minutes or less. One major tip is that once you bring your mouth to your woman's pussy, don't ignore the delicate design and function of her beautiful clitoris. If you do, shame on you. The clit serves no other purpose than to bring your woman to orgasm, which causes secretions. But I've got you. Watch my movies or hang with me here every month. We'll get you understanding what I said before: when a man gives, a woman will give back gladly.

And remember, when choosing a video or getting intimate at home with your lady, use the Ladies First theory.

Mahalo!
Your Sexcort,
Leilani

PYNK DARES YOU TO BE SEX-SEE

*The following suggested activities contain mature subject
matter—reader discretion is advised.*

Twenty-one and over, please! Practice safe sex.

1. Read chapter 10 or 18 to your lover and check him for
   hardness or her for wetness as the hot scenes unfold.
2. Get up close and personal to your man's penis while it's
   flaccid, and watch the beautiful process of its growth before your eyes.
3. Get up close and personal to your woman's clit, insert
   your finger inside of her, and see if you notice her clit
   swell from the excitement.
4. Put your man's soft penis in your mouth and keep it deep
   inside, feeling it in your mouth while it reaches full erec-
   tion. Try Leilani's technique from chapter 3.
5. Masturbate him with a penis sleeve.
6. Masturbate her with a dildo or bullet.
7. Have your guy put on his tennis shoes (Timberlands, Jordans, or whatever provides traction) and literally run up
   in you along the edge of the bed so he doesn't slip.
8. Late at night, open your garage door and have sex in your

own garage while she leans over the hood or trunk of the car, or have sex in the car.

9. Let him or her take a picture of your vagina from his or her point of view, look at it together, and ask them to talk you through which parts they give attention to when they eat you. (Delete the photo.)

10. Have sex while sitting on patio chairs on a secluded balcony (not up against the railing—your ass might fall off).

11. Have Skype sex from another room in the house.

12. Let him watch you suck on a dildo while he's inside of you.

13. Let him pick out the lingerie and high heels he wants you to wear and leave it on while having sex.

14. Ride him while you're completely nude with the lights on so he can watch your shape as you do all the work. Be confident. They don't see or care about half the stuff we think we see on our own bodies.

15. Lie next to each other and masturbate, but don't touch your partner.

16. Have sex using play names or sex names that you create for one another, like Dexter and Becky.

17. While watching a porn movie together, act out your favorite scene, position by position.

18. While he's inside of you, ask him to whisper in your ear as to what it feels like; every nook, cranny, and bump.

19. FF only: Do the 69-position with one person leading, and the other following each and every vaginal tongue movement.

20. Meet at a bar and pretend you're strangers, one asking the other to meet at a hotel. Have stranger sex at that hotel and then go home separately. Go for round two as if neither of you know about round one.

21. Go to a strip club together, then come home and fantasize verbally to each other.

22. Cook him dinner, make her favorite dessert—feed each other and then have sex in the kitchen. Be creative.

23. Buy a book of sexual positions, and each of you pick at least five positions to try.

24. Have sex every day for thirty days straight, no matter what—make time daily.

25. Don't let him or her fall asleep after sex (after the orgasm). Keep your partner awake by talking and cuddling for at least thirty minutes. This increases bonding after the hormones prolactin and oxytocin are released into the brain post-orgasm.

26. Try Tantric sex foreplay: Talk to your partner with a sexy voice about all that you're going to do to please him or her, but don't touch your partner. Blow on the areas of his or her body as you talk about each specific part.

27. Have a cuddle party before sex for about fifteen minutes, just hug, smile, laugh, talk, listen, and of course, kiss. Women, especially, love to kiss. Kissing brings about extra lubrication downstairs.

28. Create a love tray: chocolate candy kisses, Altoids (suck on these before going down), edible body oil, grapes, orange slices, strawberries, cherries, and kiwi (nothing sticky or too messy).

29. Get in a spooning position and work to help your mate climax without genital penetration—hands and mouth are okay, but no sex toys.

30. Send your man's libido into overdrive with the sun—fifteen to twenty minutes of sunlight can increase his libido by 120 percent. Maybe a nude beach, maybe sunbathing, maybe a summer concert in the park, but make

sure he wears sunscreen, then take him home and let him ride you like he's in a rodeo.

31. Give each other deep-tissue butt massages, hand-massaging the glute muscles.

32. Allow him to blindfold you while giving you a Yoni massage (*Yoni* is the Sanskirt word for vagina—also, *Yoni* is what the Y in *Pynk* stands for).

33. Record yourselves having sex (each person must be fully aware—nothing sneaky) and play it back for your own joint pleasure. Maybe a good time to play it back would be on a day when he's just watched football, when his testosterone level is high. Then delete it.

34. Give each other erotic chair dances. Start off fully clothed and strip down to nothing.

35. Suck on ice cubes and then go down on him or her. Also, drink a hot beverage like tea or coffee and do the same. Cold head—warm head.

36. Use a fleshlike tongue vibrator on your clitoris while your partner sucks your nipples. A tongue vibrator is shaped like a mouth but it has a bumpy, tipped tongue that licks and flicks back and forth.

Hitting the big 4-0, three women vow to let loose like never before...

*Please turn this page
for an excerpt from*

SIXTY-NINE

Prologue

"The Way We Were"

Girlfriends

MIAMI DADE COLLEGE—MIAMI, FLORIDA
1989

She really did love her best friends, but less than twenty years ago she slept with one of her best friends' man and got pregnant.

Magnolia Butler, Rebe Palo, and Darla Humphrey were the epitome of BFFs way before the term *BFF* ever came into popularity. In fact, they were so tight and so meant to be, they were all born in 1969, Magnolia and Darla on January 1, and Rebe on February 14.

Magnolia and Darla were juniors at Miami Dade College in Miami, Florida, and Rebe was a sophomore, since she graduated from high school a year late. They no longer lived in dorms. Magnolia and Darla were roommates in a small two-bedroom apartment down the street from campus. Rebe lived less than a mile away in a rented house with her high school sweetheart, Trent. They had a three-year-old girl together named Trinity, yet still managed to maneuver through the rigors of college life, even though their relationship was rocky.

Magnolia and Darla were not only childless, which was just how each of them wanted it to be, but they were still virgins. Magnolia, who was Trinity's godmother, just hadn't made the right connection with any of the guys she'd met so far. Not enough to share her body with anyway. So she decided to wait. Darla made a serious connection and was saving herself for marriage. She was dating a fellow student who was a starting pitcher on the college's baseball team, named Aaron Clark, and Darla and Aaron were set to be married the summer after they graduated. They'd both agreed to wait, postpone consummating their relationship, just to make sure the night was extra special. Aaron had been around the block a few times, but Darla, who was raised with Christian values by conservative parents, witnessed every girl in her family get pregnant by the time they were sixteen. She wanted to be different. Not only did she want it, but her parents required it. "Save yourself for marriage. A man wants a virtuous woman. Sex is not recreational. Sex is between a husband and a wife. No man will want you if you're sullied. Not as a wife anyway. Sex before marriage is a sin." And Darla believed it. It was important to her to honor those puritanical values in the name of her mother, who passed away in a car accident while driving to pick Darla up when Darla was a high school freshman. Darla's father vowed to never remarry. Darla had witnessed a true-love example, up front and in living color. And she wanted the same. But fate, as crazy as it can be, had other plans.

Magnolia was the child of a mistress to a married man. She never met her father. Her mother had been his chick-on-the-side before getting pregnant. When she broke the news to him, he simply stopped seeing her. One night when Magnolia was a baby, her mother went out to have a final conversation with her married lover, leaving Magnolia alone. She didn't come back. She had suffered a nervous breakdown in a hotel room where they'd met to talk, and when he left, Magnolia's mother flipped out and tried to kill herself by jumping off a fifth-floor balcony. The next morning, when Magnolia's grandparents found out, they rushed to baby Magnolia and took her in, ending up being the only mother and father she'd ever know. Her mother had been a drifter since then. And Magnolia made no bones about telling everyone she could care less about her mom. Nothing else mattered other than making sure she never turned out to be like June Butler.

Born in Maui, Rebe Palo, half-black and half-Hawaiian, and her family moved to Ocala, Florida, when she was four. She grew up in a not-so-nice neighborhood, where her older brother was in and out of what his mother called gangs. Her mom and dad divorced when she was seven. Her dad ran off, being a rolling stone enjoying his newfound freedom, so Rebe and her brother were raised by her black mother who was so overbearing and bossy, she could have turned the tide on Donald Trump and fired him. Rebe dealt with watching her temperamental mother always preaching what she never practiced, so much so that her mother charmed her way into becoming pastor at a small Baptist church by the time Rebe was twelve. Five years later, Rebe got pregnant, but by then, her whole life had changed. By then, Rebe and her brother would be victims, and her life would never be the same.

By Magnolia and Darla's graduation day nearly two years in the future, it would turn out that Rebe and her baby's daddy broke up after she accused him of being an addict, and he spread rumors that she was not only crazy, but so moody he'd almost have to rape her to get her to have sex with him.

Darla and Aaron would end up taking a spring-break cruise to the Bahamas to elope before their senior year just so they could finally have sex.

And Magnolia would date a hot Italian guy her senior year named Gabe Pastore. That is, until she'd catch him cheating on her in the backseat of his car at a drive-in movie. Magnolia had followed him. She always was the snoop.

During that year, one of them would end up pregnant.

And would have an abortion.

Yet her BFFs would never know about it.

Or maybe they would.

And the father was either Rebe's man, Trent, who'd die from a drug overdose four years later; Darla's man, Aaron, who'd have a fatal heart attack in 2004; or Magnolia's ex, Gabe, who ended up marrying a well-known porn actress in Hollywood.

One of them was the father of an innocent baby that never ever had a chance at this thing called life.

A life that has a funny way of paying people back.

Payback that in an instant would flip these best friends' worlds from a six to a nine by the time they were forty, coming to a literal head all in the name of sex.

One

"A Sexier Side of Me"

Girlfriends

INT.—LIV NIGHTCLUB INSIDE THE FONTAINEBLEAU
HOTEL—LATE EVENING
December 31, 2008

It had been the coldest winter in ten years in Miami,
though the temperatures were on a slight upswing lately.
The sharp, beachfront chill that lingered in the Florida air on
the outside was still no match for the three hot girlfriends
who'd checked their coats, sporting their sexy, skimpy
evening wear for a celebration of *out with the old and in with
the new*, like no other year of their lives. It was a recognition
of necessary crossroads.

Divorcée Rebe Palo-Richardson said, with a millisecond
smirk on her chocolate face, the face she got from her
mother, "Girl, on my wedding night with Randall, I started
my damn period. That should've been a definite warning sign
that my marriage would not last through the ebb and flow, so
to speak, of holy matrimony." Her micro-braided head rolled
toward the two best friends she'd known since high school.

She tried to speak at a level just above the blaring celebratory music in the background.

She sat on the contemporary purple leather stool at the fully packed bar with her long, bare legs crossed like a prima ballerina. Her stately gams, formed from her days as a dancer, extended far beyond the hem of her little black dress. A scripted tattoo was etched along her right ankle, one of a few that served as life-messages upon her sexy body. Darla Humphrey, now Darla Clark, sat on the other end, and Magnolia Butler was in the middle.

The trendy hotspot, called LIV, inside the Fontainebleau Hotel on the Miami Beach strip, was deliciously decorated in pale blues and lavender, with dark wood bar tables, draped private VIP rooms, and two mirrored, elongated bars. Oversized plasma TVs graced every wall, showing last-minute countdowns from most major cities.

Magnolia and Darla both lived nearby in Miami Beach. Rebe lived in Coconut Grove.

It was New Year's Eve.

The well-promoted, well-attended bash was wall-to-wall packed.

The sounds of Whitney Houston's "Exhale" serenaded the disco-like, neon-lit room. The soft mixture of pink and blue LED flashing-light designs bounced along the walls and from the ceiling. The glass dance floor was a pastel menagerie of light grids that grooved to the beat of the popular R&B music.

And it was 11:46 p.m.

"What? So after that you didn't have sex because of your monthly visitor?" Extra thick and curvy Darla, a widow, leaned toward her friends with her light brown, precision-cut hair with bangs that covered her high forehead. She wore platinum hoop earrings, and a liquid silver minidress, looking like a lady disco ball. She picked up her fluted champagne glass and took a tiny sip of the yellow label Brut, extending her manicured pinky as she swallowed. And she still wore her princess cut diamond wedding ring on her ring finger.

Rebe scrunched up her nose, and her smoky eyes squinted like a foul wind had blown by. "Ewwww, yes, of course it stopped me," she said, squirming in her seat.

"All I know is he turned out to be a player, just like all the rest." Magnolia knew all too well from the way Randall would always look at her, checking her out whenever Rebe would turn her back. She frowned like she took his infidelities personally, and gulped her vodka and peach schnapps. Her scarlet nails matched her knee-length strapless chiffon dress. Her gold slingbacks were high and sexy.

Darla added, "There are ways to slow down the flow. That's all I'm saying. Even I know that. I mean, it was your honeymoon."

Rebe paused with a hold-up look for them both. "Oh, you, the one who hasn't had sex in what, six years? I can't believe you've got the nerve to be giving me tips on anything." She gave a snarl.

Darla raised her threaded brows. "It's been five years, thank you very much, and I'm proud of it." She gave a long blink. "Anyway, you're the one who started this topic of conversation, not me."

"Yeah, well I wish I hadn't. I was just trying to laugh off why my marriage may have failed, that's all. Feeling a little reflective." Rebe twisted her generous lips and raised her glass, tipping a swallow of Perrier water into her mouth.

Magnolia kept her hands on her cocktail glass. "Hell, at least you had a wedding night. I think my man-picker is broken. It has been as long as I can remember. And it's probably a good guess that I'll never find out what it's like to even have a wedding night. I mean, after all, thirty-nine will be gone in, ah," Magnolia peeked at her diamond watch, "twelve minutes and counting."

Darla, a dental technician, tilted her head toward Magnolia as her lips gave way to her to-die-for bleached teeth. "Me too, girl. I'll be saying good-bye to thirty-nine right along with ya."

Rebe added, "I'm right behind both of you. Remember when we were younger? We thought forty was damn near elderly. I mean, all of our parents were the very age we are now." She thought back for a minute. "Tell me, where in the hell did the time go? My Lord." She shook her head and gave Magnolia a reflective gaze.

Magnolia said, "That's true, huh? Back in the late eighties in college we just swore by now we'd have all the answers. Was that more than two decades ago already?"

Rebe nodded. "Yes, it was." Her eyes shifted to Darla. "And then you and Aaron ran off and eloped. You came back married and I was like, excuse you."

Darla ran her fingertips along the back of her closely tapered neckline. Her full face showed her displeasure. "Oh please. Don't bring him up. Not tonight."

Magnolia spoke right up, "Oh Darla, we love you. I know it's been five years since he passed, but you had a solid marriage and a man who loved you. A faithful man. My relationship with Neal lasted a little more than one damn year before he got with old ghetto girl. Aaron loved you for you, Darla. He told me that himself. And for that, you're blessed."

Darla's shoulders dipped. She leaned her full-figured body back and then forward, and exhaled. "I do miss him. Lord knows I do. But one day, I'm gonna need to move on and get me someone, or should I say, get me some, period." She looked like she was almost joking.

Rebe gave a look of wonder. "But Darla, come on now. I still can't believe you haven't had even one dick in you in all that time. Not a one?" She held up a solo index finger.

"No. And?" Darla waited like she was prepared for battle.

"And, how do you do it?" Rebe asked.

"I mind my own damn business, that's what I do. Just like you don't want us all up in your stuff." She cut her eyes from Rebe to Magnolia. "And we know you get more dick than all the ladies up in this club tonight put together. Fast ass."

Magnolia gave a half-gasp and put her hand to her chest. "Me? Oh please. Talk about minding someone's business. So now I'm the slut? Where'd that come from? All because Rebe shut down the pussy on her wedding night."

Rebe shook her head and managed a snicker.

Darla put her hand up. "I'm just saying. I mean honestly, you've been in more relationships than we have."

"I have. Yeah. You're right. But don't trip just because I can catch, now. That hasn't been the problem, catching. But damn, if I'm so successful in the bedroom, then why did Neal leave my ass? A man who wasn't even that good in bed anyway." Magnolia readjusted her long black ponytail, which hung down the middle of her back. Her scent was her usual gardenia. It was always sprayed over the cherry ladybug tattoo on her neck.

Rebe said, "I did hear on television that it's not only about how much sex you have, but also what kind of sex you have that matters. And I'm not trying to say I'm any expert, because I am surely not." Rebe's eyes were suddenly distracted by nearby testosterone. "They said we women should get off our backs and get on our knees, so to speak. It's about open-ing our minds and our legs. I mean, I remember they talked about not only having safe sex, but having great sex, too."

Darla stared squarely at Rebe. "Did you hear about that before or after you got stingy on your own honeymoon?"

Rebe kept her sights on the vision of a hunk behind Darla's back, a few barstools away. "Very funny," she said without even a snicker. "I'm just saying, Randall cheated on me just like Neal cheated on you, Magnolia. And when Ran-dall left, he left me and my daughter. Trinity took that hard, especially after not having a father figure since her dad died. So, like I said, I know how you feel." Rebe uncrossed her legs and offered a demure smile, but not to Magnolia.

Darla added, "I know one thing. I don't care what those women out there are doing in this crazy-ass world nowadays. I'm not about to die over a moment of pleasure. I'm sorry but I've just gotta be me."

Rebe batted her eyes and inched her sights back to her buddies. "Yeah, but think about it. Haven't you ever won-dered what it would be like to just totally let go and freak out like there's no tomorrow? To have sex with a stranger or have an orgy or buy all the sex toys you can and just screw yourself all night long? Haven't you even been the least bit curious? Come on."

Magnolia said immediately, "Not even."

Rebe sucked her tongue. "Please. Yes you have."

"Orgy. Hell no. Masturbate all night, maybe." Magnolia took a drink, fighting her urge to laugh at herself.

Rebe eyed the view behind Darla again. Her cheeks began to blush. "Well heck, I'll be the first one to break beyond my boundaries. Shit, I might just walk right up to him," she nod-ded toward the man she'd been eyeing and then looked down toward her water glass, "and ask him to take me home and fuck me like the new freak I need to be. Like he's mad about slavery and shit. I mean do me like it's 1999, instead of 2009. Take me like I'm the last screw of his life and he's about to get hit by a Mack truck in the morning." She shook her brain, and her torso like she had shivers running up and down the slit of her vagina.

Darla gave Rebe a side angle stare and turned around to see a big man, very long, like he could be maybe six-seven if he stood, with a low-cut fade, perfect goatee, and light skin, deep dimple in his chin, eyeing down Rebe like she was the last corner of grandma's secret recipe macaroni and cheese on Thanksgiving Day. "Damn," she said, turning back around to give Rebe a high five with her eyes.

Magnolia glanced behind Darla, too. "Yeah, right. You do that. And then, and only then, I *will* have an orgy," she said with sarcasm.

"No, you won't," Rebe said as a dare.

Magnolia shrugged her shoulders. "I don't have to worry about a damn orgy because you're not about to say one single solitary thing to that man. Not darling Rebe. And yes, he is a hunk now. I will say that. Oh, yes I will."

Rebe straightened her back. "Yeah, well, I guess you really don't know me like you think you do."

"Please. You don't know yourself." Magnolia looked assured.

Rebe said, "Maybe none of us knows ourselves the way we should." She turned her body all the way toward them and recrossed her legs. "I'll tell you what. Dare. How about for 2009 we turn up our libidos and make some real resolutions? Some sexual resolutions. Something different. How about if we go into the new year shattering our beliefs about sex? Living our sexy dreams, out loud." She used her hands to assist her words. "I just think we've set these boundaries for ourselves, and maybe they've limited our ability to really experience the sexual side of us. I mean, these comfort zones are getting tired if you ask me. Honestly, I've had enough of this frigid adulthood. I've never been excited about sex much anyway, but for some reason lately, I'll be honest with you, I'm on fire." Eyes agreeing with her words, she circled the rim of her glass with her fingertip, like moonshine was inside versus sparkling water. Darla looked at her like she was on something.

Rebe continued, "I don't know about you two, but I've been thinking about this a lot. We are not getting any younger. And physically, I can see myself starting to age." She pointed under her eyes. "Right around here. Like little crow's-feet, and dark circles."

"I don't see anything," Magnolia said, squinting her eyes to see.

"Yeah, well I do. First of all, I think I'm perimenopausal. But in spite of that, I'm about to cross over the erotic line and dive off the edge for real. I'm about to say good-bye to my inhibitions. Hell, it's a new year." She leaned closer toward them. "I say we lighten up like we should've twenty years ago." She sipped her water.

Darla shook her head. "Rebe, girl, please. We're not twenty anymore. We can't go back."

"Who says?"

Magnolia reminded her, "We're forty. Hello." Her eyes said *hello*, too. "Our biological clocks are ticking just like yours. I don't even have a kid, you do. Hell, I've never even been married. But I've got the bridesmaid thing down, between you, about two cousins, and one of my old co-workers. Enough."

Rebe smirked and glanced up at the time on the television screen over the bar. "Hold up now. We're not forty yet. And for the next five minutes, I'm about to dare even myself and open my mind in a way I've never done before. I'm about to take back my sexual freedom, and my first step is—get ready for this—I'm gonna start stripping."

Darla looked amazed. "Stripping. Oh Lord, are you sure that's seltzer water or whatever the heck it is you're drinking? I know you were a dancer years ago and all, but who's gonna hire a forty-year-old stripper?"

"I already have my pole-dancing class set, if you don't mind."

"What?" Magnolia watched Rebe's eyes, which were again focused on the big man to the left.

The crowd started to get louder.

The buzz was more intense.

Folks' glasses were being filled to the rim.

People moved closer together.

Rebe moved her eyes back to Magnolia and Darla. "Anyway ladies, what about you? What is it that you've always wanted to do but never had the nerve to do?"

Magnolia took a long gulp as the bartender walked up. She smiled and pointed toward her and her friends' glasses for fill-ups. The bow-tie-wearing lady nodded and walked away. Magnolia spoke as if she were telling the FBI's most classified secret. "Well, actually, a few months ago I was talking on the phone to this guy, and he told me I sounded like a phone sex operator. I mean he pissed me off a little, but later I actually thought of what it would be like to do that. You know. Turn someone on over the phone while they play with themselves." She dropped her sexy smirk and sat up straight. "Maybe even strange men. Like online."

Darla waved her hand at Magnolia. "See, you trip me out. Your banker look, with your hair always pulled back, wearing suits and carrying briefcases just doesn't match with that madness." She shook her head. "I know you meet guys, but, I can't even picture you doing that."

Magnolia nodded to the bartender as she set down their drinks. She asked Darla, "Well what about you? Like we'd ever be able to picture you doing anything."

"To tell you the truth, I've been thinking about opening a business. I mean, I think maybe it's about time for me to do something with what's left of this life insurance money." She heard her own words and knew it was her overbearing pride that was bigger than her honesty. "And, I was wondering what it would take for me to open an adult store."

"An adult toy store? You?" Magnolia asked, looking baffled. "And you can't picture me online?"

"Well, you know I love lingerie. I was thinking about a lingerie store, and adding in some toys, videos, things like that."

Rebe spoke with energy before Magnolia could say anything else. "That sounds good, Darla. If that's what you wanna do, then I think you should do it." Her eyes flipped between her friends. "I'm shaking off all that 'what we can't picture' crap. So what do you say? Three of us? I mean, it's just sex. It's not gonna kill us. Let's do it."

Magnolia tapped her fingernails along the bar and looked left and then right at her friends. "Shit, might as well."

Rebe smiled, noticing the time. "Then the challenge is on. Grab your glasses, ladies."

Just then, just as the BFFs agreed to their sexploration rules, the boisterous countdown began around them. They all rose to their high-heeled feet, standing side-by-side on the concrete flooring, and raised their glasses high in the air.

"Ten."

"Nine."

"Eight."

"Seven."

"Six."

"Five."

"Four."

"Three."

"Two."

"One."

As everyone began to yell, "Happy New Year," Magnolia said extra-loud, "Here's to girlfriends never being farther away than the arms of our hearts can reach." It was the threesome's sisterhood mantra.

Rebe and Darla nodded and smiled, and all three said together, "Cheers," as they clinked their glasses.

A few of the people along the bar and those who stood behind them offered a touch of their glasses, too, each saying, "Happy New Year," and the ladies saying it in return. Groups of strangers hugged, loud horns blew and noisemakers cranked, and turquoise balloons drifted slowly from the ceiling downward among the many bodies, making a trail to the floor around them.

"Happy Freaking New Year," Rebe said out loud like she started to really get the 2009 feeling, just as she looked over at the big man with the perfect goatee. He stayed seated as people hustled about. His eyes were only for her. Hers met his and stayed. She read his lips: *Happy New Year*.

Rebe heard him loud and clear and mouthed it back with sexy.

She had a new look on her face.

And Magnolia and Darla noticed.

They watched Rebe watch him and then she smiled toward the big man. She spoke with volume. "Freaking New Year is right. And I'm about to start right now." She took hold of her black clutch from along the bar top and pulled on the hem of her short dress. "Listen. I love you both, but I gotta go."

Magnolia placed her hand on Rebe's wrist. "No you're not."

"Watch me." She placed her glass back down on the bar. "And I might even suck his dick."

Darla's forehead was pissed. She warned, "Rebe. Be careful. You don't even know him."

"That's the whole damn point."

"I'd swear you were on something. Not a drop of alcohol?" Magnolia asked over the loud blare of feel-good voices.

"Nope. Not even a little bit."

Darla spoke close to Rebe's ear, "Look, you text me in ten minutes, and then if you leave, you text me an address. Don't play now."

Rebe acted as though she was deaf. Magnolia and Darla watched her simply sashay away, with her elongated back, and long legs strutting like she was on a runway. She gave a girly fling of her skinny braids and stood before the big man, shook his hand, and brought her lips close to his left lobe. Magnolia and Darla could see Rebe shut her eyes as she spoke.

They could see his chin dimple deepen.

"Celebration" by Kool and the Gang played as folks joined in to sing along, some heading to the dance floor.

In thirty seconds flat, after the big man whispered back to Rebe, he stood tall, proving that he was indeed six-seven, towering over her by a foot. He placed some money on the bar and grabbed Rebe's hand, stepping away with an ear-to-ear smile, while she femininely followed, looking back at her buddies, winking and grinning like a teenager.

Fully checking them out, Magnolia said, "Well I'll be damned," almost giving off a smirk of envy. "The nerve."

Darla's mouth was stuck on open. She swallowed hard and blinked three times fast, looking at Magnolia as though prompting her to do something quick, and then darting her worried eyes back toward Rebe's exit. "Oh my God. She did it. She's leaving. Is she leaving, or are they headed to that private room? Where are they going? That child cannot be serious." She turned toward the bar and looked at Magnolia, who was now holding her BlackBerry Pearl, reading a text message. Darla said, "I guess I'm the only one worried. You know we've got to watch that girl. I just wanna know, what happened to the squeamish girl who just used the word *ewwww* a minute ago? She has lost her ever-loving mind at the stroke of midnight." Darla turned back toward Rebe's departure and lost complete sight of the big man and Rebe. She stood on her tiptoes. "Heck, where'd his tall ass take her?"

Magnolia sat down and put her cell back in her purse. She wore a casual grin. "Rebe's truly taken this forty-year thing to a whole new height. And I guess that means our butts need to get serious too, girlie. Like she said, we just made three sexual resolutions. And I don't know about you, but I'm in." Magnolia again raised her glass for a toast. "Happy fortieth birthday, Darla."

Darla cut her eyes away from the crowd and plopped her body down on the bar stool next to Magnolia. "Happy fortieth birthday," she said as though weak. She and Magnolia leaned toward each other for a hug, and Magnolia patted her on the back. Darla glanced at her tiny barrel purse and opened it, snatching her touch-screen cell, eyeing it with a frown. "That newly freaky girl had better text me. Trying to shake the missionary and get all sixty-nine on us with the Mr. Rick Fox wannabe. Let her hair down, my ass. She ain't forty yet, dammit."

READING GROUP GUIDE

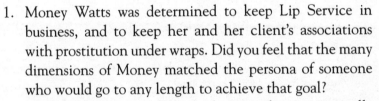

1. Money Watts was determined to keep Lip Service in business, and to keep her and her client's associations with prostitution under wraps. Did you feel that the many dimensions of Money matched the persona of someone who would go to any length to achieve that goal?
2. Midori Moody was a love junkie, yet she was tragically wounded. Did you think it would have been possible for her to find Mr. Right and move past her demons?
3. Leilani Sutton had a certain "skill at giving skull" that made her very popular. As you read her scenes, did you find any particular aspect of her techniques that intrigued you to the point where you would want to mimic her processes? If so, what in particular intrigued you?
4. Kemba Price was in an open relationship with Beryl, who had her men on the side. Do you think Beryl had a right to be so upset when she found out what Kemba was up to?
5. Were you surprised that a pimp like Romeo could have such an attraction to men? Have you ever heard of a story

or movie where the pimp was bisexual? Is so, what is the title?

6. Which sex scene turned you on the most, if any? What was it about that scene? Which scene turned you off the most, and why?

7. Have you ever been in an intimate situation where there were two dicks in the room?

8. Does penis size matter to you? Have you experienced a Kemba- and/or Virgil-sized penis? Would you continue to date a man who you found out had a micropenis?

9. If you found out that one of your parents patronized hookers, would you tell the other parent?

10. Would you consider a part-time career as a phone sex operator?

11. Do you think prostitution should be legalized? Why or why not?

12. In your everyday life, does dating a man who buys you dinner, gifts, trips, and so on, equate to being a prostitute if you sleep with him in return?

13. Why does it seem that so many politicians take risks when it comes to sex on the side of their relationship/marriage?

14. Is there a particular character in *Politics. Escorts. Blackmail.* that you would like to follow up on in a sequel? Why?

15. Is there a certain power of the pussy that men cannot resist? Is the old saying true that, "Women rule the world because they've got half the money and all the pussy?" Either way, please give examples.

ABOUT THE AUTHOR

Pynk is the bestselling author of *Erotic City*, *Sexaholics*, and *Sixty-Nine*, and a contributor to the anthology *The Heat of the Night*. Pynk won the 2008 YOUnity award for Fastest Rising Literary Star, and Disilgold.com's Most Outstanding Author of the Year award for 2009.

Erotic City, which centers around a fictional swingers club in Atlanta, was voted one of the Best Reads for 2008 by Black Expressions and was a finalist for a 2009 African American Literary Award in the category of erotica. *Sexaholics*, about four women addicted to sex, was voted among the 2010 Best Books by the Sankofa Literary Society. *Sixty-Nine*, about three sexually repressed women born in 1969, was nominated for a 2011 African American Literary Award and was a Top 20 Black Expressions Bestseller. *The Heat of the Night* was written by five bestselling female authors, offering sizzling stories that empower women to take control of their climax. *Politics. Escorts. Blackmail.* tackles the topic of politicians and their not-so-undercover connection to the call-girl industry in New York City.

Each steamy Pynk title is set in a different city—Atlanta, Los Angeles, Miami, Dallas, and New York City. Pynk's mission is to encourage women to freely live their sexy dreams, responsibly and without guilt.

Born and raised in Los Angeles, Pynk now resides just outside of Atlanta, Georgia. For more information on Pynk, you can visit her website at http://www.authorpynk.com/ or find her on Facebook.

Can't get enough of Pynk? Then make sure to pick up her other erotic novels.

Now Available from Grand Central Publishing

(03/11)

Hitting the big 4-0 is not all Magnolia Butler, Rebe Richardson, and Darla Clark have in common as they vow to let loose like never before. For these women, living on the erotic edge is challenging everything they believe about lust, sinning, and betrayal.

(03/10)

Miki, Valencia, Teela, and Brandi share one thing—they are all addicted to sex. United through Sexaholics Anonymous, these women try to recover from their dependence on wild, spontaneous, and even sometimes dangerous sex. And they have a long, wrenching road ahead of them.

(11/08)

Erotic City has become Atlanta's best-kept secret, a private club where the wealthy can live out their wildest sexual fantasies. But now, one of its frequent patrons threatens to close the club's doors forever, and the nights of hot fun and cold cash are about to culminate in a dangerous clash of passions and wills.

If you loved POLITICS. ESCORTS. BLACKMAIL., then you're sure to enjoy these steamy favorites as well!

Now Available from Grand Central Publishing

(08/11)

Packed with frank and meaningful discourse, contemplative advice, and page-turning hot-and-sexy fun, *SATISFACTION: Erotic Fantasies for the Advanced & Adventurous Couple* offers something for everyone. By combining erotic fiction with advice and instruction on how to incorporate these fictional erotic adventures into your committed relationship, Karrine Steffans will teach you how to leave your inhibitions at the bedroom door.

(06/11)

London Reed needs lots of cash fast, and when handsome tycoon William Thorne shows her just how to bend the rules, she finds that the cost of doing business is guilt, lies, betrayal, and an addiction to the high-end call-girl life that she can't shake.

(04/11)

Sisters Foxy, Victoria, and Déjà run a prosperous bakery by day and fulfill their clients' adult fantasies at Crème Fantasyland at night. Business is booming, but life at home is another story. As the women try to work through their professional and personal lives, an unexpected threat may cause them to lose their business or, worst of all, their freedom.

For information on GCP African American titles, find us on Facebook: http://www.facebook.com/#!/GCPAfricanAmerican